DARK HUNT

A Ryan Weller Thriller

EVAN GRAVER

CHAPTER ONE

Sea Tiger
Caribbean Sea

Captain Kristoffer Barsness wasn't a superstitious man, but if ever there was a voyage full of omens, he was on it.

Nothing seemed to have gone right since leaving port, and now the teeth of a tropical storm were gnashing at their stern. They were halfway across the Caribbean Sea, dragging the defunct cruise ship *Galina Jovovich*, named after a Russian actress, from the Port of Miami to the breaking yard in Bluefields, Nicaragua, where they'd cut her up for scrap.

Barsness stared out of the water-streaked rear windows on the bridge of his ocean-going X-Bow tug, *Sea Tiger*, as it plowed through the driving rain, its thick tow cable disappearing into the darkness. This was the *Sea Tiger*'s first tow, but Barsness couldn't count how many tows he'd made in the fifty years he'd been plying the seas.

The old Norwegian ran a hand over his stubbly gray hair, cut short to the scalp to disguise where it was thinning on top. He was tall, with powerful shoulders and a thick chest sculpted from years of deck work as he'd made his way up through the ranks to command his own tug. He'd just come on for the midnight watch, and he sipped from a mug of coffee as he listened to Martin Aadland, his short, pudgy first mate, as he gave a summary of the previous four hours.

But Barsness's mind was on the *Galina*. With the collapse of the Iron Curtain, a Canadian firm had purchased the ship, designed by the Soviets to weather the brutal environments of the Baltic and North Seas, and moved her to Argentina, where they ran cruises to the polar ice caps of Antarctica. When the owners took the *Galina* to Miami for a much-needed retrofit, they'd mismanaged their funds and the vessel had gone into receivership. They'd left the ship to rot at a dock on the Miami River, where she was an eyesore to developers and owners of high-end condos. Eventually, the City of Miami had seized the vessel and auctioned her to the highest bidder to pay the crew and to recoup the government's costs. The winning bidder decided she wasn't worth saving and hired the Norwegian firm, Stavanger Marine, to tow the forty-five-year-old *Galina* to the breakers.

The *Galina Jovovich* had a stout bow for breaking ice, and she contained a lot of extra steel to strengthen her hull, perfect for breaking and recycling, but, so far, the trip to Bluefields had been fraught with danger and inexplicable complications.

Before they'd even left the Port of Miami, *Sea Tiger*'s tow cable had snapped. Fortunately, the harbor escort tugs had quickly corralled the wayward ship before the *Galina* could do any damage. The crew of the *Sea Tiger* had rigged the backup cable, but Barsness had his doubts about its strength. Stavanger might have provided him with a magnificent ship, but they'd cut corners, and one of those was the used backup cable. Even though it had been inspected and certified, it wasn't the same as the original, which, in hindsight, Barsness thought, wasn't that great either. Now, with the coming storm, there would be even more strain on the cable.

Aadland finished his report by saying, "The tropical storm should pass to our west, but we're in for a rough ride."

Barsness sipped his coffee, pondering the situation.

When the captain didn't speak, Aadland continued. "Seas are building to two meters and the winds are holding steady at a three, with gusts up to four."

As a young officer, Barsness had memorized the Beaufort scale, an empirical measurement of wind speed. A three was between twelve to nineteen kilometers per hour, and a four registered between twenty and twenty-eight.

"What does the radar show?" Barsness asked, picking a piece of lint from his pressed white shirt. As always, the epaulets with the four gold bars remained fixed in place on his shoulders. He preferred to wear coveralls to prevent his uniform from becoming dirty and to avoid his wife's curses when she had to remove a stain, but Stavanger Marine wanted their captains dressed for the part.

Aadland moved the mouse on the computer and refreshed the screen. "It's on track to cross the Virgin Islands, enter the Caribbean, and turn toward Jamaica."

No one had told Mother Nature that hurricane season had yet to start. She clearly had a mind of her own, and she'd created an early May storm.

"We should cross ahead of it," Barsness said, looking over his first mate's shoulder.....

"Aye, Captain," Aadland replied.

It would have been faster to cross through the Windward Passage between Cuba and Haiti, but, given their current problems, Barsness had decided to use the Mona Passage between Puerto Rico and the Dominican Republic to avoid maneuvering around the Windward Passage's heavier traffic. The extra time in transit now put them dangerously close to the storm's track, and the decision seemed to put everyone on his ship in peril. Barsness shuddered at the thought of being caught in a hurricane with the cruise ship in tow.

He ordered the mate to turn them onto a new course that would swing them farther south and wide of the storm, avoiding the worst of the pounding waves and driving winds. He glanced through the window again at the ship under tow. Its black hulk was lit with battery-powered running lights to prevent collisions, but he could barely make them out. Were the batteries dying already? There was no way he could put crewmen on the *Galina* to change them, not in this weather. He shuddered again. The old ship was spooky.

As *Sea Tiger* changed course, turning broadside to the mounting waves, the tow cable sagged and creaked as the *Galina* took the tension, like a giant dog shaking on a leash. Barsness had never seen anything like it.

"Keep it steady," he snapped at the helmsman, Erik Sorbo, a skinny, fresh-faced man with blond hair and blue eyes who was a recent graduate of the Merchant Marine Academy. Despite Sorbo being in his early twenties, Barsness still thought of him as a kid.

"Aye, sir, I'm trying," Sorbo said. "The waves are making it difficult."

"Stand aside," Barsness barked.

Despite the captain's struggle with the controls, even he could not keep the tow cable from sagging. The cable's pop was audible on the bridge each time the tension returned. Barsness cursed, wishing he had a wheel to control the tug, instead of these bloody joysticks.

"She's not going to make it if this keeps up, sir," Sorbo said.

Barsness relinquished the controls back to the helmsman and allowed him to wrestle with the two ships while he kept his mouth shut. The joystick controls on this modern ship just weren't his forte.

Once Sorbo had completed the turn, the tension on the cable lessened. Barsness hoped the currents of the heavy following sea would give them an extra push on their way across the Caribbean. Their transition of the Mona Passage would have allowed them to make a straight run for Bluefields, but now they were dipping south toward Venezuela, making the voyage longer and less profitable due to the extra fuel being burned by the *Sea Tiger*'s powerful engines.

He picked up his coffee mug and sipped again, gazing out at *Galina Jovovich*'s weak running lights. *Had the starboard light gone out?*

With luck, the seas would smooth out and they'd make it to the breaking yard with only a day or two of delay. While the winds were still blowing hard, the waves didn't seem as tall, lessening the pitch and roll of the *Sea Tiger*.

They monitored the storm as it continued to form in the east. Capt. Barsness retired from his watch to sleep for four hours before he would spend the coming day on the bridge. He yawned as he walked to his cabin. He hung his shirt on a hanger in his closet and washed his face in the sink.

Stepping to his bunk, he dropped into bed, worried about the storm, the delay in delivering the ship, and his wife, Ruth, being home alone. He concentrated on the pleasant days they had spent together, sitting on their porch and watching the ships on the Vesterelva River sailing to and from Fredrikstad.

His alarm clock woke him from a fitful sleep, and a rising sun greeted him, streaking the sky with brilliant reds. Overnight, the waves had increased, and he could feel the *Sea Tiger* plunging and tugging at her cable. He jammed on his shoes and tugged on his shirt, buttoning it as he raced to the helm.

"What's happening, Martin?"

"The storm track has changed. It's heading right for us. I've already made a course correction, but we'll just have to ride it out. We can't move fast enough to get out of the way."

Barsness cursed and glanced at the *Galina*. She crested the waves uneasily, her bow plummeting up and down, straining against the tow cable. There wasn't anything to do but ride it out and pray for the best. He would stay on duty all the way to Bluefields if needed.

Outside, the waves continued to mount as the clouds obscured the sun and day turned into night. Rain lashed the windows, driven sideways by the high winds. With one hand on the back of the pilot's chair, Barsness continuously scanned the stormy sea beyond the front and rear windows, then checked the radar screens and instruments. They would get the worst of it; of that, he had no doubt.

It was late evening when Aadland came on deck. "You need to rest, Captain."

"Not now, Martin. I must see the ship though this storm. Then I'll rest."

The tropical storm tracked right along their course, as if sensing the *Galina* wanted nothing to do with being towed to the breaking yard. She seemed to fight them at every step. Barsness continued to fret about the integrity of the cable and the tow harness. He looked back, the *Galina*'s bow just visible, the rest of the ship shrouded by the heavy rain and fog. *Had the batteries in the running lights died?* he wondered.

In the middle of the Caribbean, the storm stalled and built into a raging hurricane, delivering force twelve winds at over one hundred miles per hour and creating forty-foot waves. Barsness ordered a further course deviation to the south, trying to skirt the edge of the storm.

His heart sank when he heard the tow cable part with a sound like a cracking whip. The loose end smacked the tug's steel superstructure with a resounding thud that reverberated through the hull.

"Ninety degrees to port, *now!*" Capt. Barsness shouted.

Sorbo jerked the joystick and the big tug responded at once, leaning hard to the left. Coffee mugs slid off consoles and shattered on the deck. Loose papers fluttered through the air as Barsness clutched the back of the helmsman's seat. The sudden maneuver would put them out of the direct path of the rudderless ship behind them.

"Straighten up, Erik," Barsness said, and Sorbo righted the tug. "Maximum speed to the south."

Barsness swore under his breath. *Sea Tiger* was a state-of-the-art ship, with the newest and the best of everything. How could this have happened? He'd never lost a ship under his tow. This would be the end of a long and prosperous career, but that was a worry for later. Right now, all that mattered was the safety of the *Sea Tiger* and his crew.

Aadland struggled across the bridge to where Barsness stood behind Sorbo's seat. "We have to track the *Galina*."

"We'll find her again," Barsness answered.

"Her AIS has been dismantled and she has no running lights," Aadland cried.

While under tow, the *Galina* didn't need the Automatic Identification System that provided course and speed along with the ship's name, as no one had expected her to break loose. Now that she was adrift in the powerful storm, there was no telling where she'd end up.

"May God have mercy on her," Barsness said, as the *Galina Jovovich* disappeared into the raging tempest.

CHAPTER TWO

Everglades Explorer
Miragoâne, Haiti

Captain Darrell Smith leaned over the middle hatch of *Everglades Explorer*, a 220-foot-long general cargo vessel, and stared into the hold. Thirty feet below, crewmen and Haitian day laborers piled bags of rice into the slings attached to the two onboard slewing cranes. He straightened and glanced around before shaking a cigarette from the half-empty pack and lit it with a plastic lighter. Smith put the lighter and the smokes back in his pocket, ran a hand through his sandy blond hair, and let the breeze cool his lean frame.

He turned and scanned the small harbor of one of the world's poorest and most dangerous countries. Low green hills rose steeply from the placid blue waters of the Bay of Miragoâne, part of the larger Gulf of Gonâve between Haiti's two large peninsulas. The town itself was a collection of bland concrete block buildings whose flat roofs seemed clustered one atop the other, leaving little room for the narrow streets and back alleys. Dominating the town's landscape was the large spire of the Saint John the Baptist Cathedral.

Smith had been to Miragoâne enough times that he knew the names of the local hookers, and his crew of Hondurans and the Estonian engineer each had their favorite. The women seemed to instinctively know when the ship would arrive, and they'd be waiting on the dock along with the usual pickpockets and thieves who were always ready to creep aboard in the dead of night and rob them blind.

White box trucks sat along the dock with a crowd of workers piling rice bags into the back of each as *Explorer*'s cranes deposited them on the quay. For every worker carrying a bag, there were five more standing around, either smoking or chatting. He couldn't wait to get this rusty tub unloaded and head back to Miami, but first he had to make a few more stops on his usual trade route.

He kept a watch rotation, but even so, his crew would get drunk on Clairin, the Haitian version of rum, and spend their evenings fornicating on the aft deck or in their staterooms. Frankly, Smith didn't mind and, at one time, he, too, had partaken in the local dalliances, but he had a wife and a baby now. He hadn't decided if he loved his new wife or not, but he loved that little girl. They'd gotten married because he'd knocked her up, and so far, things were working between them.

Robenson Girard came up the gangway and approached Smith. He was the local fixer, and he was tall and lean with a shaved head and a death's head grin. Smith liked the man, and he often brought a few extra goods not listed on the manifest for Girard to sell, and they'd split the profits. He'd brought everything from rolls of used carpet to discounted mattresses. Once, Smith had given Girard an old Honda CB750 motorcycle as a present. It was Girard's most prized possession, and it had won his loyalty to Smith.

"Cap'n Darrell," Girard said, "the port officials want you to move as soon as the holds are empty."

"I figured," Smith replied, smoke trailing from his nostrils. "There's three more ships on the hook, waiting to offload."

"What did you bring today?" Girard asked.

Smith grinned. "Bolts of cloth, but I have something special for you."

Girard raised his eyebrows, and Smith motioned for him to follow as they walked to Smith's cabin. Smith unlocked the door and they stepped inside the cramped room, equipped with a bunk, fold-down table, and two hanging lockers. Smith removed a red three-drawer toolbox from a locker. He'd bought it at a pawnshop, and it contained a wide assortment of mismatched tools covered in a fine patina of rust.

The Haitian's eye widened when he opened the drawers, and he dropped to his knees to examine the tools. "It's too much, Cap'n Darrell."

"Don't complain to me that you don't have enough tools to fix your motorcycle anymore."

"And if I complain that I don't have any money?"

"We'll work on that on the next load. I'll have more mattresses ready."

Girard grinned and hefted the toolbox. "And I'll have more buyers."

The two men emerged on deck and found the first mate, Charles Navard—a squat, thick man with forearms like Popeye—leaning over the open hold, shouting at the workers to sweep up the spilled rice and stuff it into bags. They could get a good price for the bag, even with the dust and rust from the hold mixed with the grain.

Navard turned when Smith and Girard approached.

"Almost empty, Captain. All that's left is your special merchandise."

"Let's load it into a sling and get it overboard. Then we need to make ready to move to the anchorage."

A frown crossed Navard's face.

"Don't worry, Charlie," Smith said. "You can party with your woman tonight. We'll leave tomorrow."

Navard rubbed his hands together and glanced aft to where, Smith guessed, she waited with a full bottle of booze.

An hour later, the crew had unloaded the unusually patterned bolts of cotton cloth that Smith had bought from a Miami wholesaler and had moved *Everglades Explorer* to the anchorage where the crew's party kicked into high gear. Smith took the late watch, allowing Navard half the night to party with his whore. Not that it mattered much. The woman would keep him occupied during his watch, and thieves would probably try to rob them as they had before, but at least at anchor, there was less of a chance for them to do so.

With the ship riding easily on the placid waters, Smith went to the kitchen where Juan, his Honduran cook, had made beef and gravy over rice. Smith gobbled it down and retired to his cabin to fill out the ship's log and to get some sleep before his watch.

The alarm clock brought Smith out of a dream and he struggled to wake up, sitting on the edge of his bunk and rubbing his face until he could keep his eyes open. He pulled on a pair of clean coveralls and slipped through the quiet passageways to the galley. He poured himself a cup of coffee and headed up the steps to make his rounds.

As he stepped onto the main deck, music from a nearby radio drifted on the breeze. He walked to the bow and back, checking the hatch covers to make sure that stowaways hadn't disturbed them. He'd once had three men hide in the hold for the journey to the States and, when he had arrived,

Immigration had forced him to keep the men under lock and key until he could return them to Haiti. Smith had felt so sorry for the pitiful-looking men. He hated keeping them locked up and vowed to never let a stowaway on his ship again, so he examined every space, locker, compartment, and hold before sailing, and he'd do it again tomorrow morning.

Smith walked aft to where his men partied on the stern. There were only a handful left on deck, and several were openly engaged in copulation. He snorted and turned away.

Eventually, the music stopped, and the ship swung silently on her anchor under a star-filled night sky. Smith liked these early morning watches, when the world was asleep, and the sky lightened in the east. He sat in the pilot's seat with his feet propped on the console. His eyes grew heavy despite the multiple cups of hot coffee. Soon his eyelids fluttered, and his chin dropped to his chest, totally oblivious to the danger he and his men were soon to face.

CHAPTER THREE

Captain Smith didn't hear the wooden pangas ease alongside the *Explorer*, nor the pirates who clamored up the ladder and crept quietly through the darkened ship, zip tying the crew and their escorts. It wasn't until the pirate leader thrust a gun barrel under Smith's chin that he awoke, and Smith stared at the man holding the Colt 1911 pistol. He thought he was Latino from his light skin and dark hair, but there was something Eastern European about his features, making it hard for Smith to accurately judge which country the pirate was from. Rugged stubble grew on his cheeks and strong chin. He wasn't much taller than Smith, and he had a determined look in his hooded eyes.

The pirates walked Smith down to the aft deck where the other crewmen knelt beside the railing. Navard and his woman lay dead, killed by a single bullet to the back of their heads while intertwined in their lovemaking. Smith felt the vomit rise in his throat at the sight and staggered forward to the rail to throw up.

Under his feet, the deck began to vibrate as the engine started. The anchor chain rattled in the hawsepipe as it came aboard. Smith realized these men were stealing his ship, and there was nothing he could do about it. He glanced at the bodies on the deck and at the blood that had drained into the scupper. The vomit rose again.

The pirate leader said something to the other pirates in a language that Smith didn't understand, but he recognized some words, and they struck fear in his heart. *Allahu Akbar*— God is greater. He thought of it as the call sign of Islamic terrorism. One by one, the pirates forced the crewmen to their knees and delivered a bullet from a suppressed pistol into the back of their heads.

Smith cringed with each wet *splat* the bullets made as they entered his crewmen's heads. He prayed they would spare his life and that he would see his baby again. The gun cycled in the cool air, making a *clack-clack* as it ratcheted another round into the chamber after each shot.

Then, as the shooter took aim at Smith, the ship lurched. He knew the anchor had come off the seabed. Off balance, the pirate missed the captain's head, and the bullet hit him between the right shoulder blade and the spine. Smith felt the hot lead tunnel through his flesh and explode out of his chest, just below his collar bone. He fell forward and passed out.

Several seconds later, the pain brought him back to reality. His right side felt like it was on fire. The ship hadn't moved, still idling for some reason. He automatically wondered if they were adrift. He lifted his head and saw the lights of Miragoâne rocking gently back and forth.

With great effort, he pulled himself forward, over the edge of the ship, and fell into the water below. He wanted to keep falling and never go back up. The pain burned through him, and he pictured his baby. With every ounce of strength, he fought through the pain and swam up with his good arm.

The deep throb made by the turning of the *Explorer*'s

propeller caused him to pause. His lungs screamed for air, and his ear drums pulsed with the sound of the giant blades that could chop his body into pieces with a single turn. When he couldn't ignore his need for oxygen any longer, he fought upward.

His head broke the surface and he drew in a deep breath of air. Fire swept through his body at the sudden expansion of his rib cage, and he almost passed out again. He saw his ship heading out the channel to the Gulf of Gonâve.

Smith lay on his back, taking shallow breaths and doing scissor kicks toward land. The incoming tide had swept him away from the ship while he was underwater, saving him from certain death when the *Explorer*'s prop had started to spin. He was alive because the idiots running the ship hadn't put her in gear when the anchor had stopped holding the ship in place.

He wasn't sure how long he'd been in the water, but when his feet touched the ground, he rolled over and tried to stand. His weary gaze fell on two men standing beside a wooden fishing boat. They stared right back at him. He waded forward, slipping in the muck and mud, falling face first into the water. This seemed to spur the men into action, and they raced to his aid.

They hooked the captain under the armpits and dragged him toward the shore. Smith screamed in agony as one of the men put pressure on his wound.

Before he passed out, he croaked, "Find Robenson Girard."

DARRELL SMITH AWOKE in a small room with tan walls and bright lights. A white man and woman hovered over him and spoke in hushed tones. The pain he was experiencing was now a dull ache. He saw the woman remove a bloody bandage as the man handed her a clean one to put in its place. When she'd finished smoothing the tape across his skin, she glanced at his face.

She nudged her co-worker and said, "He's awake."

The man leaned in closer. "How do you feel, Mr. Smith?"

"Bad," Smith croaked. He licked his lips and swallowed, trying to clear the hoarseness from his throat. "Everything hurts."

With a smile, the man said, "You've been shot, so that's to be expected. I'm Dr. Murphy, and this is Sister Barb. You're at the Catholic clinic."

"Am I still in Haiti?" Smith asked.

"Yes. Your fixer brought you here. We patched you up and called for a medivac flight to take you back to Miami. It should be here in a few hours."

Smith nodded, and his eyes fluttered before he passed out again.

He was going home.

CHAPTER FOUR

Caribbean Sea
Bluefields, Nicaragua

The only sounds Ryan Weller could hear in the ink-black water were the hiss of the regulator as he breathed in, the rumble of bubbles as he breathed out, and the thrusters of the cable-laying barge, *El Paso City*, as she labored to stay in place ninety feet above him.

Rafted to the side of the barge was the salvage vessel *Peggy Lynn*, where a compressor and blending station provided him with a constant supply of nitrox—oxygen-enriched air—which flowed through the umbilical hose that connected the compressor to his yellow Kirby Morgan dive helmet. Affixed to the helmet were powerful lights that illuminated the dark seabed and the thick submarine cable he was inspecting after being rousted from bed in the dead of night.

Ryan threw the control valve forward on a water-jet trenching tool and immediately cut his visibility to zero as the water jet blasted a deep groove in the rock, sand, and mud, throwing up a thick cloud of particulates. The lights on his helmet barely cut through the gloom.

Ryan was investigating the reason why the subsea cable trencher had stopped dead in its tracks. The trencher was a twenty-five-ton, sled-like device fitted with a single nine-foot-long plowshare, which, together with a multitude of high-pressure water jets, carved a furrow in the seabed for the cable to lie in. The sled now hung suspended from the *EPC*'s crane cable, with just a foot of the plow share still in the trench as Ryan worked underneath it. It was an older model on skis and sled runners instead of the newer robotic trenchers that ran on treads, like an underwater combat tank.

In the early 2000s, New World Network had laid ARCOS, the Americas Region Caribbean Optical-Ring System, a fiber-optic cable which circled the Caribbean, touching twenty-three ports in sixteen countries between its start and end in southern Florida. Technology had rapidly evolved in the twenty years since NWN had first laid the cable.

As traffic on the ARCOS had increased and slowed the capacity of the aging line, NWN decided to run a newer, larger cable capable of accommodating hundreds of terabytes. The Cloud wasn't in the sky with satellite networks, but on millions of miles of subsea cables that crisscrossed the oceans, often at depths over eight thousand feet and under pressure so great it was like holding up a car with only a thumb.

It was the job of divers like Ryan to not only install new cables, but to inspect the old ones to ensure they remained operational. On occasions where they did fail, the divers fixed them as rapidly as possible to limit Internet blackouts.

He worked with a group of free spirits, operating from the *Peggy Lynn*, a ninety-foot-long converted fishing trawler.

Their primary employer was Dark Water Research, a worldwide commercial dive and salvage conglomerate. Because of *Peggy Lynn*'s size, they often found themselves in tiny foreign ports doing jobs a larger DWR crew and vessel could not. They also took on bigger roles like this one, trenching a new branch of the ARCOS trunk line to Big Corn Island off the coast of Nicaragua.

Satisfied with his work, Ryan shut off the water and the current carried away the silt, allowing him to see the hole he had dug. Once he had an unobstructed view, he stepped down into it, asking for slack in the umbilical from his tender.

The umbilical was the life support system of a commercial diver. Not only did it deliver life-sustaining air, it also consisted of a synthetic line, acting as a strength member and attached to his dive harness by a D-ring just behind his head, a pneumofathometer hose, used for measuring depth, and fiber-optic video and communication lines, allowing topside control to maintain comms and view and record everything the diver did. They had wrapped those four lines together at short intervals with colored tape to mark the depth.

With his tender handling everything topside, all Ryan had to do was concentrate on the dive and uncover the mystery of the stalled trencher. He blasted away again with the jet and found an enormous boulder that had damaged the trencher's plow teeth and water jets.

After adjusting the nozzle on the trenching tool, he used the power of high-pressure water to slice through the boulder, clearing the way for the trencher to resume operations.

"Well, shit," Ryan said, after letting the silt clear again.

"What?" Stacey Wisnewski asked. She was sitting at a computer station on *Peggy Lynn*'s bridge, watching his helmet cam footage on a large monitor.

"I just cut through another cable. I thought we were supposed to be paralleling the old one."

"Did you just say you cut another cable?" Stacey asked, with hope in her voice that she had heard wrong.

"Sorry, Purple, but you heard right. I cut through another submarine cable." Stacey had dyed her brunette hair purple long before Ryan had met her at a dive shop in Key Largo where they'd both worked as dive instructors. Now she was a jack-of-all-trades on the salvage vessel. "It was on the back side of this boulder. Can't you see it?" He moved his helmet nearer to the cable, so the camera had a close view of the frayed fiber-optic strands.

"I see it," she said with annoyance.

"I hope your insurance is paid in full," Capt. Dennis Law said into the topside microphone. It didn't surprise Ryan to hear him. He was always on the bridge during diving operations, even during the long decompression stops. Dennis was in his seventies, with a thick head of white hair and a trimmed white beard. Ryan had never seen the old man in anything other than khaki pants, tennis shoes, and a faded red T-shirt with the name *Peggy Lynn* arched above the left breast pocket. He was owner and master of the vessel, named in memory of his late wife.

"Hey, I just work here," Ryan said. "You need to ask Travis about the insurance."

Travis Wisnewski had stepped into Ryan's old role as the salvage crew's leader while Ryan often worked on other projects for DWR.

"Hold on. I'll ask *EPC* what they want to do," Dennis said.

Ryan sat on the edge of the pit and let out a lengthy sigh. He hoped this was the old branch line, or they would have a long night pulling the cut cable out of the dirt so *EPC* could haul the severed ends aboard and have her engineers splice the cable back together.

If it was the cable they were replacing, he figured they'd

leave it alone and finish running the new one. The islanders could live without Internet for a few days. *Well*, he smiled ruefully as he thought to himself, *they'll have to, no matter what.*

He propped his elbows on his knees and let the heavy helmet sag onto his balled fists. "How much bottom time do I have, Anthony?"

"Ten minutes," the skinny black youth replied. Anthony had become a part of the crew eight months ago when they'd needed help to recover shipping containers that had spilled from a freighter in the U.S. Virgin Islands.

It's only been five minutes since the last time check? It seemed like forever. Ryan stared at the groove in the boulder and the frayed cable, watching a fish swim into his light to search through the debris he had stirred up while cutting the boulder. Both the light and the swirling silt attracted fish which the divers sometimes speared for food. Mostly, the fish were curious about what the intruders were doing in their natural environment. On occasions, larger predators like sharks and goliath groupers swooped in to investigate.

Stacey's voice came back through the speaker. "*EPC* wants you to mark the cable ends with locator beacons. They're not sure which cable you cut, but we'll find out soon. Anthony will drop the beacons to you."

The acoustical beacons dropped down a line to his position. Anthony had rigged them with short lengths of cord, and Ryan tied one to each end of the severed cable. Next, he covered them with an inch of dirt to keep them in place. The beacons would emit a ping for thirty days, allowing the repair crew to use a sonar locator to find the break in the cable.

This was one of the most boring dives Ryan had made in a long time, and he wanted a little action to liven it up.

Later, he'd realize that that was a thought he wished he'd never had.

CHAPTER FIVE

As Ryan rigged the acoustical beacons on the seabed, Capt. Law stood on the bridge of the *Peggy Lynn*, holding a cup of coffee. He peered out the window into the heavy fog that reflected the bright glare of the overhead work lights as they shone from both *EPC* and his own vessel. He hated being rafted to the barge, but it saved them fuel and they could take advantage of the larger vessel's stability as his divers worked in the mist. Despite the *EPC*'s heavy fenders and the massive tires chained to *Peggy Lynn*'s rails, the waves still slammed the two boats together, sending shudders through the smaller vessel.

The wind had picked up to increase the wave height, as predicted by the weather service. Rain squalls tore through the area, decreasing visibility and slowing their work. A tropical storm was moving in on the tail of the earlier hurricane, which had stalled in the middle of the Caribbean before churning northward over Cuba and eventually flooding Louisiana. The weather hypothesizers hadn't forecasted that the storm would become a hurricane, and Dennis had no illusions that this coming storm would do as they claimed.

Meteorology's the only job in the world where you can be wrong all the time and still get paid, he lamented to himself.

The radio crackled behind him. "*Peggy Lynn*, we're reading the acoustical locators, but we have something funny on the radar. Can you take a look and tell me what you see? Over."

"Roger, *EPC*," Dennis replied and stepped to his radar. Their radar dome wasn't as high as the *EPC*'s, which sat atop the barge's five-story structure, and he doubted he would be able to see whatever they were looking at. He zoomed it out to the maximum setting and stared at the sweep arm. After several passes, he spoke into the mic, "All I can see is rain and storm clutter. Over."

"Roger that."

"What are you seeing?" Dennis asked.

"It looks like a ship, but it's not responding to AIS inquires or radio hails."

"Probably a local fishing or lobster boat."

"Roger that. *EPC* out."

———

CAUGHT in the current and concealed by the burgeoning storm, the *Galina Jovovich* hid in the violent rain, limiting the radar's ability to detect her. She swept toward the unsuspecting crews and slammed into the side of *El Paso City* with deadly force, T-boning the cable layer's bow just ahead of *Peggy Lynn*'s position.

EPC's dynamic positioning system switched off with the sudden impact, and the boats began to drift. The *Galina*'s bow sheared away a substantial section of the barge's outer skin, allowing seawater to flood her compartments. With her bow jammed against the *EPC*, the *Galina*'s stern drifted toward the *EPC*'s stern, threatening to pinch *Peggy Lynn* between them.

The impact threw Anthony, the dive tender, backward. He landed hard against the air compressor and gashed the back of his head open. He staggered to his feet, paying out Ryan's umbilical as fast as he could to relieve the strain and help his diver while ignoring the hammering pain in his skull and the blood pouring down his back, soaking his shirt.

Emery Ducane, *Peggy Lynn*'s octogenarian cook and handyman, fell from his perch on a stool beside the recompression chamber where Travis Wisnewski waited out his scheduled stops after his long dive. Emery lay flat on his back, staring up at *EPC*'s crane arm, now listing over the smaller salvage vessel.

The pounding coming from inside the chamber brought Emery out of his daze, and he slowly shook his head to clear it. He glanced up to see Travis's face pressed against the tiny porthole. Travis stopped pounding on the chamber hatch and shouted something, although Emery couldn't make out what he was saying through the ringing in his head.

As *El Paso City* listed to the right as she sank, she pulled on the lines holding *Peggy Lynn* to her, dragging the smaller vessel down with her.

Gary Bartwell, the backup diver on *Peggy Lynn*—a bear of a man with long brown hair and a beard—sprang from his place on the dressing bench and grabbed the ax mounted to the bridge's bulkhead. With a mighty swing, he severed the stern rope and ran toward the bow. An explosion aboard the barge knocked him off his feet, and the ax skittered out of his hand.

Stacey Wisnewski shook in her seat as she monitored Ryan's dive through the camera feed displayed on a large flat-screen monitor. She glanced at the screen and saw nothing but gray mud, then twisted to see Capt. Dennis sprawled on the floor, his eyes closed and his mouth open. She jumped from her chair and checked his jugular vein for a pulse while putting her cheek close to his mouth. His pulse was strong, and his warm exhalations moistened her skin. Satisfied he didn't need more urgent care, she stood, determined to find out what had caused the commotion.

The exterior work lights on the salvage vessel illuminated a macabre scene. Not only was the barge on fire and sinking, but the high steel hull of the ghost ship and that of the barge would collide and trap them in a deadly pincer movement.

Stacey couldn't let that happen. She jumped to the wheel, flipped the switches to start the vessel's two diesel drive engines, and threw full reverse power to them. *Peggy Lynn*'s stern had swung free, but the bow was still being pulled down by the barge.

Gary appeared and attacked the bow line with his dive knife. The rope separated with a crack like a snapping whip.

Suddenly, the RPM gauge for the starboard engine bounced into the red zone, accompanied by the screaming of the engine. She slapped the kill switch to keep it from destroying itself. With one good engine left, Stacey backed the boat out from between the other two vessels and watched as the ghost ship collided with the *EPC*, then slid metal on metal in a ghastly scream like nails on a chalkboard that set her teeth on edge and made her cringe.

Clear of the two ships, Stacey put the drive into neutral. They would need to ensure their diver was safe, then give aid to the survivors. She turned to see Gary standing in the bridge's door, panting.

"You wrapped Ryan's umbilical in the prop," he said.

CHAPTER SIX

Ryan finished securing the beacons to the subsea cable. Just as he rose to his feet, the trencher plunged down, smacking him in the back of the helmet and driving him into the ground. At the same time, he heard the teeth-gritting sound of metal against metal as something on the surface sheared and popped. He was struggling to wiggle out from under the trenching rig when the hydraulic shockwave from an explosion rippled through the water.

Fortunately, the seabed's soft sediment, distance from the detonation, and the water's depth all combined to save him from most of the initial, and subsequent, rapid-gas expansions in a non-compressible environment. In short, he was lucky to be alive.

Ryan tried to get onto all fours, but the trencher's plow kept him from moving. Twisting to discover what the problem was, he felt the crushing weight of the plow settle even further until it covered the hole, trapping him. He couldn't roll to his left without the eighty-cubic-foot aluminum dive cylinder strapped to his back hitting the plow's frame, and rolling to his right, the bailout bottle collided with the side of the hole. The plow's sword jet, designed to help soften the mud and sand for the plow shear, allowed Ryan to lift his head just a couple of inches off the seafloor. When he tried to back out again, his butt hit the shear, confirming that it had fallen between his legs.

"Guys?" he asked tentatively as the shrieking of metal died away.

When no response came, he reached over his shoulder and grasped the umbilical. He pulled on it to ensure it was clear of the plow. The holographic Diver Augmented Visual Display, or DAVD, projected onto the faceplate of his dive helmet, allowing him to see blueprints and three-dimensional terrain mapping as well as life support status. It told Ryan that he was still breathing from the overhead compressor, but with all the topside commotion, he had no idea how long it would last.

He jerked the umbilical toward him, trying to stretch it taut, and gave it five sharp tugs to tell Anthony he was in trouble. Ryan closed his eyes as he concentrated on dragging the umbilical in one-handed. He'd had Anthony keep it tight while he worked, but now all he was getting was a pile of umbilical beside him.

Opening his eyes, he saw the tiny tank icon on the DAVD flashing, indicating he was now breathing from the bailout bottle.

He now only had twenty minutes to extricate himself from the hole before he ran out of air.

CHAPTER SEVEN

Stacey wanted to vomit. Not only was the *EPC* sinking before her very eyes, but she had just severed Ryan's umbilical and fouled *Peggy Lynn*'s starboard propeller.

"Get us over him, *now*," Dennis commanded. He'd sat up and was cradling his left arm in his lap.

Stacey came out of her fog and shouted at Gary, "Get suited up. Prepare to dive on my command."

Gary raced to the aft deck to gather and don his equipment, and Stacey turned to the GPS screen, pushing the button to guide the ship over Ryan's last known coordinates.

"What's going on with the *EPC*?" Dennis asked.

"She's going down."

"Send Gary down on the doubles and get the workboat in the water."

"Get up," Stacey said. "You need to take the helm."

"I can't. I think I broke my arm."

Stacey picked up the microphone for the speaker mounted on the bridge bulkhead. "Gary, dive on doubles, and take a spare cylinder. Anthony, get in the SeaArk and rescue the survivors."

Once the *Peggy Lynn*'s position matched the coordinates for the hole Ryan had been digging, she set the ship's dynamic positioning system. Linked to their GPS, the DPS would use the bow and stern thruster to make continual adjustments to stay over the diver.

"Can you watch the wheel?" Stacey asked Dennis. "I need to make sure everyone is all right."

Dennis nodded. Stacey helped him to the captain's chair and grabbed the first aid kit that hung on the wall. She wrapped his arm tightly with ACE bandages before fashioning a sling.

"Do you want some pain medication?"

"No." Dennis pushed her away. "You've got work to do. I'll be fine."

She jumped over the door coaming and raced down the steps to the main deck. She saw Emery rigging a round fender with a long rope and an anchor to act as a downline for Gary and to mark the location of both Ryan and the plow. He dropped the anchor over the side, and the rope ran overboard as he turned to help Gary shrug into his back-mounted double cylinders.

Stacey stepped over to the recompression chamber, checked the time, and kissed the porthole where Travis had his sunburned face pressed against the glass. His sandy blond hair stuck out at odd angles, and he still reminded her of Zac Efron, just like the day they had met in the parking lot of a Key Largo dive shop. She laid two fingers of her right hand on her upper left arm, showing he had twenty minutes of decompression time remaining. She pressed the talk button and said, "A ship ran into *EPC*, and I accidentally cut Ryan's umbilical when I threw the ship in reverse. We're mounting a rescue."

"Let me out!"

She shook her head. "No." Letting him out now would

subject him to the bends. He needed to remain in the chamber for the allotted time to eliminate the nitrogen from the tissues of his body.

"Stacey, give me a hand," Anthony called. Reluctantly, she turned away from her husband's troubled face and helped to lower the twenty-four-foot SeaArk center console workboat from its davits into the water.

"Are you okay?" she asked, seeing the blood on the back of his shirt and the towel wrapped around his head.

"I'm good," he replied without stopping.

Once Anthony was in the SeaArk and racing toward the sinking cable layer, barely visible above the waterline, Stacey asked Emery, "What do we need, Grandpa?" Everyone on the crew called the old man Grandpa, not just because he was old enough to be their grandfather, but because they respected him and his experience.

"I won't know until Gary finds Ryan."

"Okay. I need to get back to the bridge. Dennis broke his arm."

"How is he?" Grandpa asked. He and Dennis had worked together for more years than either of them wanted to remember, and they were practically family.

"He'll be okay, but he needs medical attention. The bone didn't break the skin, but I could feel it moving when I splinted it."

Emery grimaced. "Make sure he doesn't over-self-medicate."

Stacey nodded, knowing that he meant she needed to keep Dennis away from the Jim Beam.

Interrupted by the speaker connected to Gary's communication unit on his OTS Aga full-face mask, both turned in astonishment when they heard him say, "I found both ends of the umbilical, but not Ryan."

CHAPTER EIGHT

Ryan had tried to bull his way forward and push his way backward to no effect. He couldn't struggle, or he'd quickly burn through the air in the bailout bottle. Diligently, he scooped out mud and sand from under his helmet and chest to force his way far enough under the sword jet arm to get clear of the plow. He wouldn't have enough air to make a complete set of decompression stops, but he would suck the tank dry to try to stave off the dreaded bends. If *Peggy Lynn* were still afloat, they could throw him in the recompression chamber and keep him from getting bent.

If she wasn't still up there?

Well, that was a thought for another time.

He kept scooping, trying to keep his breathing slow and controlled. What he wanted to do was frantically scoop away the sand that kept backsliding into the hole he was excavating. After several large scoops, he was able to slide forward and bring his leg around the plow blade. With both legs together, he backed out from under the plow and found he had to dig at the edge of the crater to get out. Just as he started pawing at the soil, the plow slowly tilted to the left, then suddenly jerked free of the hole, and landed on its side.

Ryan stood transfixed, watching the plow dig a wide furrow through the muck before stopping fifty feet away. The sound of crushing and twisting metal reached him, and he looked up to see the hull of the *El Paso City* crash onto the seabed one hundred feet away from him, some of its powerful lights still glowing brightly.

"That's not good," he muttered to himself.

The tank display flashed on his faceplate, and he focused on it. He was down to fifteen hundred pounds of air. He had two choices: stay on the seafloor and die of asphyxiation, or swim to the surface and suffer the bends, and he had no idea if there was still a ship there, awaiting his return.

As he continued to steady his breathing, Ryan settled on a third choice. *EPC* had dive gear aboard, and he'd been in her dive locker on several occasions. He started swimming toward the barge and stopped when he heard the sound of engines laboring overhead. Ryan hoped it was *Peggy Lynn,* and that they would send a rescue diver. It should be their top priority and knowing Dennis like he did, he would be doing everything possible to help him and the survivors of the shipwreck.

Swimming toward the *EPC*, he could see that she lay on her starboard side. Tools, wreckage, and parts lay strewn across the seafloor. Part of the subsea cable had fallen out of the massive basket that traversed the width of the barge and now lay in a tangle beside the wreck.

"I know what we'll be doing next," Ryan said to himself.

The wreck was both an environmental hazard and a danger to the shipping lanes. It would be Dark Water Research's top priority to raise the *El Paso City* and recover the subsea cable, saving the network company and DWR millions of dollars.

Now, as Ryan stared at the *EPC*, he knew he needed to

find a supply of air, or the crew of the *Peggy Lynn* would be recovering his body.

Not wanting to drag the umbilical, he sawed through it with his dive knife, leaving just a three-foot length attached to his helmet, and tucked it into his belt. He set off for the barge again, visualizing the steps he would take once he found a gas supply. First, he'd have to doff the helmet, put on the mask he carried in the thigh pocket of his wetsuit, and rig two cylinders to breathe from. At least he could sit on the barge's rail and, according to his computer, be at the forty-foot mark for his first decompression stop. It also told him that he'd been underwater for thirty minutes, ten of which he'd been on bailout.

The bailout bottle was two-thirds depleted when Ryan reached the barge. He wasted no time examining the wreck, instead swimming quickly to the dive locker. Once inside the cramped room, he had to orient himself to the ship's sideways tilt. He spotted a regulator beside a harness-style buoyancy compensating device, or BCD, both of which he mounted on a tank. Next came the hard part. He unlatched the helmet from the watertight ring around his neck. The air pressure in the helmet kept the water from flooding in, but once he'd pulled it off, a wave of water would swirl around his head and up his nose.

He drew in a deep breath and pulled the helmet off. Moving quickly, he shoved his dive mask against his face and exhaled just enough to clear the water before seating the strap on the back of his head. Next, he took a breath from the regulator on the tank he'd rigged and removed his working harness and bailout cylinder, setting them and the helmet out of the way. He'd be back for them soon.

Ryan pulled on the BCD and tightened the waist and shoulder straps. He rigged two more bottles with pieces of rope and hung them on his harness. Finally, he made his way out of the locker and swam toward the superstructure. On the way, he spotted one of the barge's mooring lines and knotted one end to a round fender which bobbed in the current, floating like a giant balloon from the ship's railing. He cut the rope holding the fender to the ship and watched it rocket upward, trailing the rope he'd tied to it. When the fender reached the surface, the rope slackened, and Ryan tied the bitter end to the railing. Now, he had an ascent line.

He sat down on the hull and watched the minutes of his safety stop tick down on his computer and his Citizen dive watch. Glancing around, he saw most of the automatic life rafts had inflated when the *EPC* sank. Above, he could hear an outboard motor, which he guessed belonged to *Peggy Lynn*'s aluminum workboat.

Through the darkness, Ryan saw a light flashing as it swept in an arc. He recognized the beam of a dive light stabbing through the darkness. Figuring someone from *Peggy Lynn* had come looking for him, he pulled his dive knife from its sheath and banged its butt against the *EPC*'s steel hull. The light swung in a circle before focusing on the source of the pounding. A few minutes later, Gary swam up and sat down beside Ryan. He said something into his communications unit which sounded like mumbling to Ryan, and Ryan flashed his deco schedule with his fingers.

Gary nodded and said something else unintelligible into his comms gear while they worked their way up the ascent line Ryan had rigged. They stopped halfway up, and Gary motioned for them to hold. The heavy sounds of prop wash carried through the water. Ryan saw *Peggy Lynn*'s bright underwater work lights as she coasted alongside the rubber fender that marked their location. The prop stopped, and the gentle sounds of the thrusters, laboring to keep the ship in position, took over.

The two divers floated in silence for another two minutes

before Gary motioned them upward again. They swam straight for *Peggy Lynn*'s stern ladder and climbed aboard. As soon as Ryan was on the ship, Anthony told him to strip and get into the recompression chamber that Travis had just vacated. Ryan left a trail of gear in his wake until he wore only his compression shorts, and he climbed into the single-man chamber where he stretched out on the thinly padded bunk, pulling a cotton towel over him as the door slammed. Within seconds, the chamber was blowing him back down to eighty feet.

Through the speaker, Grandpa said, "We'll bring you up slow."

Ryan tapped the tank's metal wall with his knuckle to show he understood and closed his eyes. He began a breathing regimen to encourage his body to relax. In for a three count; hold; out for four. He soon drifted into an uneasy sleep, troubled by the work ahead.

CHAPTER NINE

When Ryan exited the chamber, *EPC* crewmen crowded *Peggy Lynn*'s deck, and the vessel was limping toward Bluefields on its single engine. He pulled on shorts and a faded DWR T-shirt and looked for familiar faces as he made his way to the bridge with Travis, who had been monitoring the chamber while Grandpa, Anthony, and Gary served coffee and warm soup to their waterlogged passengers.

On *Peggy Lynn*'s bridge, Mike Wetzel, *EPC*'s captain, sipped coffee as he stared out the rear window at his personnel gathered on the aft deck. Stacey stood at the wheel, and Dennis sat in the captain's chair, cradling his arm.

Ryan found his coffee cup, wiped it out with the tail of his T-shirt, poured hot coffee, and took a sip before asking no one in particular, "What happened while I was playing in the dirt?"

Stacey gave him a blow-by-blow description. She finished with, "We found sixty-five souls. Five are unaccounted for."

"It's my fault," Wetzel said. "I should have been more attentive when my radarman told me about the mystery blip."

"It's not your fault, Mike," Dennis said. "It's one of those freak things that can happen at sea."

Wetzel shook his head. "No. I'm the captain. I'm responsible. I should have paid attention when Jeff told me he had something suspicious on radar. I assumed it was the weather. I was too distracted by everything else."

"What could you have done?" Travis asked. "You were tethered to the seabed. There was nowhere for you to go."

Wetzel stared down at his crew. Dennis waved his hand to silence the conversation and said, "Tell us about your dive, Ryan."

Ryan recounted the harrowing tale of being caught beneath the plow and how he'd managed to escape. Pouring more coffee, he asked, "Has anyone called Greg?"

"Not yet," Dennis said, "but Captain Wetzel called Chatel."

Ryan knew Dennis meant retired Admiral Kip Chatel, current CEO of Dark Water Research, a man Greg Olsen had selected to succeed him when Greg had stepped down. He still helped with special projects, but his new focus was on his private military contracting company, Trident. He'd asked Ryan to join him at the PMC, but Ryan had wanted to remain with his crew.

The crew watched as Stacey guided *Peggy Lynn* through the deep-water channel between the city of El Bluff on the El Bluff Peninsula and the tiny island of Isla Casaba Cay. It was a relief to enter the protected waters and end the constant battering from the waves and wind. While Ryan had been in the recompression chamber, Gary had tried to cut the umbilical from around the prop and shaft, but the waves had made it too difficult and Dennis had ordered him out of the water to prevent further injury.

Stacey had to be careful to stay within the navigational beacons on the way to Bluefields, fighting the pull of the single engine as it pushed them to starboard. The wide bay shoaled to just two to three feet deep on either side of the dredged channel. When they reached the ferry dock, Ryan, Travis, and Gary secured the ship to the dock bollards.

Even though it was late, the Nicaraguan Army troops who guarded the dock flocked to the pier, guns drawn.

Ryan threw his hands up and said in Spanish, "These people are survivors of a shipwreck. We'll offload them and moor the boat in the bay."

The lieutenant in charge of the troops stepped forward, his hand still on his sidearm. "What shipwreck?" He was a short, stocky man with a wrinkled, sweat-stained shirt, whose name badge said, 'Baltazar.'

Ryan explained what had happened and asked if there were accommodations available for the crew in town. Baltazar demanded to see the ship's papers, visas for everyone, operational permits, and declarations of firearms and money.

"We have several people who need medical attention," Ryan told the man. "Can you call a doctor for us?"

"I must see the paperwork first."

Ryan retreated to the bridge and returned with the permits from the Ministry of Trade, Industry, and Development in Managua, along with passports and paperwork for *Peggy Lynn*'s crew. He also slipped several one-hundred-dollar bills into his passport and handed it over first. He didn't declare any weapons or cash, even though the vessel had an abundance of both hidden in various compartments.

Lt. Baltazar glanced up sharply when he saw the bills, but then a smile creased his face. He gave a cursory glance at the other paperwork. "Welcome to Bluefields, *Señor* Weller. My men will escort your people to a local hotel and call a doctor."

"*Gracias*." Ryan motioned for the *EPC* crewmen to follow the lieutenant.

The crew were split between two hotels. Ryan carried a Mastercard Black Card in his name and embossed with the DWR logo, which he used to pay for the hotel rooms and purchase meals for the crews.

When he returned to the *Peggy Lynn*, Ryan found the crew ready to cast off. Dennis remained in his chair on the bridge. Ryan paused at the door. "I got you a room, Captain."

Dennis narrowed his eyes. "I'm staying with my ship."

"No, you need to get your arm looked at," Ryan said. "Go ashore, see the doctor, and spend the night at the hotel. We'll get you in the morning."

Stacey and Travis agreed. Grandpa leaned over the rail and spat a stream of tobacco into the water. He was usually the one to sway Dennis. "You're no good to us with a bad wing, whippersnapper."

Ryan laughed. He and Travis were the ones Grandpa usually called 'whippersnapper' when he wanted to correct or admonish them.

Dennis grimaced as he stood. "Fine."

Grandpa sped below deck, and by the time Dennis stepped onto the pier, he'd reappeared with a gym bag and Ryan's backpack. He handed both to Ryan, who then guided Dennis up the street to the hotel.

As they walked, Dennis glanced over his shoulder to see *Peggy Lynn* easing away from the pier. "Treat my boat right, Stacey," he mumbled.

"You know they will. They love her as much as you do."

"What about you?" Dennis asked.

"She's carried us through a lot of rough water," Ryan said.

"You're choosing your words, son. I'm grateful for you getting me off my ass and out of Key West, but every time you show up, I'm holding my breath, waiting for the other shoe to drop."

The words startled Ryan, and he didn't have an immediate

answer. He liked the crew and working the underwater jobs, but Dennis was right: he had a habit of disappearing.

"I know you like chasing bad guys and whatever else you and Greg cook up, but it's hard on us when you're always coming and going. We have to rotate divers from DWR when you're not here. Maybe you should go be part of his little army."

"Are you giving me the boot, Dennis?"

"No. I'm just asking you to think about the ship and crew first."

"Roger that, Captain."

Ryan took Dennis to the triage area the doctor had set up in a hotel conference room and went to get a room key for the captain. After giving it to Dennis, he left to find the bar. He needed a stiff shot of tequila and some time to figure out his next move.

CHAPTER TEN

The second-floor hotel bar and restaurant of the Hotel Casa Royale was full of the *EPC*'s crew, but Ryan wanted a quiet drink to reflect on his ordeal and celebrate his escape. Unfortunately, it was early morning and he figured none of the local bars would be open, so he settled for a drink at the hotel's bar which offered a view of the docks below, lined with local fishing boats, and in the bay he could see *Peggy Lynn*'s mooring lights.

He ordered a shot of tequila and a Toña, a pale lager made in Nicaragua, before slamming the shot and carrying the beer to a table where he knew several of the crewmen. They talked about the ghost ship that had rammed and then sank the *El Paso City*.

Ryan couldn't help but wonder where the ship had come from, where it was headed, and what other tragedies would befall unsuspecting vessels before someone corralled the wayward vessel.

The satellite phone in Ryan's backpack rang, and he excused himself to answer it.

"Tell me what happened," Greg Olsen said.

"Did you talk to Chatel?"

"I did, but I wanted to hear it straight from the horse's mouth."

"So now I'm a horse?"

Greg snickered. "More like a jackass, but that's another subject."

Ryan laughed as he moved onto the wide veranda. "Takes one to know one."

"Yeah, it does. Now give me the details."

Ryan recounted everything Stacey and the crewmen of the *EPC* had told him.

"Any idea where the ghost ship went?" Greg asked.

"No clue. I was underwater."

"She's probably caught in the northbound current, heading for the Yucatán Straits."

"That's as good a guess as any," said Ryan.

"I'm on my way down there, anyway, because we're bidding on the shipping port the Nicaraguan government wants to build in Bluefields."

"Really? Where are you now?"

"We just left Cozumel."

"Who's with you?" Ryan asked.

"Shelly, Rick, and Erica Opsal. You're not going to believe this, but she and Rick are dating."

"When did that happen?"

"Shortly after you guys came back from Mexico."

"I'll be damned. I thought she had some class."

Greg laughed again then called out, "Hey, Erica, Ryan said he thought you had more class than to go out with Rick." Into the phone, he said, "Rick just told you to do something that is anatomically impossible with your small dick."

Ryan laughed and changed the subject. "I assume you're bringing engineers to give you their opinion on the port project?"

"Chuck is flying them down in the Beechcraft."

"You're going all out on this."

"It's a major contract, and I think we can get a piece of it. Chuck is supposed to land tomorrow morning—well, this morning. I want you on the plane as soon as it lands. Tell him to fly you to Roatán and we'll hunt for the ghost ship. I'm smelling a salvage contract."

"Can't you do it with just Rick?"

"I need two people. You're my guy."

"I was afraid of that."

"What's that supposed to mean?" Greg demanded.

"Nothing. Dennis just gave me a speech about putting *Peggy Lynn* and her crew first."

"I'm your boss," Greg countered.

"No, you're not. I'm an independent contractor, and I put that crew together."

"You put them together to pull the gold out of the *Santo Domingo*. After that, it was something completely different. Do you want to be a glorified mechanic and an underwater welder, or do you want to do something fun every day with your best friend?"

"What about the tropical storm? It's heading your way."

"We're on our way to Roatán right now, and the storm is veering northeast. Stop worrying and get on the plane. Either way, I want *Peggy Lynn* over *El Paso City* as soon as the weather permits, if not sooner. I don't want someone else trying to salvage my equipment."

"You really think someone is going to horn in on salvaging your boat?"

"I don't think the good citizens of Nicaragua are well-versed in the Merchant Shipping Act of 1995, stating that all jetsam, flotsam, lagan, cargo, and wreckage remain the property of the original owners. Let's get the team over the wreck just in case."

"I'll call Travis now." Ryan thumbed the End button.

The sky was turning pink and red on the horizon, and fishermen were working around their boats, preparing to go to sea. The stench of rotten fish and garbage pervaded his senses. With the dawning light, he saw the plastic litter and trash floating at the water's edge. Despite the smell and the trash, the place had a romantic feel to it and, looking at the ancient wooden boats, he almost felt that he was with Bogart and Hepburn on *The African Queen*.

Ryan rubbed his face with both hands. He wanted to talk to *Peggy Lynn*'s crew before he took off again, and he needed to sleep. The nap in the recompression chamber had refreshed him, but his body demanded more. And now he had a sudden craving for a cigarette. It was like that when he felt tired or he'd had a beer or two. For too many years, he'd depended on the nicotine to get him through his exhaustion, particularly during multiple deployments as a U.S. Navy Explosive Ordnance Disposal technician and as a solo sailor, crossing the world's oceans.

He called Travis's sat phone and the commercial diver answered in his Michigan Upper Peninsula drawl. "Geez-o-Pete, Ryan—do you know what time it is, eh?"

"Tell me you're actually from Canada."

"Just 'cause you're on the beach having a *cole* one, doesn't mean you need to call and harass me."

Ignoring the man's regional slang for a cold beer, Ryan said, "I just talked to Greg. He wants *Peggy Lynn* over *EPC* as quickly as possible."

"Yeah, I reckoned he would." He yawned. "Where're you going?"

"Nowhere."

"Normally, you say Greg wants *us* to do this, or Greg said *we* should do that. This time, you said Greg wants *Peggy Lynn* over the *EPC*. So, I'll ask again—where ya goin'?"

"Greg is on his way down here on *Dark Water* to make a bid for work on a new port facility in Bluefields. He wants me to fly to Roatán so we can look for the ghost ship."

"When?"

"This morning after Chuck Newland lands with the engineers."

Travis was silent.

"Do you want me to stay?" Ryan asked.

"If you leave, we'll be short-handed again. We'll need everyone on this project."

"Greg is sending more people and equipment," Ryan assured him. They hadn't talked about it, but raising the *EPC* was a bigger job than the five divers on *Peggy Lynn* could handle.

"Do what you want to do, Ryan. You always do, eh?"

The call ended, and Ryan took the phone away from his ear. Did they all feel the same as Dennis? It wasn't fair that he was always jetting off on some adventure and leaving them to pick up the slack, but it was his crew, damn it. He'd put them together.

They couldn't vote him off the boat.

CHAPTER ELEVEN

Ryan went to the bar and ordered another Toña. He returned to the balcony, watching the fishermen depart with the rising sun, and bummed a cigarette. Neither the beer nor the nicotine helped him to decide what to do. He was torn between staying with the crew and leaving to help Greg. He flicked the cigarette butt away, disgusted with himself for having broken a nine month 'no smoking' streak. After washing the taste from his mouth with more beer, he ordered coffee, eggs, toast, and fruit from a passing waiter.

By the time the waiter set the coffee on the table and asked if Ryan needed cream or sugar, the diver's foul mood had worsened. Ryan shook his head and the waiter left, leaving him to stare at the brew in his cup. How many times did he have to joke that he liked his coffee black like his soul before he manifested it in his life? Ryan was always a believer in manifestation. What he visualized would come true, and now his soul was as black as the coffee, and when he took a sip, he realized it was just as bitter.

He buttered his toast and piled scrambled eggs onto it before taking a bite. The food settled his stomach and helped to put his dark thoughts behind him, but he still needed to make a decision.

Ryan was just wiping his mouth with a napkin after his last bite of fruit when his sat phone rang again. "What's up?" he asked, seeing Greg Olsen's name on the caller ID.

"I had Chuck fly along the coast on his way down to see if he could spot our mystery ship," Greg said. "He says there's an old cruise ship grounded on a coral atoll called Compass Reef about forty miles north of your position. Get there now."

"What about *El Paso City*?"

"Command decisions, Weller."

"Roger that, boss." He ended the call and waved for the check. After signing for it, he jogged to Dennis's room and knocked on the door. The captain answered it in boxer shorts and a T-shirt. He had a plaster cast encircling his left arm from his wrist to halfway up his bicep.

Ryan said, "Get dressed, old man. We've got work to do."

"What do you mean?"

Ryan explained their priorities while Dennis pulled on his pants and hunched sideways to button and zip them, accommodating for the arm cast.

"Take Travis and Gary and find a boat to take you to Compass Reef," the captain said. "I'll get *Peggy Lynn* over our cable layer."

Ryan dialed Travis's number again.

"Geez-o-Pete, Ryan," Stacey said angrily.

"Shut up and listen," he barked, amused that she had picked up her husband's vernacular. "Send the workboat for me and Dennis. Have Travis and Gary pack gear to board an abandoned ship and get Anthony in the water to clear the left prop. We've got work to do."

"Oh, *now* it's we—"

Ryan hung up before he could hear the rest of her

sarcastic retort. He and Dennis walked to the dock at the end of Calle Municipal where a line of people stood by the gate, waiting for the ferry to El Bluff. The two Americans flashed their passports to the soldier, and Ryan pointed toward the SeaArk as it drew alongside the wharf.

The sentry allowed them through the gate, and as soon as they were in the SeaArk, Stacey spun the wheel and headed for *Peggy Lynn*.

As they approached, Ryan saw the surface supply umbilical snaking over the side of the salvage vessel and the bubbles coming up from the water at her stern. They tied off the SeaArk and clambered aboard *Peggy Lynn*.

Grandpa was leaning against the gas blending station, a pair of headphones clamped over his ears, pinning down the black watch cap that covered his long white hair. He'd let it grow since they'd left Key West almost two years ago, and now it was almost to his shoulders. He could have been a double for Willie Nelson. When Ryan had asked him to sing "On the Road Again," Grandpa had spat a long stream of tobacco beside Ryan's bare foot as his way of saying no.

"How's he doing down there?" asked Ryan.

"He says he almost has the umbilical cut away. In thirty years of running this boat with Dennis, we never had a problem like that."

Ryan chuckled. "Blame it on the woman driver."

Grandpa grinned. "I wouldn't say that to her face."

"Me neither."

Grandpa smiled and nodded his head, indicating something behind Ryan, who turned and saw Stacey standing with her hands on her hips, head cocked, and eyebrows furrowed.

Ryan grinned at her. "Oops."

"Next time," Stacey said, "I'll cut your hose on purpose." Then she smiled sweetly. "How come I don't get to chase the ghost ship?"

"I want you to drive *Peggy Lynn*. You're the second-best captain we've got aboard."

"After you?"

"Uh, no, Dennis is the best."

Gary and Travis carried gear bags from below and set them on the deck.

"What do you think we'll need?" Travis asked.

"Rope and a grapple."

"Got those," Gary said.

"Water, food, a change of clothes, and some firepower," Ryan added. "We're going to camp out on the derelict that sank the *EPC*. It'll take a few days for the tug to arrive." He turned to survey the harbor, and his gaze settled on a white twenty-three-foot Trophy Walkaround with a hardtop over the cuddy cabin.

"I'll be right back." He hopped in the SeaArk and motored to the Trophy, where a black man was puttering about on the aft deck.

Ryan came alongside and asked in Spanish, "Is your boat for hire?"

The man smiled. "Yes," he replied in English. "I take you to de best fishing spots on the coast."

"I wanna go to Compass Reef."

"That's a long run, *amigo*, but good fishing."

"I don't care about fishing. How much for you to take me and two friends up there?"

"Three-fifty a person."

Ryan whistled. "Kinda steep, ain't it?"

"Is the price, *amigo*. You do not like it, find another captain." The man turned away to work on the boat.

"You take cash?" Ryan asked.

The boat captain turned back, a broad smile on his weathered face. "American dollars?"

"Yes." Ryan nodded. "Move your boat to the port side of

the red salvage vessel over there." He pointed at *Peggy Lynn*. "We'll be ready to go in a few minutes."

The Miskito leaned over the rail and extended his hand. "I'm Wyn."

Ryan shook the man's hand and introduced himself.

"I will need to get bait, ice, and refreshments for you, *mi amigo*."

"All I need you to do is run us to Compass Reef. You get whatever you need and meet us alongside *Peggy Lynn* in a half hour."

"Yes, sir," Wyn said.

Ryan pushed the SeaArk away from the Trophy and raced back to the *Peggy Lynn*. He tied off the workboat, climbed aboard the larger vessel, and went below to his room. From a compartment under his mattress, he pulled his Glock 19 handgun and a KRISS Vector submachine gun, with plenty of high capacity magazines crammed with hollow-point cartridges. After he'd changed from shorts into gray cargo pants and holstered the Glock on his hip in an inside-the-waistband holster, he put the Vector and the spare magazines into a duffle bag with a load-bearing tactical vest. On top of those he put several pairs of underwear, socks, and pants.

On deck, he added his bag to the pile of gear the others had accumulated, including ropes, a grappling hook, canned food, cases of bottled water, and a camp stove. Gary had decided upon a Remington 870 pump-action tactical shotgun with a pistol grip and folding stock to complement his own Glock, and Travis sported a pistol, even though he didn't want to and wasn't as well-trained as either Ryan or Gary.

Anthony climbed the stern ladder and announced he had cleared the prop and shaft of all the umbilical hose, but the prop had sheared the key holding it to the shaft. He would need to remove the prop to check for further damage.

Grandpa handed the necessary tools to him, and Anthony disappeared once more over the side.

"Probably what caused the engine RPMs to shoot up," Dennis said to Stacey. "The shaft was spinning inside the prop. Hopefully, you shut off the engine before there was too much damage."

"I hope I did, too," she replied, nibbling at the tip of her left index finger while glancing between Travis and Ryan.

Travis gave her a kiss. "It'll be all right, honey. Even if you gotta run on one engine, you can still get over the *EPC* like Greg asked."

Wyn pulled his Trophy alongside *Peggy Lynn* just as Ryan had instructed, and the men transferred their gear into the smaller fishing vessel before piling into the boat. Wyn put the single outboard into drive, and they made their way across Bluefields Bay, past El Bluff, and into the broad Caribbean Sea beyond.

The dark blue waves were running about two feet high, and the Trophy bashed through them as they sped northeast toward the tiny reef. Using the travel time effectively, Ryan looked at the coral structure using an overhead satellite view on a tablet. The imagery was blurry, but it showed Compass Reef as a line of waves breaking over barely visible coral. The reef was part of a group of eighteen islands known as the Pearl Cays, designated as a wildlife refuge even though there were several privately owned islands in the archipelago. According to the navigation chart, the water around the reef dropped sixty feet to the seabed below.

It took two hours for them to make the run to the grounded ship, and it came into view ten minutes before they arrived. Wyn slowed as they neared the ship and motored slowly around it, keeping well clear of the coral heads.

The 328-foot-long ghost ship had grounded bow first, then the waves had pushed her to the west. Written on the stern of the rust-streaked hull were the faded white letters of the ship's name, *Galina Jovovich*. Her coat of dark blue paint didn't hide the giant red stars on either side of the bow, indicating the ship had once belonged to what President Reagan had called the 'Evil Empire.'

As they circled the ship, Ryan saw that most of the lifeboats were missing from their davits, and even though she'd been built for enjoyment as a cruise ship she had a silent, eerie quality to her, causing a shiver to run up his spine.

"Is this what you are fishing for, *amigo*?" Wyn asked.

"Yeah," Ryan replied, staring up at the ship towering above them.

"Greg wants us to board that thing?" Travis asked.

"Yeah," Ryan said again. Even he remained unconvinced. "Wyn, go around to the lee of the ship."

Wyn goosed the Trophy into the clear water west of the breakers booming against the reef.

"This area is normally very calm, but the storm is making it rough," Wyn informed them.

Ryan pulled out his sat phone and dialed Greg. When the boss came on the line, Ryan said, "She's right where Chuck said she'd be."

"Are you aboard?"

"No, and we don't really want to be, either. She looks like she'll roll over any minute."

"You'll have to hold the fort until the tug gets there."

"How long will that be?"

"*Star of Galveston* is on her way, but it'll take three or four days."

"You're kidding. We have to stay on that dump for that long? When will you get here?"

"Tomorrow."

"All right. We'll see you then." Ryan hung up and glanced

at Travis and Gary. Both men nodded their assent, but neither looked happy. "Wyn, take us to the starboard stern. Gary, ready the grappling hook and rope."

As Wyn drove them to the *Galina*'s rounded stern, careful to stay in the lee where the hull blocked the waves and wind, Ryan removed his tactical vest from his bag and pulled it over his head. He didn't think there was anyone onboard, but it was better to be prepared.

The ship's bulbous bow had run up on the reef, giving her an upward angle and a list to port which allowed Gary to easily toss the grappling hook over the handrail on the captain's deck, two decks above them.

Ryan went first, scrambling up the rope with practiced ease and climbing through the accommodation ladder opening onto the main deck. When he was aboard, he pulled the KRISS from his bag and slung it on its three-point harness.

He signaled Wyn to bring his little craft closer to the *Galina* and Gary climbed the rope. He tossed the end to Travis, who tied on their gear bags. Ryan and Gary pulled the gear up, making several hauls to get it all aboard. They stacked everything along the railing, keeping their bags containing the guns and ammunition handy.

There were locals who lived on several of the nearby islands, and Ryan suspected they'd been aboard already. If not, they might notice the newcomers and be curious to see what the strangers were doing. Ryan doubted they would be a genuine threat, but he also knew his team would have to stick around until help arrived, regardless of whether the islanders were friendly or not.

Once the gear was aboard the *Galina*, Travis climbed the rope and dragged it up after him. Wyn waved, backed the Trophy out of the *Galina*'s shadow, and headed for home.

Travis sat on the deck and pulled out a bottle of water. He looked up at Ryan and, in a deep voice, he said, "Rambo, kill."

"I know it's not in your nature because you're Canadian."

Travis held up his middle finger.

"Let's store our kit in a locker so it doesn't grow legs," Gary said.

The men spread out and found a small utility room just inside the main passageway door. They put their gear in it and moved up the stairs to the upper deck, heading for the aft observation platform on the captain's deck where a deflated twenty-five-foot rubber boat lay beside two rows of picnic tables bolted to the floor.

Ryan put his Vector to his shoulder and kept moving. It was strange being on such a quiet ship. Usually there would be people talking, an engine running, or some other noise to be heard. All he could hear now were the boom of the waves on the coral heads and the whistle of the wind. He was often the only person on his sailboat and it never bothered him but being on this massive rusting hulk was almost intimidating.

Making his way up the wide stairs to the bridge deck, he saw no one, but still he kept swinging the snout of his gun from side to side.

From the rear of the group, Gary said, "You know they make horror movies about this shit."

"This is crazy," Travis said. "There's no one here."

"Then why do you have your gun out?" Gary asked.

CHAPTER TWELVE

Ward and Young Insurance
Tampa Bay, Florida

Emily Hunt stood at her office window, overlooking Old Tampa Bay, her arms folded across her chest. It had become a ritual for her to watch the morning boat traffic for a few minutes before starting work if she was in the office. Lately, she preferred to be more out than in.

As a lead insurance investigator, she had an excellent vantage point from her fifteenth floor office in the modern steel-and-glass building that housed Ward and Young, an insurance agency that had its roots in the early 1900s when they'd covered the automobiles, yachts, and houses of the rich young industrialists who had made Florida their winter playground. The company had flourished following the post-World War II economic boom and was now a leading insurer along the Gulf Coast and the U.S.'s southeastern seaboard.

The company was one of the largest underwriters of

vessels in the United States, specializing in protection and indemnity insurance, or P&I, for shipowners who wanted to cover open-ended risk such as cargo damage during carriage, terrorism, and environmental disasters. Not only did Emily investigate claims made against hull and machinery damage, but she worked to prevent fraud through the surveillance of clients, auditing of accounts, and working with law enforcement to prepare criminal prosecution.

Her background as a former Broward County sheriff's deputy and current holder of a private investigator's license helped her to seamlessly navigate between the staid coat-and-tie world of insurance and the seedy underbelly of criminal activity along the world's waterfronts. She also wasn't above using her good looks and feminine wiles to solve a case.

A knock on the door startled her from her reverie, and she turned to see Kyle Ward standing in the doorway. As always, the CEO of Ward and Young wore a tailored suit, and not a strand of his brown hair was out of place. Emily had told him that his well-trimmed beard made him look more like a bum than the head of an insurance agency, and she hated how it scratched her cheeks and lips when they kissed.

He stepped into the room, pushed the door closed, and set a manila folder on her desk before walking to where Emily stood beside the window. Placing his hands on her shoulders, he took in her dark blue slacks and white blouse before saying, "Is that a new outfit? It looks good on you."

At five foot ten, she could look her boss and boyfriend in the eye. She continued to stand with her arms crossed, even as he leaned in to peck her cheek. Their relationship was outside the company rules, but Kyle thought they could get away with it because he was, after all, the one who made the rules. Emily hadn't fully committed to the relationship, even though she was sure Kyle probably carried a ring in his pocket, waiting for the opportunity to propose.

"I was thinking about taking you to dinner tonight," he said, "but the board called a meeting. You have a new case as well."

She raised her eyebrows.

Kyle dropped his hands and continued. "Our friends at Dark Water Research have run into problems in Nicaragua."

"What are they doing there?" Emily asked.

"Apparently, they were laying subsea cable when one of their divers cut a fiber-optic line. Then a ghost ship struck their cable layer and sank it." He held up his right hand, palm out. "Before you ask, Ryan Weller is part of the crew."

She leaned back, eyebrows furrowing. "What do you mean, 'ghost ship'?" She let the comment about Ryan slide for a moment to make him feel like he'd dodged the implications of dropping her ex-boyfriend's name into the middle of their conversation.

"An old cruise ship was being towed to the breakers in Bluefields when the tug got caught in the hurricane a few weeks ago. The tug's cable broke, and they left her to drift."

"And it hit DWR's cable layer?"

"They've claimed salvage rights to the derelict ship, and your ex is on it right now." He slid his hands into his pockets and looked out at the bay. "I can see the Gulf from my office, but I've always thought this was a better view."

They stared out the window for a few moments.

"Anyway," Kyle said, breaking the silence. "The DWR case is pretty straightforward, ex-boyfriend or not. Find the owners of the ghost ship and get them to pay for the damages. You probably won't have to leave your desk."

"Why do you keep mentioning his name every time something comes up that involves Dark Water Research?"

He faced her again, leaning against the glass. "You two have a complicated history, and I don't want you to get hurt again."

"I'm over him."

It was Kyle's turn to raise his eyebrows. "Really?"

Emily turned to look at the picturesque bay. Crisscrossed with boat wakes, the water sparkled in the morning light. She tightened her arms around her body. "I can do my job."

Kyle rubbed her shoulder and gave it a gentle squeeze. "I know you can, Em."

"Have you talked to Greg Olsen?" she inquired.

"He's in Nicaragua. DWR is preparing a bid to build a new port facility in Bluefields. He drove his boat down there." Kyle shook his head. "I'd rather fly."

"What about dinner?" she asked to be polite.

"Unfortunately, it's going to be a late night for me." He kissed her cheek again on the way out of her office, closing the door behind him.

Emily sat behind her desk and opened the file. After a quick read-through, she did a search through the insurance databases and on the Internet for the *Galina Jovovich*. She was able to identify the ship's owners, except they had signed their rights over to the towing company, Stavanger Marine, which had won the bid to move the ship from Miami to the breakers in Bluefields. Emily compiled the necessary paperwork and filled out the forms to file a lien against the *Galina* and the towing company with both the U.S. courts and the Norwegian Secretary of State, where Stavanger had its headquarters. It would be up to the DWR lawyers to file a suit against Stavanger Marine for any other compensation.

With the paperwork done and half the morning gone, Emily walked down the two flights of stairs to the law offices and turned her file over to a clerk at the front desk. She was eager to get back to her office and finish the paperwork she'd come in to do before Kyle had dumped the ghost ship in her lap. For some reason, if the Ward and Young agent in Houston couldn't handle something for DWR, the problem fell into her lap. She wasn't sure if it was because she knew the owner personally or because they had requested her to do the work. Whatever the reason, she was glad to be done with today's assignment. Checking her watch, she smiled. If she could get through her backlog quickly, she might be able to make it to Fort De Soto Park to do some paddleboarding.

When Emily got back to her office, the desk phone was ringing. She picked up the receiver and said, "Hello, this is Emily Hunt."

"Ms. Hunt, this is Marcie in reception. There's a Mr. Lorenzo Spataro here, asking to speak to you. He says it's about a claim he's filed with us for one of his ships. He only wants to talk to you about it."

"Did he say why?"

"No, but he seems pretty adamant."

"Okay," Emily said. "Send him up."

A few minutes later, a heavyset man with an olive complexion and wavy black hair knocked on her door. He wore a blue guayabera shirt, tan slacks, and brown loafers. He held a white Panama hat in his hand.

Emily met him at the door and ushered him in. She introduced herself and extended her hand. "What can I do for you?"

"I'm Lorenzo Spataro. I own Spataro Shipping in Miami."

He shook her hand before he produced a handkerchief from his pants pocket and wiped his forehead. "My ship has been stolen. I filed a claim, but I was told to come see you."

"Have a seat, Mr. Spataro."

He sat across from her at the desk.

She leaned forward, folding her hands on the desk blotter. "Who sent you to see me?"

"Greg Olsen."

Emily cocked her head. "Why?"

He dabbed at his forehead again. "Forgive me. I have a

glandular condition. Several days ago, my freighter, *Everglades Explorer*, was stolen from Miragoâne, Haiti. A group of pirates boarded her and killed the crew. The captain barely survived and he's in a hospital in Miami. The crew were good men who didn't deserve to die. As the shipowner, it was my responsibility to make sure they were safe. I failed, and now I would like to get justice for them, and to get my ship back."

She nodded for him to continue, but she wondered why Greg had sent Spataro to her instead of his favorite troubleshooter who normally handled these kinds of situations. Maybe they were too busy with bidding on the port facility and salvaging their wrecked ship?

"I want someone to look for her. Mr. Olsen said that you do this as part of your job." Spataro dabbed his forehead again and, when Emily didn't say anything, he continued. "He told me to talk to you because he believed the cost of finding her would be less than what your company would pay out in coverage and I would not be without a ship."

"Do you have anti-piracy coverage?" she asked.

Lorenzo Spataro nodded. "I do. I would be a fool to sail in and out of Haiti without it."

"I'm sure the company will look at your claim and pay it out."

"I know, but I don't want to lose my ship, and who will bring justice for my men?"

"What do you think *I* can do, Mr. Spataro?"

"Help me find her."

Emily leaned back in her chair. The Caribbean had many ports and even more hiding places. That was if the pirates even stayed in the Caribbean. If they changed the name of the vessel or changed her features in some way, she might never be found. "I think it would be best if you waited for your claim to come through and then bought another ship.

Most likely, they've taken her to a breaking yard to sell her for scrap."

Lorenzo frowned and fidgeted with the handkerchief before wiping his forehead again. "The *Explorer* was the only ship my father and I ever bought together before he passed away, so it has some sentimental value." He wrung the cloth in his hands. "I spoke to the Coast Guard and to U.S. Customs. They said there was nothing they could do. I called Mr. Olsen and he told me that you specialize in this for Ward and Young. I had no idea the company had such a division. You are my insurance agents. Please, there must be something you can do for my men."

"Can you wait here for a few minutes, Mr. Spataro?"

"Yes, I can do that."

Emily strode down the long hall to her boss's office on the other side of the building.

His secretary, a young brunette, looked up from her computer and smiled. "Hi, Emily."

"Is Kyle available? I need to talk to him."

The secretary used the intercom to speak to their boss, and a moment later, Emily stepped into his office. Kyle stood by the window, a golf club resting on one shoulder while he talked into a speaker phone. He quickly wrapped up the call and asked what she needed.

"We have a client who's lost his ship to pirates."

"So, tell him to file a claim." His tone was cold and indifferent as he planted his feet shoulder width apart and positioned himself over his club as if he were about to drive a ball straight through the window.

Emily continued. "He's asked me to help him look for it because he heard I do recovery for the company."

Kyle didn't look up as he worked his feet into the carpet to find the perfect stance. "That's your job."

"You're right. I'm going to go look for a stolen freighter."

He looked up suddenly. "What?"

"I said, 'I'm going to look for a stolen freighter.'"

"Okay." He nodded and went back to working his hands on the club, swinging it back and forth a few inches at a time.

Emily stepped out of the office and closed the door. She stopped by the secretary's desk and asked her to make a note of the date and time and add it to Kyle's calendar to indicate that he had agreed to her mission.

The office door opened, and Kyle stuck his head out. "Are you going to Nicaragua?"

Emily pondered the question. Bluefields was one of the largest shipbreakers in the Caribbean, and she could survey the damage to DWR's ship while she was there. "Maybe."

Kyle's eyes narrowed. "Come inside."

Emily returned to the office and closed the door behind her. Kyle took a few practice putts, and she waited for him to say what he had to say. She crossed to the window. He was right; she could see the Gulf of Mexico between the condos on the far beach.

"You're going to see *him*, aren't you?"

She turned to face him. "Mr. Spataro from Spataro Shipping is in my office right now, Kyle. His freighter has been stolen, and the pirates killed the crew. I'm going to help him find it."

Kyle gave her a look that said he wasn't stupid and shouldered the club.

Emily knew why he had concerns. Maybe helping Spataro was a ploy to help her get to Nicaragua. She did have a history with Ryan, and, even though she had tried to put it behind her, it haunted her every day.

It haunted her because, in truth, she was still in love with him.

CHAPTER THIRTEEN

Galina Jovovich
Compass Reef, Nicaragua

The *Galina Jovovich* had been the pinnacle of Soviet luxury at the time they had built her, and the exterior doors were made of oak and leaded glass, set into steel bulkheads that had grown cancerous with rust.

"The Russkies sure didn't care about watertight integrity on this boat," Gary Bartwell said.

"They had to make it pretty for the passengers," Ryan replied.

The three men pushed through the heavy doors and stepped onto the bridge. All the electronics, radios, and navigation gear were still in their proper places. Everything had metal labels with Cyrillic writing on them, and someone had used a label maker to create English translations, sticking the blue-and-white stickers under the original tags.

Ryan walked to the bank of windows across the front of

the bridge, above the console containing the navigation equipment, letting his Vector dangle from its sling across his chest. He looked down at the foredeck below, where two fixed cradles remained, empty of their motor launches. A crane had its center post near the bow, and its boom tip rested in a frame on the port side of the ship. He surmised that the crew had used it to launch the smaller boats and to load supplies.

"Geez-o-Pete," Travis shouted.

Ryan and Gary both spun on their heels, bringing their weapons to bear.

Travis pointed to a corner where a rat sat on its haunches, staring at them.

"It's a freaking *rat*, Yooper," Gary said, using the nickname for someone from Michigan's Upper Peninsula.

Travis's voice shook with fear. "There was a herd, or pack, or whatever the hell you want to call them."

"It's a pack," Gary said.

"This *is* a cruise ship," Ryan said. "Maybe they booked Frank Sinatra and Sammy Davis, Junior for the after-dinner show."

"Very funny, Weller," Travis barked. "There's a whole rat pack on this turd boat."

"You mean Dean Martin and Joey Bishop are here, too?" Ryan asked. "Maybe they'll show *Cannonball Run Two* for the evening movie."

"Why do you have to be such a wiseass?" Travis asked. "It really gets on my nerves."

Ryan grinned. "Since I'm getting on your nerves, I'll tell you one more fun fact: a group of rats is called a mischief."

"And how the hell would *you* know that?" Gary demanded.

Ryan shrugged. "Something I picked up along the way."

"Freakin' *Encyclopedia Britannica*," Travis mumbled.

"Nah, he's more like Google," Gary said. "He thinks he knows it all."

"Well, excuse me for being a fount of knowledge," Ryan said sarcastically, moving past the two men and heading for the stairs to the deck below. He paused to study the ship's deck plans, which hung in a wooden frame screwed to the bulkhead. Again, there were both Russian and English versions.

With a wicked grin, Ryan said, "Do you suppose they call these 'stairs' and not 'ladders' on a cruise ship?"

"They are civilians," Gary said. "We can't expect them to speak in Navy lingo."

"Would you Department of the Navy assholes shut the hell up?" Travis muttered.

"I'm with the men's department," Gary smirked.

That joke made Ryan mad every time he heard it. He hated that the Marines had claimed that mantle. "Travis, did you know the Marines invented sex, and sailors introduced it to women?"

"I heard it was the other way around," Gary said.

"I don't care which one of you guys invented what," Travis said, glancing nervously around.

"Look at that giant rat!" Gary pointed behind Travis, and the Yooper spun, bringing his pistol to bear.

Ryan and Gary burst out laughing.

"Shut up!" Travis shouted when he saw there wasn't a rat. "It's not funny. I *hate* rats."

Still chuckling, Ryan said, "We know."

They made their way down to the captain's deck, cleared the six staterooms there, along with the chief engineer's and captain's quarters. Again, they found nothing of interest, other than the ship looked like it had just set sail, minus its passengers and crew.

A circular staircase delivered them to what the plans

called the upper deck. They worked their way through all the rooms, including an auditorium where the rats had destroyed most of the seat cushions, a ship's store, an office, a library complete with moldy old books and green sofas, an exercise room, five staterooms, and a lounge with a full bar.

Gary pointed to the half-empty bottles of liquor. "I've found where I'm spending the rest of this dreary duty."

"I agree," Ryan said. "We should bring our bags up here after we tour the rest of the ship."

The last unexplored area on the deck was a spacious dining area filled with rectangular tables and a long buffet station on the port side. After they cleared it, they descended the stairs to the main deck, moved through the kitchen and the crew and passenger berthing areas, and continued to the lower deck, where they found more berthing. The air in the passageway was hot and stank of rat feces, mold, and waterlogged carpet. They used their flashlights to illuminate the dark passages, the only other light came through the tiny portholes.

As they retraced their steps to retrieve their gear bags and move them to the lounge, they heard voices. Gary and Ryan rushed up the stairs, with Travis trailing behind. Ryan guessed he didn't want to get into a confrontation or use a firearm to defend himself, and he accepted that Travis knew his limits.

When they strode onto the open aft observation deck, they saw four men dressed in ragged shorts and T-shirts, standing beside the door. On the water alongside the *Galina*, another man sat in a long wooden panga equipped with a high horsepower outboard, waiting for his companions.

"*Alto*," Ryan said. *Stop*.

The men turned his way, surprise registering on their faces at being confronted by white men with guns. They put their hands in the air.

"What are you doing here?" Gary demanded.

A man stepped forward and held out his hand. "I'm Eddy. We are Miskitos and live nearby." He was tall and skinny, wearing only cutoff jeans. "We look for things we can use."

Ryan lowered his weapon and shook Eddy's hand. "Nice to meet you. I'm Ryan."

"What are you doing here?" the native asked.

"We've secured salvage rights. A tug is on its way to pull her off the reef and take her to a breaking yard in Bluefields."

"Good. She is damaging the reef."

"There's a machine shop with plenty of tools still onboard. Are you interested in them?" Ryan asked.

Eddy spoke in Creole to the other men, who nodded their heads.

Ryan led the men to the shop. Eddy and his compatriots entered the room and began filling sacks with tools and spare parts.

"Why are you letting them do that?" Gary whispered.

"It's good relations. Besides, we've got no use for that stuff. Let them have it."

Eddy came out of the room with a heavily laden sack slung over his shoulder. "How long you stay?"

"The tug should be here in five days."

"You like fresh fish?"

"*Sí, señor*," Ryan said.

Eddy pointed at Ryan and grinned. "I bring you some."

"That would be awesome."

"You like cold beer?" Eddy asked.

"Absolutely," Gary chimed in.

"I bring you cold beer and fresh fish. We work together."

Ryan smiled at Gary. His plan had worked.

The Miskitos made several trips to empty the tool room, loaded it all in the panga, and raced across the water toward a distant island. Eddy brought them fresh fish and cold beer on their return.

Ryan, Travis, and Gary sipped the beer while Eddy's crew pillaged the cruise ship, taking books, chairs, silverware, pots, pans, and anything else they thought they might use. Then they helped the Miskitos load their loot into the panga.

As the Miskitos shoved off for the last time, Eddy said, "I'll come back tomorrow. Bring more fish and beer."

With a salute, Gary called, "We look forward to it."

"Let's light the stove and grill some fish," Ryan said.

They trooped to the bar, only to discover a mischief of rats had attacked the fish.

Gary brought his Remington up. "Cover your ears, grunts."

The booming blast echoed through the lounge, and the rats disintegrated into a pink mist.

"Let's move to a cabin with a door so we can keep the rats out," Ryan suggested.

They settled on a stateroom on the starboard side, carried their gear inside, and closed the door before trooping to the foredeck, where they lit the camping stove and heated three cans of beef stew. The divers washed their meal down with more of Eddy's cold beer, frequently shooing away the rats that were attracted to the smell of their food.

Gary threw his empty can across the deck, and a mischief immediately converged on the bouncing can as if being called by a dinner bell. He raised the shotgun and sent a wave of buckshot through the mobbing horde. The blood pouring from the rats brought even more, and they began cannibalizing the dead.

Travis turned away from the frightening scene, his face turning green and his throat constricting as he fought to hold his food down.

"Holy shit," Gary said. "I think we need to find a watertight compartment to sleep in or the rats might eat us."

"I can't do this," Travis moaned.

"Suck it up, buttercup," Gary said. "We're getting paid big bucks for salvaging this ship. If we're lucky, we'll get a Lloyd's Open Form for saving the environment from this piece of shit."

They carried their rat-gnawed gear bags to the tool room. Ryan shut the door, but the room quickly grew stuffy with three bodies in it, and there was nowhere comfortable for them to lie down.

"This isn't going to work," Gary said, pushing his bulk up from his seat on the floor. Before he'd joined the Marines, he'd played tight end for the Appalachian State Mountaineers and had been part of the team that had beaten the Michigan Wolverines in 2007. After that, he'd done several tours in Iraq as a combat engineer, earning the rank of captain before getting out to pursue another career. His degree in quantitative geoscience led him to a commercial dive school in Houston, where he popped up on Greg Olsen's radar. Greg and his company made a habit of hiring former military, and after Gary earned his hat—moving from tender to full-fledged diver—Greg had sent him to work for Travis.

"*Sonofabitch!*" Travis shrieked and snapped on his flashlight. A rat skidded to a stop and glanced back at them before jumping across the workbench and scrambling its little feet on the bulkhead as it escaped through a ventilation shaft.

"Watertight, but not rat-proof," Ryan said. "Let's head up to the observation deck. One of us can keep watch while the others sleep."

"Are you kidding me?" Travis exclaimed. "I can't sleep with rats running around. Plus, we'll have to drag all these bags up three decks again. I'm sick of moving them."

"Last time, I promise," Ryan said. He shouldered three of the bags and let Gary and Travis carry two each so they would only have to make one trip. The bags were heavy, and the canned goods slammed into his back with every step, but he kept going just to get it over with.

When they reached the aft observation platform on the captain's deck, they set their gear down under the overhang. Travis lay down on top of a picnic table, and Gary sacked out in the deflated rubber boat. Ryan leaned against the rail and drank a bottle of water. He didn't think he could sleep, either. The thought of having rats racing across his body was revolting, and now he wished he had a cigarette.

"Come on, Greg, get here fast," Ryan muttered. "I don't know if we can do this for five days."

CHAPTER FOURTEEN

Mercy Hospital
Miami, Florida

It was eight-thirty in the evening when Emily parked her car in the parking garage at Mercy Hospital. Sitting right on Biscayne Bay, the old building had the most picturesque setting for any hospital she'd ever been to, and in the evening dusk, the lights of the houses on Virginia Key and Key Biscayne glowed against the dark sky and blue water.

She got out of the car and shouldered her purse before crossing the street to the hospital. At the reception desk, she asked for Darrell Smith's room number and got into the elevator with an elderly couple. The old man was leaning on a walker, and his wife held his arm as if helping to support his weight.

Emily stared straight ahead at the doors as they closed, and the car rose upward. After leaving Kyle Ward's office, she had told Mr. Spataro that she would help him. They had caught the last non-stop flight of the day to Miami and she'd rented a car at the airport. She kept a travel bag packed with extra clothes and essentials in her Jeep just in case she ever needed to head out at a moment's notice, as she had today. She could have gone home and packed, but she wanted to get away from the office and concentrate on something other than Ryan Weller and Kyle Ward, but the whole time she'd been on the plane, all she could think about was going to Bluefields to check the breakers for Spataro's ship, and maybe bumping into her ex.

She had originally blown Ryan off because he had put her life in jeopardy twice. It had angered her then, but the more she thought about it and the more she pursued criminals through her own line of work, she slowly came to realize that their lives weren't all that different, after all. Both of them liked the excitement and danger of confronting lawbreakers, but hers seemed to require more paperwork and less gunplay.

The elevator stopped on the floor she needed, and she stepped off. She walked down the hall, smelling antiseptic and heavy-duty cleaners. She found Smith's room and poked her head in the door. The man in the bed closest to the door looked at her expectantly.

"Are you Darrell Smith?"

"He's over there." The man nodded his head toward the bed on the other side of the curtain.

Emily walked to the curtain and peered around it. A lean man with blond hair lay in the bed. His skin was pale, and his eyes were sunken. Beside him, an IV machine dripped fluids from multiple bags into clear tubes which snaked over the bedrail and into the man's arm. "Mr. Smith?"

He gazed at her for a long moment before he said, "Yeah."

Her voice was just above a whisper when she spoke. "Hi, I'm Emily Hunt. Can I come in for a few minutes?"

Smith nodded.

She slipped around the curtain and sat in the chair beside his bed. "I represent Ward and Young, Mr. Spataro's insurance agency. I spoke to him this morning and he told me what happened."

"Can you get me some water?" he asked.

"Sure." She rose and picked up the pitcher, but it was empty. "I'll be back in a minute."

Emily went to the nurses' station and asked where the water and ice dispenser was located. The nurse pointed down the hall to a small alcove. Emily filled the pitcher half-full of ice and topped it with water. The actions reminded her of being in the hospital with her father before he had passed away. He'd gotten bladder cancer after years of smoking, and he'd drank a lot of water before he'd … She squeezed her eyes shut and tried to push the thoughts from her mind, but the smell of disinfectant reminded her of those unhappy days.

She carried the pitcher back to Smith's room and filled his cup. He took long gulps just as her father had done. Her skin crawled and she wanted to run away; to get out of the hospital and to breathe fresh air again.

"Can you tell me what happened?" she asked, reaching into her purse for her phone so she could record the conversation.

Smith cleared his throat. "We were in Miragoâne. I had the late watch, and we planned to sail at first light." He gave her a blow-by-blow description of the events of that day, from unloading the rice to him being shot in the back. He'd made it to the beach, but he couldn't remember much after that.

"Can you describe the pirate leader?"

The captain took another long drink of water, and Emily refilled his cup again. He stared up at an old game show on the television. Emily saw Steve Harvey guffawing at a contestant's answer.

"He was a white guy with black hair," Smith said. "The

only time I got a decent look at him was right before he led me out on deck."

"Is there anything else that you can tell me about him?"

Smith laid his head back on the pillow after another drink. He stared at the television for such a long time that Emily didn't know if he had fallen asleep with his eyes open or if he was thinking.

Finally, he said, "They spoke English, but, right before they shot us, two of them were muttering in a foreign language. I heard one of them say, '*Inshallah*,' and the one who did the shooting cried, '*Allahu Akbar*.'"

The insurance investigator sat in stunned silence. After a moment, she said in a low voice, "You're telling me the men were Arabic?"

"I don't know who they were; just that they killed my men and stole my ship."

"I'd like to send a sketch artist by to talk to you. Are you up for that?"

"Sure, I'll try."

"Good. I'll arrange it for in the morning. Get some rest, Mr. Smith. Tomorrow, we'll get a look at your pirate."

CHAPTER FIFTEEN

Galina Jovovich
Compass Reef, Nicaragua

Morning dawned with spectacular reds in the gap between the ocean and the thick clouds stacked above it. Ryan sleepily recited the sailor's ditty, "Red in the morning, sailors take warning. Red at night, sailor's delight."

"Let me guess—the storm's heading our way," Gary said, joining Ryan at the rail.

Ryan drew his sat phone from his chest rig and opened an Internet browser. He scrolled to the weather app and checked the storm's track. "It's turned toward us."

"That's not good."

"No, it isn't," Ryan admitted. He dialed Greg Olsen's number. When the owner of DWR came on the line, Ryan said, "When're you gonna get here? The storm is coming, and this piece-of-shit boat is infested with rats."

"We'll be there in an hour."

"Good. We'll see you then. Have the beer on ice."

"Roger that."

Ryan ended the call and glanced at the eastern horizon. A cloud bank now blanketed the sun. Even the ocean was restless, rolling in deep blue waves to slam against the ship or burst apart on the coral reef, flinging spray high into the air.

"I don't like this," Travis said. "The ship is moving too much. I'm afraid she'll slide off the reef."

"We'll deal with that if it happens," Ryan replied.

They lit the stove and ate more canned stew for breakfast, chasing it down with hot coffee while fending off the starving rats.

Greg arrived as promised and stood off to the west, letting the *Galina* and the coral protect his Hatteras GT63 sportfisher, *Dark Water*, from the harshest waves. Rick and Shelly slung the rigid-hull Zodiac off the bigger boat's long nose, and Rick ran it across to the *Galina*, coming in on the protected stern.

When Ryan glanced down at the reef, he saw the ship had changed position. He slid down the rope to the Zodiac and had Rick take him to the cruise ship's bow. The bulbous nose had left a deep groove in the coral where she had slid onto the reef and then shifted with the waves.

Rick weaved their way through the coral heads back to *Dark Water*. Erica Opsal, one of DWR's pilots, stood in the cockpit, wearing khaki shorts and a red bikini top. She smiled as Ryan tossed her the Zodiac's painter. She was several inches taller than Rick's five-feet-six and kissed him when he and Ryan came aboard *Dark Water*. Ryan could see why the ladies would like the short fellow, even if his shaved head reminded Ryan of television police detective Kojak.

Ryan climbed the ladder to the bridge, expecting Greg to be at the helm, but Shelly Hughes, Dark Water Research's chief operations officer and Greg's girlfriend, sat behind the wheel instead. She wore a blue one-piece swimsuit over her curvy five-feet-five frame. Her brunette hair was in the normal ponytail, and Costa del Mar sunglasses shielded her brown eyes.

He found Greg in the saloon. The Hatteras always amazed him. It was one of the most beautiful and luxurious boats he'd ever had the privilege of using. Everything was stainless steel, marble, beautiful hardwoods, and expensive fabrics. Greg sat in the settee behind the table with his laptop open before him beside a cold beer. His wheelchair looked strangely empty without him in it.

The two friends bumped fists before Ryan pulled a Mountain Dew from the fridge and closed his eyes as he took the first long drink. Between the icy drink and the air conditioning, he felt like he was in heaven compared to the primitive conditions on the ghost ship. He gave Greg, Rick, and Erica a situational update before he asked them to go to Bluefields to collect as much rat poison and traps as they could find so they could deal with the *Galina*'s rat infestation.

"Shelly and I have a meeting this afternoon with the Nicaraguan Ministry of Transport and Infrastructure and Arcadis Nederland, the Dutch company they've hired for feasibility studies," Greg said.

"Well, have Rick come back with my supplies. Take Gary and Travis with you so they can get started on salvaging the *EPC*. I'll stay here with Lady *Galina*."

"By yourself?"

Ryan shrugged.

"Are you sure?" Rick asked. "I wouldn't want to be on that tub when the storm hits."

"Just make it fast."

Ryan collected a six-pack of Mountain Dew and a case of water before Rick shuttled him back to the *Galina*. Travis and Gary gratefully traded places with him in the Zodiac. By the time Ryan climbed to the aft observation deck where they'd left their gear, the Hatteras was a speck on the horizon as she raced south at maximum speed.

He wasn't worried about being alone, but he should have been.

CHAPTER SIXTEEN

Three hours later, *Dark Water* was back, with Rick, Erica, and Gary aboard. Gary and Erica launched the Zodiac while Rick idled the Hatteras in the lee of the *Galina* but well off the coral reef.

During the time it had taken for the men to run to Bluefields and back, the storm had drawn closer. The wind had freshened and was backing to the southeast and the waves had built to four-foot swells. Ominous black clouds had completely blotted the sky, and, in several places on the horizon, patches of rain fell.

Gary ran the Zodiac to the *Galina* and tied off with the line Ryan handed down. In the bow were three cardboard boxes. Ryan lowered another length of rope, and Gary tied on the first box. Ryan hauled it up and read the Spanish lettering on the outside—Rodilon. Rat poison pellets. The second box contained the same and the third held a dozen large rat traps along with a six-pack of Stella Artois.

"You sure you want to stay?" Gary shouted.

"Someone has to keep our salvage rights," Ryan yelled back.

Gary flashed a thumbs-up and untied the rope. He maneuvered the Zodiac away from the cruise ship and headed back to *Dark Water*. They struggled to get the Zodiac into the blocks on the Hatteras's bow. When Rick turned the sportfisher south, he waved from the bridge.

Ryan walked along the upper deck toward the *Galina*'s bow, staring over the railing at the frothing sea below. He climbed onto the pulpit. The bulbous bow seemed to have slipped farther down the reef since earlier that morning. A sudden fear took hold, making him feel hollow. It was possible that the ship would slide off this tiny rock and drift again, this time taking him and the rats along with it. He shuddered at the thought and headed back to where he'd left the industrial cartons of poison.

He tore open a pack of pellets and poured them around the gear bags. Then he stuffed pellet packs into his backpack and spent the rest of the afternoon dumping them throughout the ship, closing and dogging every watertight hatch on his way back to his gear. When he got there, he saw the rats had consumed many of the poisonous pills he'd left for them.

While heating a can of chicken soup, Ryan read the safety sheet included in the packages of Rodilon. The rats would take three to five days to die after ingesting the poison. He had hoped it would work faster. He hadn't slept since before he'd gone into the water to cut the rock that had stopped the subsea cable plow, and now he felt utterly exhausted. Just thinking about taking a nap made him yawn. Then he remembered seeing the enclosed cabin of the crane on the bow, mounted on a six-foot-high pedestal.

He picked up the box of rat traps and beer before trudging to the bow. The crane cab was small, barely large enough to accommodate a padded seat and the controls, but it was the only place the rats hadn't entered because they couldn't climb the slippery, salt-encrusted steel. Ryan set the traps around the outside of the cab, baiting them with scraps of canned ham. He hadn't even finished laying the traps before he heard the first one snap. Then the second and the third. Each contained a dead rat.

Instead of emptying the traps, he left them and crawled into the crane cab. He closed the door, locked the latch, and opened a beer. In the box, he discovered a package wrapped in a brown paper sack. Greg had written a note in blue pen on the sack, which read: *Because you're bored*.

Ryan smiled as he opened the wrapper and found a pack of Camel Blues and a lighter. He cracked the vent windows and felt the moisture-laden air swirl through the cabin. He lit a cigarette and breathed deeply. The guilt he'd felt earlier about breaking his streak wafted out the window with the smoke from this cigarette. After he'd smoked it down to the butt, he flicked it out the open window, finished his beer, and slouched in the seat with his arms crossed. It didn't take long for his chin to droop to his chest as he drifted off to sleep, jerking awake with each snap of a rat trap. Eventually, he fell into REM sleep and dreamed about swirling sharks and beautiful blondes.

As he slept, the ship broke free from the coral and continued her way north.

CHAPTER SEVENTEEN

When Ryan jerked awake, he immediately sensed something was different.

Besides the rain that streaked down the windows and hammered against the crane cab's roof, the ship had a different motion. He suspected that she had broken free of the reef and was drifting again.

He decided to stay in the cab because there wasn't a damned thing that he could do about the wayward ship. While waiting for Rick to return on *Dark Water*, he'd moved the gear bags up to the bridge to keep them dry from the approaching storm, figuring he would go there if she broke loose from the reef. While the *Galina* had no ability to maneuver and no power left in her batteries, she had a large compass and Ryan had a handheld GPS receiver to track their movements. If there was real trouble, he would break into one of the remaining lifeboats and activate the Electronic Positioning Indicator Radio Beacon, or EPIRB, which would send a distress signal to assemble search and rescue forces.

After lighting a cigarette, he pulled the sat phone from his pocket to call Greg. Then he decided there was no point, put the phone back in his pocket, and opened another beer.

While being stuck on the ghost ship wasn't ideal, it was a vacation compared to the last six weeks of constant activity on the *Peggy Lynn*, providing diver support to the cable layer. This working lifestyle was tough. He could call it quits, pick up his sailboat in Grenada, and keep chasing the sunset. There was more money in his Cayman Islands bank account than he could spend in a lifetime, so why was he busting his ass? Maybe having those thoughts meant he shouldn't be out there. Any doubts about his place on *Peggy Lynn* told Ryan there was truth in Travis and Dennis's accusations.

The *Galina* pitched and rolled beneath him in the heavy seas and high wind, which sang through the crane cables and rigging. The Russians had built the *Galina* to tour the Arctic, and she'd been to Antarctica as well, surviving the Drake Passage and bulldozing through ice, so Ryan had no doubt she would come through this storm. He smoked and drank warm beer as he looked out the window at the slate gray water covered in spume.

Then the ship shuddered. Ryan heard a loud screech of metal above the wind, signaling contact between the *Galina*'s hull and the unforgiving coral. He stayed put, feeling the ship grind along the rocks before breaking free and continuing on her way, caught in the current and the blowing storm.

He decided he needed to check for leaks and pushed open the cab door. The rain instantly soaked his clothes, chilling him to the bone. On the deck, the rat traps had shifted with the restless movements of the ship, and watery blood stained the places where their cannibalistic brethren had gnawed the dead. Ryan ran past the traps to reach the cover provided by the port promenade deck, an outside passageway enclosed with large vinyl windows. At the open stern, he glanced over the railing at the hull plates. He couldn't see any damage, so he made his way inside and down the stairs to the lower deck. His flashlight offered a small cone of illumination in the complete darkness.

In the engine room, he swept the beam over the outer skin, checking for any breaks in her watertight integrity. *Galina* was an ice-strengthened ship, meaning her hull had extra thickness and the girders, beams, and bulkheads that reinforced her were thicker than what other ships possessed. Despite all the additional steel, a jagged rock could still puncture her skin.

Not spotting any water coming in, Ryan double-checked that the watertight doors were locked on his way to the bridge, a narrow room with a straight console running the width of the deck. Above the console were windows, the tops of which slanted outward. In the console's center was the ship's engine telegraph, and surrounding it were a blizzard of controls and gauges. He checked his GPS and glanced at the compass hanging from the ceiling.

Ryan stared out the windows, watching the bow dip into the waves and throw spray high into the air. The storm was driving the ship forward on a following sea. He called Greg, and the owner of DWR gave him the satellite phone number for the captain of the *Star of Galveston*.

After consulting the tiny GPS screen that showed the *Galina* had drifted about five miles before hitting the submerged rocks, he called Anders Mikkelsen on the *Star*.

Ryan was familiar with the ocean-going tug and her Danish captain. It was Ryan who had helped Anders get a job with DWR, and they had worked together on two previous operations.

"Ah, Ryan. How are you, my friend?" Anders asked.

"Not so great, Captain. I'm on the *Galina*. She's broken free of the reef and we're drifting north."

"I see," Anders said, worry in his voice.

"She just hit some rocks. I didn't see a breach in the hull, but I dogged all the watertight doors on the lower level. How soon will you get here?"

"We're transiting the Yucatán Strait and making ten knots toward your position. I'm afraid it will take me over two days to reach you."

"If I stay on this course, we'll ground in the Miskito Cays."

"I have studied this problem. There is a chance the current will carry you out to sea."

"It depends on what the storm does," Ryan said. "If it turns north, then maybe, but if it goes ashore behind me, I'm pretty sure I'll run aground again."

"According to the latest from NOAA, the storm will hit Nicaragua behind you and turn north. They're predicting that it'll gather quickly into a hurricane when it crosses into the Gulf of Honduras."

Ryan tried to visualize the storm's track in his mind as Anders continued. "It's about seventy miles wide and moving at eight miles per hour. We should miss most of it when she weakens over land. Do you have access to radar?"

"I have my sat phone and a handheld GPS."

"I will pray for you. As you Yanks like to say, 'Fair winds and following seas.'"

Ryan laughed. "I've got the following seas all right, but the winds aren't fair."

"It is good you laugh. I'll see you soon."

Ryan ended the call and plugged the phone into the charging pack. There were only a few charges left on it. Fortunately, Travis had also left him his charging pack. He lit a cigarette and leaned against the console. His beer was warm and the Mountain Dew barely cold in the cooler. He chose the soda, drinking it between surges in the ship's motion.

He checked the GPS plot regularly over the next few

hours. The *Galina* was making two knots of headway, and the radar app on his phone told him the tropical storm had crossed onto land, just as Anders had predicted. The winds were now blowing from the northwest, pushing the *Galina* offshore. If he extended the ship's track, he figured that the storm should carry him clear of the Miskito Cays and into the Caribbean Sea.

At least he wouldn't run aground again.

CHAPTER EIGHTEEN

During the hours Ryan spent pacing the bridge, the *Galina* had become sluggish in the tall waves, wallowing at the stern. He now stood at the door of the engine room with the beam of his flashlight glinting off the water sloshing in the hold beneath the deck grates. Running aground was the least of his worries now.

He walked along the engine room catwalk, shining the light into the oily water, looking for the tear in the ship's hull. There were still plenty of mattresses, blankets, and timbers aboard that he could use to plug the hole, but first he had to find it.

The *Galina* had struck the coral reef on her port side, but, despite his best efforts, he couldn't spot the hole. He decided it must be close to the keel, and with the water already sloshing around in the hold, he wouldn't find it without a dive mask and scuba tank.

Ryan left the engine room and spun the wheel in the center of the door, causing four rods, called dog arms, to move outward over the door's frame, pulling the door tight against a rubber gasket thus forming a watertight seal.

These watertight doors sealed off the various compartments, preventing the floodwater from invading the whole ship.

In the library, he perused the shelves, looking for something of interest to take his mind off the storm and the fact that he was on a sinking ship.

The first book that struck his fancy was *Vastness of the Sea* by Bernard Gorsky. It told the tale of Gorsky, a Frenchman, and his three partners, who explored and photographed the undersea wonders beneath their sailboat, *Moana*, in the mid-1950s. Gorsky kept a running commentary of the things they saw, both above and below the water, and documented their struggles to cross the oceans, eat from the sea, and record their story.

Ryan read the book in one sitting and wanted to know what happened to the men after they left Tahiti. Had they circumnavigated the world and returned to France? He stowed the book in his bag to take with him and walked to the library to find another. He tried various books, but none of them satisfied him the way Gorsky had. Despite the weather, the rats still peeked out at him as he sat on the green sofa. He would stomp his feet or yell at them, but they ignored his gestures and continued to point their noses toward him and sniff the air. Ryan found it most unsettling.

He finally landed on *Endurance* by Sir Ernest Shackleton, a paperback covering Shackleton's exploration of the Antarctic and how his ship had become locked in ice, forcing the crew to escape in small boats across a storm-tossed sea to a whaling station on a distant island.

Startled awake by the ringing sat phone, Ryan sat upright, knocking the paperback off his chest, and sending the rats scurrying away before he could grab the phone.

"What's going on?" Greg asked when Ryan finally pressed the Answer button.

"Nothing much, just taking a nap and reading some books they left in the library."

"Glad you're enjoying your cruise."

"It's a little rough. I've put in a complaint with the captain."

"What's the situation?"

"Situation Normal ... you know the rest."

"Anders tells me you're adrift and hit some rocks."

"Yep, and there's a hole below the waterline amidships, near the engine room. She's taking on water, but I can't find the leak."

"Keep a close eye on it," Greg said.

"I'm not hanging out down there, if that's what you mean."

"Damn, can't you be serious for two minutes?"

"Probably not, but this shit isn't life or death. The ship will stay afloat until *Star of Galveston* gets here and we can get some pumps to dewater her. What's the storm doing?" Ryan asked.

"It's tearing up the coast on its way north."

"Well, it's pushing me out to sea, and we should avoid the rocks around Miskito Cay."

"I'd be happy if she grounds again," Greg replied. "I'm worried about you."

"Isn't that sweet? I've got an inflatable life raft all picked out. The CO_2 charges are full, and the EPIRB batteries are working."

"Glad to hear it. Call me if you need anything."

"What's the latest down there?" Ryan asked.

"This storm has everything screwed up. All my salvage equipment coming from Texas City has had to reroute to the east because of it. Which puts us behind schedule even further, and the cable company is charging the hell out of me for that cable you cut, even though it wasn't properly marked on the charts. Plus, we're getting penalized for every day we aren't laying cable."

"Can't you claim perils of the sea?"

"We are. I have a whole passel of attorneys working the phones and charging me exorbitant fees."

"Seems about right."

"Perils of the sea works for the *EPC*," Greg said, "but my insurance doesn't have a perils of dumbassery clause for people who cut subsea cables."

"Ha ha, you're hilarious," Ryan said. "I'm not the one who didn't mark it correctly."

"I'm just messing with you. I gotta go," Greg said. "Stay safe, brother."

"Will do."

Ryan shut off the phone and walked to the engine room. The water had barely risen, according to the mark he'd left on the ladder from the catwalk down to the deck grates. He swung the beam of his flashlight across the water, watching it slosh back and forth, its surface covered in a sheen of oil from the bilges and shining with the colors of the rainbow under his beam. After marking the water level again by scratching the paint with the tip of his tactical folding knife when the ship rolled upright, he went back topside.

The compass said he was heading northeast, but he didn't know if he would clear the Miskito Cays yet, as the ship was still many miles away. To his eye, the waves were still the same height, but the wind looked to be dying. The radar app confirmed the storm had moved ahead of him and his ground speed had decreased, moving the ship at just over a knot.

Night fell, and he ate more canned stew before he ensconced himself in the crane cab again, drinking warm beer and smoking another cigarette. The ship was riding a little lower, but Ryan thought she'd hold until the tug arrived. He really hoped she grounded herself on another shoal to keep from sinking.

He woke up several times during the night, but he didn't leave the cab. Ryan accepted that he was just a passenger on this ghost ship. Again, he thought about what his future held as he flicked ash out the window. He had options. He could get in his sailboat and never look back or go to Texas and work with Greg at Trident. Maybe he could start his own firm and continue to be a salvage consultant, or he could just say, 'to hell with all of it,' and go live in the mountains somewhere. When he thought about the cold, wet snow sifting down from leaden gray skies, he shivered and concluded that he wasn't a mountain man. Maybe he could find a woman to go with him and live like Gorsky and his friends had, making the sea their life on a little boat as they sailed the globe. There were plenty dating sites he could try.

Ryan put his chin down, crossed his arms, and tried to sleep, but his thoughts turned introspective again. There was only one woman he wanted to sail into the sunset with. The last time he had seen Emily Hunt, he'd rescued her from an international arms dealer who'd held her hostage in exchange for gold Ryan was salvaging from a sunken freighter. When the ordeal was over, Emily had stalked up the accommodation ladder to a waiting airplane without looking back at him and had sent his DHS handler to tell him that she never wanted to speak to him again.

Despite the time that had passed since they had parted, he could still remember the curves of her body, the way the sun shone on her thick mane, the color of ripened wheat—what he liked to call her Viking hair——and how her cornflower-blue eyes sparkled when she smiled. She was the only woman he ever believed he would marry, and she'd become the measuring stick for all others.

He lit a smoke. It was a habit Emily had found disgusting

and had asked him to quit. And he had. Now here he was, imbibing again.

"What a sad sack you are, Weller," he muttered to himself. He shifted in the seat, trying to get more comfortable. Idly, he flipped the knobs and switches inside the cab, toggling the joystick in a circle. Nothing happened, just as he knew it wouldn't.

He settled in and closed his eyes. Somewhere out there, in the darkness, the *Star of Galveston* was racing toward him. After a few moments, he walked to the bridge. When he was standing behind the console, he checked the compass heading, used the GPS to verify his location, and removed the hot and cumbersome load-bearing vest. He went to the library, wearing a headlamp, picked up an old, dog-eared thriller novel by John Buchan called *The Thirty-Nine Steps*, and returned to the crane cab.

He awoke with the sun, as its rays burned through the cab. The paperback had slipped from his hands and lay on the floor, and his headlamp's batteries were dead. He cursed himself for not turning it off, but he only had one more day before the *Star of Galveston* arrived on station and he could flee this rat-infested tub.

As he luxuriated in the sunshine and puffed on a cigarette, he noticed two things. One, the seas had fallen to two-foot-high rollers; and two, there was a panga racing straight toward the *Galina Jovovich*.

He stepped out of the cab and ran along the deck and up the steps to the bridge to get his binoculars, keeping low to avoid being spotted by the men in the boat.

That was when he heard voices.

CHAPTER NINETEEN

Everglades Explorer
Jamaican Channel, Caribbean Sea

The *Everglades Explorer* slowly steamed across the Caribbean, making eight knots toward the town of Puerto Cortés on Honduras's eastern coast. Masoud Sadiq, the pirate leader, stood on the bridge with his captain, learning how to maneuver the freighter. It was the captain's fault the ship hadn't been ready to move as soon as they'd upped anchor, because he was unfamiliar with the ship's controls. After several long seconds, the man had gotten a handle on the situation and they'd headed out to sea.

Once they were underway, they dumped the bodies of the dead overboard, and the computer specialist hacked the Automatic Identification System, or AIS. By law, the ship needed an AIS, which broadcasted the ship's position, course, and speed to various tracking websites via satellites. Sadiq's specialist had spoofed the system so the information changed to mirror ships close to them. Now, there wasn't much to do until they reached Honduras.

Sadiq stepped onto the bridge wing and took deep breaths as he stared across the vast expanse of rolling blue sea. He was no stranger to the salt air filling his lungs, having grown up on the banks of the Mediterranean Sea in the town of Latakia, Syria. His father was a contractor, building housing units on the coast, and his mother was a beautiful homemaker, who had taught him the Shia faith mixed with Alawis, a doctrine incorporating other forms of religion, including the celebrating of mass, drinking wine, and reincarnation.

He'd joined the Syrian Arab Army at eighteen to serve his mandatory two-year conscription, and he quickly caught the attention of the 14th Special Forces Division. There Sadiq had received training in air assault tactics and conducting counter-insurgency operations. For ten years, he bounced around Iraq, Syria, and Lebanon, conducting sabotage, kidnappings, assassinations, and terrorist attacks against the Americans and the Jews.

It was during this time that he began to resent the Americans for interfering in the Middle East, pushing their democracy and capitalism around like a new form of religion; one many young Muslims were swayed by. They watched American television shows via satellite dishes and wanted to dress like American actresses and actors. Not only was the Great Satan a threat to their way of life, but the United States also tore at their religion and demanded that Muslims not adhere to the strict tenets of the Quran. When the Quran said to attack infidels, the Americans said it was outdated and misunderstood. Sadiq had seen them strip religion from their own lives, and he believed that if the Americans had their way, they would take it away from the Muslims as well.

In 2011, when civil war had broken out in his country, he'd chosen to stay with the Syrian Arab Army. He was an Alawite like the president, Bashar al-Assad. He had fought the rebels and then the Americans and the Russians. Again, he saw their interference as problematic, and no one was willing to stand up to them and protect his homeland. They'd imposed sanction after sanction on his country and derided it for being a hotbed of terrorism.

The turning point for Sadiq had been when an American cruise missile attack had killed his father. Sadiq was the eldest son, the one who shouldered the burden of his mother's care. He joined the Islamic State of Iraq and Syria, or ISIS, the burgeoning movement intended to recapture the land and bring about the return of the caliphate. They wanted to kill all the infidels, and Sadiq wanted nothing more than to do the same. He sent money home to his family, even after ISIS cut their fighters' pay in half.

For him, joining the movement was not so much about spreading ideology as it was about revenge. During his initial indoctrination, he realized that revenge and ideology were twin driving forces. Kill the infidels, or make them repent and pay the *jizya*, or tax, as ordered by the Prophet Mohammed in the Quran until they did so by willing submission and felt themselves subdued. Then, and only then, would he receive his vindication.

He had conceived of this attack against the United States many years ago and had approached several ISIS leaders with the plan, but they were too busy conquering land in Iraq and then trying to defend it. When they had turned him down, he didn't know if they were uninterested or if they thought the plan was unfeasible. But when the group's founder, Abu Bakr Al-Baghdadi, had killed himself by detonated a suicide vest during an American raid, Masoud Sadiq's phone had rung.

Sadiq had briefed General Golnar, the new head of ISIS, and Golnar had given him the green light. Because of his dedication to the cause, the leaders trusted Sadiq to carry out his vision. It had taken months for him to find the men he needed. Most of ISIS's fighters had no experience aboard an ocean-going vessel, and thus he needed to train them accordingly. The logistics had taken even more time to arrange, and then he'd had to find the right ship. Spotting the pattern in the *Everglades Explorer*'s route from Miami to Miragoâne, Haiti, to Puerto Cortés, Honduras, then to Santo Domingo, Dominican Republic, and finally back to Florida, he knew he had his ship.

Once they knew which ship to use, things had snowballed quickly from there. Sadiq and his men had a final meeting with General Golnar, where Golnar introduced the last man in the team. That man had one job.

To launch the missiles.

CHAPTER TWENTY

Galina Jovovich
Off the coast of Nicaragua

Ryan ran quietly along the bridge deck to the open bridge door. He crouched and peered around the corner, watching four skinny black men examining the gear they'd dumped from his kitbags.

One had put on Ryan's load-bearing vest and was pulling everything from its pockets. Another had traded his rusty AK for the KRISS Vector, while the third ate cold soup from the can Ryan had been saving for his breakfast and the fourth examined Gary's Remington shotgun.

Sliding back out of view, Ryan made his way to the main deck. He crept to the rail, looking for the panga that had brought the men. It was holding station off the stern, the driver barely making headway as he kept pace with the *Galina*. A second boat carried five more men through the two-foot swells, and it was now close enough for Ryan to see that they all held some type of firearm.

He drew back from the rail and moved into the ship's interior. Ryan patted his pockets, taking stock of his remaining equipment. He had the sat phone, a tactical folding knife, LED flashlight, his Glock 19 pistol with two spare fifteen-round magazines, a lighter, five cigarettes, a set of keys with a bottle opener, and, most importantly, the highly trained brain between his ears. He had more than enough ammo to take out all the bad guys, but he didn't know their intentions yet. They could be scavengers like Eddy, but he thought it was more likely that two boats of heavily armed men boarding a vessel at sea meant pirates.

Either way, he needed to wait and see what they had planned for the *Galina*. They couldn't tow her with their little pangas, despite the 225-horsepower Yamaha outboards hanging on their sterns. He dove for the deck when he heard gunfire, recognizing the sound of the KRISS.

He strode to the window and saw the second boat had veered away. Maybe the two boats were rivals? If that was the case, they might take each other out. If they weren't, then he needed a plan to get rid of the boats so he could isolate the pirates and take them out one by one.

Taking the inside stairs to the library, Ryan collected the four empty beer bottles he'd stuffed under the couch cushions, and jogged to the engine room. The water in the hold had risen almost an inch, and his shoes became coated with the watery oil mixture as he moved along the lower catwalk to the bank of diesel fuel filters. A small spigot projected from the base of each filter housing so the engineers could take samples of the diesel to determine if water had mixed with the fuel. Since water's density was greater than the diesel, the water would settle to the bottom of the filters, and a crewman could siphon off the water until only pure diesel remained.

He twisted the tap, letting out a trickle of fuel that sparkled in the beam of his flashlight, pinched between his neck and shoulder so he could work with both hands.

A glass jar sat beside the testing station, and he partially filled it with fuel. After shutting off the tap, he swirled the jar and held the light up to it. When the fuel stopped spinning, he saw a layer of water at the bottom. He let the filter drain more and tested the diesel again until there was no water in the jar, then he filled the beer bottles.

Once he had all four filled, and his hands were completely soaked from overfilling them, he went to a workbench.

Ryan dumped some of the liquid from each and topped the bottles with oil from a nearby jug before cutting strips of old rags and stuffing them down the long necks. Now he had Molotov cocktail party favors.

The engine room sat amidships, and he used the aft door to make his egress. Before he opened the door, he set his Molotov cocktails against the bulkhead, shut off his flashlight, tucked it into a cargo pocket, then undogged the hatch by feel in the cave-like darkness. Slowly, he cracked the door open and checked the passageway. It was empty, so he stepped out, moved his precious cargo, and spun the door's wheel to lock the dogs in place. He picked up his bottles and went up the steps that led to the small open stern area where he, Travis, and Gary had first climbed aboard.

He eased the heavy oak double doors open and crawled out, two beer bottles clutched in each fist.

Just as he made it to the railing, he heard shouting in Creole, immediately followed by the rattle of automatic gunfire.

CHAPTER TWENTY-ONE

Ryan pressed himself flat to the deck of the *Galina Jovovich*. He scrambled forward to the perceived safety of the solid steel railing that surrounded the open deck as bullets ricocheted above his head and shattered the glass of the door. The shooters in the bobbing boats must have spotted him as he crawled past the open transom door. Even though it was notoriously tough to be accurate while shooting from a moving object, these asshats had managed to do a fair job of pinning him down.

Slowly, he edged to the railing, trying to see through the hawsehole, a hole cut in the transom through which crewmen passed the dock lines, or hawsers. The panga loaded with men was now on an intercept course with the *Galina*, heading for the line dangling from the upper deck.

Ryan snaked his way past the cruciform bollards welded to the deck behind the hawseholes, stuck his hand through the hole, and pulled the rope out of the pirate's reach. This earned him a withering blast of gunfire which pinged harmlessly off the metal sides of the ship.

He rolled to look down the promenade deck. Surely the

pirates on the bridge would investigate why their compatriots were shooting? Damn, he wished he had his KRISS, or at least the suppressor for his Glock, but the suppressor had been in his load-bearing vest, and it and the KRISS were now in the hands of the pirates.

Turning back to the transom door, Ryan saw the panga come alongside the *Galina*. A man in the panga's bow swung a grappling hook in a slow circle. Ryan waited a moment longer for the panga to come alongside the ship, crouching behind the solid steel railing around the transom door. He glanced at the panga again. It was almost there. Another moment more, and the boat would be abreast of the door.

He took that moment to light the first Molotov cocktail. He heard the grappling hook clatter against the railing one deck above, rose to his feet, and hurled the bottle into the twenty-eight-foot wooden fishing boat. The bottle bounced off the seat and plunged into the ocean.

"*Shit*," Ryan muttered, ducking down, and lighting the second bottle.

As soon as the gunfire died, he stood, targeted the open bilge in front of the driver's feet, and threw the Molotov cocktail with all his might. This time, the bottle shattered on impact, spraying diesel and engine oil across the wooden boat and the men in it. The flaming rag ignited the fumes with a *whoosh*, and screams erupted from the burning men. Ryan ducked below the railing, not wanting to watch the men dive into the sea or burn to death, but he couldn't blot out their shrieking voices. Moments later, a secondary explosion ripped through the air.

Ryan looked over the railing to see that the panga had a hole in her stern where the gas tank had been, and the boat blazed brightly as it sank. He aimed his pistol at a man alight with flames and clinging to the bow. Ryan shot him in the head to end his horrible screaming, then he swung his sights to the driver of the second boat, steadied the gun on the rail, and put two rounds into the man's chest. The driver toppled out of his boat. The engine lanyard attached to his wrist jerked the tiller hard to port and popped free of the outboard, killing the motor.

Ryan's antics had drawn the attention of the four men who'd been on the bridge, and one fired his AK as he ran toward him on the promenade deck. Ryan kicked the remaining cocktails overboard and rolled behind the bulkhead. Shards of glass from the broken door dug into his back, forearms, and palms. He kept moving despite the pain and pushed through the double doors into the interior.

He held his Glock in the low ready position as he moved forward. Now it was time to hunt.

CHAPTER TWENTY-TWO

Through the windows, Ryan saw two pirates race along the *Galina Jovovich*'s promenade decks, one on either side of the ship. He ran forward to the spiral staircase at the front of the ship and continued up to the bridge. He pointed his Glock upward as he ascended.

The bridge was empty, but the pirates had left behind several items he could use: the suppressor for his pistol, which he quickly screwed into place, and the GPS unit, which still lay on the console. Ryan pocketed the GPS. He'd need it to coordinate the meeting with the *Star of Galveston*.

Cans of food and various other items rolled about the deck with each passing wave. As Ryan scanned the bridge, he noticed that the bastards had drunk the last of his Mountain Dew. There was half a case of water left, and he pocketed two plastic bottles before mounting the steps to the roof of the bridge deck.

Ryan crept along, pistol up in outstretched arms. He knew the *Galina* fairly well by now, and that was an advantage he had over the attackers, who would need to go door-to-door to find him. After taking out one of their boats and two of their fellow pirates, Ryan was confident they were scouring the ship for him.

A freshening easterly breeze cooled Ryan. He instinctively considered the subtle shift in the wind, which had been pushing the ship northward with the current. If the wind continued from the east, it would take him toward the coast, but he didn't have time to worry about it now.

He ran to the massive smoke funnel in the center of the deck and looked up the steel ladder rungs welded to the funnel, leading to its top. If nothing else, he could climb into the funnel and hide, but that wasn't Ryan's nature. This was *his* ship, and he wanted the men off it with as little fuss as possible. He skirted the funnel on the starboard side and approached the wide stairs leading down two decks to the aft observatory and the empty swimming pool.

The head of a pirate appeared as the man jogged up the steps. Ryan froze, bringing his pistol to bear on the lean brown man, slick with sweat beneath an open white guayabera shirt and dirty red shorts. His black hair was short, his ears large and wide, and he wore a pencil-thin mustache on his upper lip.

Behind him was a taller man, his thick afro bobbing with each step. His collarbones and sternum stood out prominently under his taut skin and sinewy muscles as he gripped an ancient bolt-action rifle. He was also shoeless like his companion and wore only blue jeans.

Ryan raised his Glock and shouted, "Stop."

Blue Jeans paused as if unsure what to do. Guayabera's rusty, wire-stocked AK sprang to his shoulder, but before he could depress the trigger, Ryan put a round through his forehead. Guayabera toppled backward, his body ragdolling down the steps.

Ryan swiveled to center his sights on Blue Jeans's chest and said, "Throw down your gun and jump off the ship."

They stared at one another—Blue Jeans still frozen in his tracks. The heat radiating from the deck made Ryan's feet hot, and sweat rolled down his forehead. He had a sudden flashback to being forced to stand on a roof for punishment while in a Venezuelan prison after breaking one man's wrist and killing another in self-defense. Those two long days had almost broken him.

"Jorge!" a man shouted from somewhere below them.

Blue Jeans opened his mouth to yell, but Ryan fired a bullet into the butt of his rifle stock. Blue Jeans dropped the antique and ran down the steps. At the railing behind the empty pool, he turned to look back at Ryan before jumping feet-first into the sea.

"Two down, two to go," Ryan muttered to himself.

Despite what Ryan liked to tell himself about enjoying his work as a commercial diver, he missed the action and a gun in his hand. Combat had always produced a certain high that nothing else could compare to, not even disarming underwater mines in pitch-black water. The *Galina* was a playground of passageways, compartments, and stairs, and the Navy had trained him to be a proficient killing machine in just such an environment.

Ryan entered the dining room and glanced around, tuning his hearing and other senses to the noises, sights, and smells that would lead him to the remaining pirates. He heard the outboard start and assumed that Blue Jeans had made it to the panga. Would he wait for his friends or leave them to fend for themselves? It didn't matter to Ryan, although a part of him hoped Blue Jeans had abandoned them. He wanted to stalk and kill as he made his way deeper into the ship's interior, swinging the elongated barrel of the suppressed pistol as he moved.

Entering the library, he saw the back of one of the pirates as he stepped out onto the promenade deck. As the door swung closed, Ryan ran across the room and stopped to peer out the window to determine which direction his quarry had gone. This man was shorter than his companions, with nappy hair, a dirty white T-shirt, and tan shorts. Like the others, his feet were bare, but he carried a brutal-looking sawed-off shotgun.

Ryan felt the tops of his feet itch. He removed his shoe and sock. The skin was red and irritated. He guessed it was from wading through the diesel and water mixture in the engine room. He pushed off his other shoe and sock and saw that foot was also red. Before pursuing his foe, he dumped half a bottle of water onto each foot to wash away the irritants, but they still itched. He forced himself to refocus on the mission and pushed through the door.

His prey stood at the aft railing, shouting to Blue Jeans. While Ryan couldn't understand the Miskito Creole, he could tell from the tone that Blue Jeans wanted his friend to jump. Ryan approached with stealth, but the man must have heard him, swinging the gaping mouth of the shotgun his way. Ryan dropped to one knee, shot the man in the chest, and continued to fall onto his right side to get below the muzzle of the scattergun.

As the Miskito jerked backward from the impact of the nine-millimeter hollow point to his chest, he pulled the shotgun's trigger. The boom was deafening in the enclosed promenade deck, and the buckshot pinged off the overhead deck and shattered the brittle vinyl windows.

Ryan was just about to put a second shot into the man when someone landed on him, pinning him to the deck and knocking the pistol from his hand. He turned his head in time to see a dark fist coming for his jaw and jerked his head back and down. The blow still stung, even though the man's fist bounced off his chin and slammed into the unyielding green deck, eliciting a cry of anguish from the attacker.

Shaking off the cobwebs from the punch, Ryan slammed his left elbow backward, connecting solidly with the man's head. The attacker roared, and Ryan hammered him again and again until he drew back enough for Ryan to roll onto his back. He wrapped his legs around the smaller man's waist, noticing a scar running across the Miskito's right cheek and that his coal-black eyes were full of anger.

Scar Face swung with both fists, trying to pummel Ryan's face, but the American held his arms up, deflecting most of the blows with his forearms. Ryan locked his ankles together and squeezed tighter. Enraged, Scar Face grabbed Ryan by his upper arms and lifted him into the air. If he clung to Scar Face, he would powerbomb Ryan into the deck. Ryan released his legs and swung them down. This threw Scar Face off-balance, and he released Ryan's arms.

Ryan stumbled backward and crashed into the railing, feeling the sharp edges of the vinyl windowpane stab him in the spine. Scar Face charged, intent on driving Ryan through the window and into the ocean below, but the nimbler, better-trained fighter squatted as Scar Face was about to slam into him and used his powerful legs to spring up, catching Scar Face in the stomach and catapulting him over the railing.

Breathless, his chest heaving, Ryan leaned out to see Scar Face swimming toward the panga. Blue Jeans gave Ryan the finger before helping Scar Face into the boat. Ryan scooped up the sawed-off shotgun from beside its dead owner, pumped a new shell into the chamber, and fired a burst of buckshot at the boat.

Blue Jeans threw the tiller over and raced toward shore as Ryan fired the shotgun until it was empty. When he'd ejected the last spent shell from the chamber, he threw the gun into the water and retrieved his pistol. Unfortunately, Scar Face had been wearing his load-bearing vest when he'd gone overboard, taking the majority of Ryan's spare magazines with him. Low on ammunition, Ryan needed to fortify his defenses, because he was certain the pirates would return with reinforcements.

CHAPTER TWENTY-THREE

The first thing Ryan did to prepare for a second pirate attack was to fill several alcohol bottles from the bar with the diesel and oil mixture and stuff the tops with rags. Next, he gathered the firearms he found on board. Along with the wire stock AK and Blue Jeans's bolt-action rifle, Ryan had found his KRISS Vector on the promenade deck near where he and Scar Face had fought. The magazine was half full, and he located a spare on the bridge deck. He used ammunition from the partially full KRISS mag to replenish his Glock.

His next chore was one he'd rather not do, but he wanted to get rid of the bodies. He found some line in a storage locker and wrapped it around the dead men, pinning their hands to their sides and working his way to their feet before tying on heavy sections of spare pipe. Then he dumped them overboard.

Finished with the gruesome task, Ryan lit a cigarette while speed dialing Greg's number.

The owner of DWR answered on the second ring. "How's life on the ghost ship?"

"I just had an encounter with real-life pirates of the Caribbean."

"What happened?"

Ryan explained how he had fended off the pirates and finished with, "What's the ETA on *Star of Galveston?*"

"You need to call Captain Mikkelsen for an accurate number."

"Okay, but I predict these guys will try again. They know I'm alone, and right now, it's a numbers game. I don't have enough ammo to sustain a prolonged gunfight."

"Okay. I'll get you some help," Greg replied.

"Get Rick and Gary on a chopper with as much firepower as you can send."

"I'll do that. What else do you need?"

"More food, beer, cigarettes—oh, and some Mountain Dew. Those lousy bastards drank all of it."

Greg laughed. "Sorry, I can't help you with the Mountain Dew. I gave you what I had, and it's hard to find down here."

"Tell me about it. How soon can I expect the cavalry?"

"I'll need a couple of hours to arrange everything and get Gary from *Peggy Lynn.*"

"Keep me in the loop."

"Will do. In the meantime, keep your head down."

After Ryan finished talking to Greg, he pulled out the GPS and turned it on before dialing Anders Mikkelsen. The Dane answered immediately with, "What's your location?"

After reading off his current GPS coordinates, Ryan asked, "What's your ETA?"

A long moment passed in which Ryan figured the captain was calculating the arrival time. Mikkelsen finally said, "Fourteen hours."

"The wind has shifted, and I think it's blowing the ship inshore. I'm abreast of Prinzapolka."

"I've had to slow down," Mikkelsen said. "My fuel burn is greater than I expected."

"I understand," Ryan said, disappointed the tug wouldn't arrive sooner. He ended the conversation by saying, "I'll see you soon."

He collected the food cans and stowed them in one of the gear bags, fired up the stove, and heated some meat with a can of mixed vegetables. What he wouldn't give for a steak or even some fresh fish. He was hot, tired, and ready to stretch out on a comfortable bed in an air-conditioned room. Beside the bag of canned goods was half a case of water to quench his thirst, but, after the excitement of the firefight, he craved a cold beer.

After eating and storing his leftovers in the locked cooler to keep the rats out, he walked to the crane cab. Ryan paused as he climbed the short ladder, looking toward the pulpit. Between the crane cab and the pulpit stairs was a raised hatch. Curiosity got the better of him. He jumped down and went forward to open it. He pulled out his flashlight and descended the ladder into the chain locker.

As Ryan stood in the small, hot locker, shining his light along the jumble of thick anchor chain links, he wondered why he hadn't had this idea before. The *Galina* was nearly three-hundred-feet long and most ships carried their length in chain, if not double. He just needed to drop her anchor to keep the *Galina* from running aground or even changing course with the wind, waves, and tide.

He'd been stupid. This was the answer to half his problems, and he should have done it as soon as the *Galina Jovovich* had slipped off Compass Reef.

"Wish in one hand, spit in the other, and see what you get," he muttered to himself as he climbed from the locker. Back on deck, he studied the anchor windlass mounted between the crane and the hatch he'd just come out from, determining how to drop the anchor.

He dialed Greg again, and when he came on the line, Ryan said, "Can you look up the water depth for my coordinates?"

"Give me a minute to get to the computer."

Ryan closed the starboard bridge door to cut down on the wind noise before leaning against the bridge console. "When's the Quick Reaction Force going to arrive?"

"The QRF is not so quick. This place is so backwater that I can't even rent a helicopter here. It has to come from Managua."

"So, when will Gary and Rick get here?"

"They're getting ready to leave on *Dark Water* right now. At top speed, they should be to your position in another three hours." Greg paused. "Okay. I've got the computer running. Give me your coordinates."

Ryan read them off, adding, "I'm about twenty-five miles off Prinzapolka."

In the background, he heard the keyboard rattling as Greg typed the numbers into his program.

"Looks like you're in water between ninety-five- to one-hundred-and-ten-feet deep."

"What's the bottom like?" Ryan asked.

"Sand and mud. Why?"

"I'm going to drop anchor on this tub and keep her from going anywhere else."

"That's a good plan," Greg said. "I should have thought of it sooner."

"You and me both. I've got work to do. I'll talk to you later."

"Do you have Rick's number?"

"Yep. Oh, have them bring a generator and a pump so we can dewater this tub."

"Roger that," Greg replied.

Ryan pocketed the phone and went forward to the chain stopper, yanked out the pin on the lashing, and flung the bar over to release the chain. At the windlass, he pulled the lever to disengage the dog clutch and turned the brake wheel. After a few fast turns, the anchor began rattling through the spurling pipe, and Ryan used the brake to slow the violent passage of the chain, but the chain only increased in speed. He hoped that the chain's bitter end was bolted to the ship or it would fly right over the side and he'd keep drifting toward shore.

Ryan cranked the brake as tight as he could, but the windlass continued to spin. Smoke poured off the brake shoes as they ineffectually pressed against the steel drum. The racket was deafening as the deck beneath his feet vibrated. Mud, dried seaweed, and rust flew off the chain, pelting his feet and legs. Unable to rein in the anchor chain, Ryan ran for cover. He didn't want to be anywhere near the windlass when the bitter end whipped through the windlass's wheel snugs.

He dove behind the safety of the steel bulkhead of the main deck cabins just as a loud *thunk* reverberated through the deck. He poked his head around the corner and saw the chain had stopped paying out. From below came a giant *pop* as metal ripped apart, followed by the sound of heavy chain beating against the inside of the chain locker as the bitter end whipped around.

Without thinking, he ran to the chain stopper, threw the bar into place, and locked it. He then threaded the stopper cable through the links and pinned it in place. The motion of the ship changed as he worked, and when he looked up, she was turning bow-on to the waves. Ryan opened the chain locker hatch and shined his light down to see the last link of the chain and its clench hanging free. It had ripped off the collision bulkhead and whipped around the locker, leaving large indents in the metal with each impact.

Stepping up onto the pulpit, Ryan saw the chain trailing off to the east, its long bend—called the catenary curve—provided a low angle of pull on the anchor flukes which would have dug themselves into the mud as the ship dragged the anchor backward. He knew it wasn't the anchor that kept the ship from drifting but the weight of the chain running along the seabed, and, with almost three-hundred-and-fifty-feet out according to the counter on the windlass, it would take one hell of a blow to move this ship again.

Now all he needed to do was wait for the pirates or *Dark Water*, and he hoped like hell that his friends were the first to arrive.

CHAPTER TWENTY-FOUR

The sun was low on the western horizon, turning the water dark-blue and black under thick white clouds shot through with rays of orange and red. Ryan stood on the aft observation deck of the Soviet-era cruise ship, *Galina Jovovich*, as she pitched in the low swells marching in from the east to crash against Nicaragua's marshy lowlands, which lacked barrier reefs to protect the shoreline and allow for deep-water ports. The seafloor shoaled quickly along the coast, and the current often changed direction without explanation.

That same current was now pushing the *Galina*'s stern south as Ryan trained his binoculars on the horizon, searching for the pirate boats he knew were coming. Now that the ship was at anchor, it was easier for them to approach and board the old vessel. He had his Molotov cocktails and his guns for protection, but if two boats approached from opposite sides, they could quickly surround and overwhelm him.

Day slipped into night as Ryan remained at the railing, searching the darkness after switching the binoculars to night vision mode. They had the latest version of software installed, which allowed the night to appear in vivid color instead of the monotone greens of the previous versions. The new binoculars were a joint effort between DWR and FRT Innovations, owned by former Navy SEAL Jacques Kilbourne. Greg had invested in the company, and, as he jokingly liked to put it, he was helping to put the research in Dark Water Research.

Ryan rolled the switch on the binoculars, changing them to a thermal imaging sensor. Coming out of the last of the setting sun were three pangas. There was too much body heat and solar energy clustered around the boats for him to get an accurate count of how many pirates were in each, but it didn't really matter.

A more helpful tool would have been a sniper rifle to pick off the pirates or to disable their engines before they could get close to the *Galina*, but Ryan didn't have such a luxury, which was making him rethink the weapons he normally carried.

Unfortunately, he had to fight with what he had, and he'd been busy since dropping the hook. He'd checked the water level in the engine room and verified it was still rising. Then he'd decided which room to sequester himself in if he had to fall back under heavy fire from the pirates. Once he had his gear stashed there, he worked to fortify the space and to provide some surprises for the invaders as they followed him into the bowels of the ship. He now had several booby traps made from fire extinguishers. None of them were deadly, but they'd help to slow his enemy.

Before he retreated to his panic room, he wanted to do as much damage to the pirates as he could, and now Ryan lay sprawled on the deck, watching the boats through the binoculars while dialing Rick Hayes's number.

"What's up, brother?" Rick asked after two rings.

"Pirates inbound to my location. What's your ETA?"

"Thirty-five minutes."

"Put the hammer down," Ryan urged.

"Look at me, saving your ass again."

"Your life would be so dull without me getting into trouble," Ryan said. "I'll let you buy me a beer or six later."

Rick laughed before turning serious again. "How many tangos?"

"Three boats full. Somewhere between fifteen and thirty guys."

"We'll limber up the old shootin' irons."

"Hurry up, Cowboy Rick." Ryan thumbed the End button while Rick was still sputtering about his new nickname. It was better than the last one: Short Rick.

Ryan pulled the KRISS snug against his shoulder. According to the laser rangefinder built into its holographic sight, the pirates were still beyond the limits of the nine-millimeter projectiles he would sling down range at them.

He settled into the ship's rhythm as she strained against her anchor. The *Galina* rode fat and heavy in the swells with her belly full of water, which helped to stabilize her as a shooting platform. As the pangas grew steadily closer in his sight, Ryan willed himself to become calm, to become one with the gun and the ship, and to remember everything he'd learned about making long distance shots.

Slowly, the range numbers counted down, and he began to distinguish features on the men as they became more visible in the low light. They looked like a rag-tag bunch of farmers or fishermen. There was little work for men like them on the marshy coastal plains of eastern Nicaragua. The fishing and lobster fleets were hiring fewer men as they overfished the waters and the lobsters moved into deeper waters, making them harder to dive for and catch.

They were desperate for jobs, money, and food to feed

their families. The *Galina Jovovich* represented a large score for them, and with just a single man guarding her, she should have been easy to capture, and they probably wanted revenge for the men Ryan had already killed.

As the boats entered the range of his rifle, two of them peeled off, one to starboard and the other to port, while the third came straight for *Galina*'s stern. Ryan moved to focus on the boat moving to his right. As it turned, it gave Ryan a shot at the high-horsepower motor. Training the sights on the engine cowling, he tracked the up-and-down movement of the panga's stern. Once he had a gauge of the boat's movement, he squeezed off a two-round burst. He waited for the sight's crosshairs to move through his mark again and depressed the trigger a second time. This burst smacked the engine and caused it to splutter.

Ryan rolled to his left as the men in the middle boat returned fire at his bright muzzle flashes. Bullets struck steel. They sparked and sang as they ricocheted away, but none hit near where Ryan had just been. He took aim at the boat racing for the *Galina*'s stern. Ryan let off three quick bursts at the men clustered on the panga's seats and gunwales, knocking several into the water before he was up and moving again, this time taking the stairs down to the main deck where he'd placed his two Molotov cocktails.

If he could eliminate two boats, it would be a productive use of resources, but Murphy always had a way of kicking his ass, just like when the cocktail he'd thrown at the first pirates had bounced out of the boat. Now he wished he hadn't dropped the others into the sea. He'd contributed to the ocean's pollution and maybe his own demise by wasting valuable resources.

These thoughts played through his mind as he squatted near the opening in the rail, waiting for the panga to draw near. He would have to wait until the last second to throw the bombs, and even then, the pirates might see the spark of flame as he lit the fuel-soaked rag and veered away from the *Galina*. It was a chance he'd have to take. He couldn't squander any more ammunition than he already had. The Molotov cocktails were the most efficient way to destroy the pangas.

The small boat drew alongside the *Galina*'s stern, and a man at its bow tossed a grappling hook over the railing and used the rope to pull the panga alongside the bigger ship.

It was now or never. Ryan shielded the flame as best he could as he flicked the lighter. The rag sparked instantly, and Ryan rose to throw it overboard. Shouts erupted from the panga as they saw the white devil holding the burning bottle over his head before slamming it down. The bottle shattered in the panga's bilge and the little boat blossomed with fire, igniting both wood and flesh.

Ryan turned away from the gruesome scene and ran to the other side of the cruise ship. She rolled heavily in the waves, shifting uneasily beneath his feet as if trying to shake off her chain to roam free once again.

Night had completely fallen and there was insufficient light for Ryan to see the pirates, save for the flickering flames of the burning panga. One panga had gone to rescue the survivors. The other had restarted its outboard and was making a run toward the *Galina*. Ryan braced his submachine gun on the rail and put several rounds into the men, hoping to deter them.

Then he saw something that made his blood run cold. A man stood in the panga and raised an iron tube to his shoulder. Ryan recognized it instantly as a rocket-propelled grenade.

CHAPTER TWENTY-FIVE

Ryan Weller stood transfixed on the deck of the *Galina Jovovich*, staring at the man in the panga holding an RPG. He didn't wonder for too long about how they'd gotten their hands on such weaponry. Nicaragua had been at war for decades, and the U.S. had armed and trained the men of various regimes in an attempt to defeat the communists trying to gain a foothold in the Central American country.

He raised his KRISS Vector, again wishing he had something with a longer range, and aimed at the man holding the RPG. He centered the holographic sight on the man's chest, let out half a breath, and depressed the trigger, sending a burst across the water.

It seemed to have no effect.

As he lined up for another shot, the night was rent by a loud buzzing sound, and the panga he'd been aiming at exploded into flames. Men flew off the boat like the hand of God had punched them.

Ryan lowered his rifle and watched in awe as Greg Olsen's Hatteras GT63, *Dark Water*, charged through the black water, a Minigun blazing on its bow, throwing a long tongue of flame into the darkness. Red tracers streaked across a sea already ablaze with two burning boats, chasing after the third panga as it sped away from the carnage.

The roar of the rotary machine gun died, and the Hatteras idled toward the cruise ship. As she passed the burning panga, Ryan saw Gary Bartwell holding the twin grips of a General Electric M134 six-barreled mini Gatling gun mounted on a post where the Zodiac's davit fit into the hull. The Zodiac wasn't on the bow, giving Gary a clean arc for the gun to swing through.

"You okay?" Gary shouted as the Hatteras came alongside the *Galina*.

"I'm good." Ryan tapped his fist against the top of his head to make the large O of a diver's okay signal.

A few minutes later, Gary had *Dark Water* tied to the *Galina*'s stern, and Ryan jumped down to its bow. He helped Gary break down the Minigun and store it in a custom case in the engine room.

When they were back on the bridge, Ryan said, "Do you have anything for long range shooting?"

"Got a Springfield M1A in 6.5 Creedmoor," Rick said. "It's a twin to the one you used in Mexico to miss the drug lord."

Ryan dismissed Rick's dig and said, "Get it."

Rick retreated into the Hatteras's cabin and returned with the rifle and several magazines full of hollow-point boat tail cartridges. "Here you go. Hope you hit what you're aiming at."

"You know I didn't take a single shot with that gun, right?"

"So you say." Rick winked at him.

Ryan had snuck into Mexico last Thanksgiving and tried to snipe the former leader of the Aztlán Cartel, José Luis Orozco. He hadn't taken the shot because Orozco had stepped out of his SUV and taken a baby into his arms. Ryan would not risk shooting an innocent kid.

"Hopefully, we won't need it," Gary said.

"I agree," Ryan said. "Better safe than sorry. Now, did you bring that pump and hose?"

"Yeah, it's in the cockpit," Rick said.

The three men built a makeshift hoist and pulled the generator and water pump aboard the *Galina*. Ryan and Gary carried the water pump to the engine room while Rick shouldered the rolls of the firehose. He made a second trip for the two-inch plastic piping equipped with a strainer basket at one end to keep debris from being sucked into the pump. They dropped it into the bilge beside the cruise ship's massive engine, connected the hose to the pump, and ran a second hose from the pump out a nearby porthole. Within minutes of starting the generator, water was pouring overboard.

Ryan wiped his hands on an old rag and said, "Now, maybe we won't sink before the tug arrives."

"I hope not," Rick muttered. "This damned thing has been more trouble than she's worth."

They took two-hour shifts, standing on the *Galina*'s stern and watching for the pirates to return. When the sun rose, all three men were eager to leave the ghost ship and return to their daily lives. Ryan wasn't sure if it was exhaustion, lack of decent food, or if his mind was playing tricks on him, but the ship seemed to have a life of her own, tugging at the anchor chain and trying to break free, even in placid waters. Even though he'd spent the last few days alone on the *Galina*, for reasons he couldn't explain, he felt more creeped out with her at anchor than at any other time. He was glad Gary and Rick were close at hand.

When Ryan climbed off the *Galina* after his last watch, Rick had coffee brewing in the Hatteras's saloon and was cooking bacon and eggs. Ryan greedily scooped the food into his mouth, having had nothing but canned goods since he'd eaten the last of the fresh fish Eddy had given him.

"Slow down there, cowboy," Rick said. "I don't wanna have to do the *hind* lick maneuver."

Around a mouthful of eggs and toast, Ryan replied, "Gary's a Marine, but even he won't let you lick his butt."

"Go ahead and choke, so I can point and laugh." Rick stopped flipping eggs and held the spatula up. "You know, last night counts as saving your ass. *Again.*"

"Are you keeping score?"

Rick went back to pushing the scrambled eggs around the griddle. "Rick Hayes: four. Ryan Weller: zero."

"That can't be right."

"Oh? Let me count the ways." Rick turned to face Ryan and held up his hand to tick off the points he was about to make.

"All right," Ryan said, cutting him off.

Gary opened the saloon door. "Got a tugboat inbound. They're hailing you on the radio, squid."

Ryan scrambled up the ladder to *Dark Water*'s bridge and snatched up the microphone. "*Star of Galveston*, this is *Dark Water*. Come in. Over."

Captain Anders Mikkelsen's voice came through the speaker. "We have you in sight and will be alongside in ten minutes, Ryan."

"What do you want us to do?"

"Standoff with your sportfisher and await further instructions."

"Roger that. I'll be aboard the *Galina* for the trip."

Mikkelsen acknowledged Ryan's last transmission, and Ryan hung the mic on the hook beside the radio. He turned to Gary, who'd accompanied him to the bridge. "I'm going aboard the *Galina*. You and Rick can haul ass for Bluefields."

"You got it." Gary started *Dark Water*'s diesels while Ryan went down the ladder to grab the M1A and to snatch a few boxes of ammunition to reload his pistol. He carried everything to the *Galina*'s bridge. The *Star of Galveston*'s crew launched their workboat, and by the time he'd finished cramming the nine-millimeter hollow points into the Glock's magazines, the crew had arrived with the tow bridle.

Ryan walked down to the bow and asked the foreman, a squat man in blue coveralls and an orange survival vest with a walkie-talkie clipped to it, if he could help. The foreman held out his hand, introduced himself as James White, and told Ryan to stand fast while they ran the tow bridle through the hawseholes on both sides of the bow, crisscrossed the heavy chafing chains on the deck, and fastened them to the bollards on either side of the anchor windlass. They worked quickly and efficiently until they had the Y-bridle situated and returned to their workboat.

"Do you have power?" White asked Ryan when the crew boat left to retrieve the tow hawser, which floated behind the tugboat.

"No, but I have a generator running to pump out the hold."

"Okay. We'll retrieve the anchor another way."

"I'm not sure the anchor winch works, anyway," Ryan said. "When I let the chain out, it smoked the brakes."

"Not a problem. We'll cut the anchor and mark it for retrieval later." He relayed the information through his radio to the *Star*'s captain.

When the workboat had the tow hawser hooked to the bridle, it retreated to the *Star* and came back with a set of portable cutting torches. The crewman attached an acoustical beacon to the chain, and the torch made quick work of the links. With a steaming hiss, the hot chain fell into the water, and the *Galina* drifted backward until the tow cable arrested her movement.

"We're ready here," White said into his radio, and he watched the bridle carefully as the *Star of Galveston* applied power and took the *Galina Jovovich* under tow.

A moment later, White radioed that everything looked good and removed his hardhat and rubbed a hand through his salt-and-pepper hair. "Got anything to drink?"

"Yeah, up on the bridge," Ryan answered, and the two men walked up the stairs.

As White sipped his water, he looked at the rifle on the console and the pistol on Ryan's hip. "Expecting trouble?"

"We've had several pirate attacks."

"Screw *that*. This piece of shit isn't worth it."

"I'm inclined to agree with you," Ryan said. "We're only doing this because this *thing* ran over and sank our cable-laying barge."

"I don't envy you."

"It hasn't been a picnic. I've been eating canned stew and shitting over the railing."

"Screw that," White said again. He glanced at his watch. "Tomorrow, we'll be at the breakers, if everything goes well."

Ryan looked longingly at *Dark Water*, wishing he were on her and zipping back to Bluefields. He wasn't because he had a job to finish and this ordeal would be over soon.

IT TOOK NEARLY eighteen hours for *Star of Galveston* to tow the *Galina Jovovich* through the channel between El Bluff and Casaba Cay, and another two to make their way up the Escondido River to a wide branch which ran to the Smokey Lane Lagoon. The branch forked at a small island where four old cargo vessels shifted restlessly on heavy anchor chains in water the color of chocolate milk. Carved out of the single canopy jungle on the muddy shores of the island was a bustling scrapyard where a bevy of workers used cutting torches and saws to strip another ship and load the steel on barges for transport.

Once they'd rafted the *Galina* to one of the defunct cargo vessels, Capt. Mikkelsen turned the tug around and headed for El Bluff, where the *Star* took a barge in tow before continuing out to meet *Peggy Lynn* to provide support for the diving operations on *El Paso City*.

Ryan wished he could have spent the night in Bluefields, drinking beers and hanging out with Greg, but Travis needed him to supplement the diving rotation while they recovered gear from the sunken cable layer.

When he climbed aboard *Peggy Lynn*, Gary was suiting up for a dive.

"You don't waste any time, do you?" Ryan asked.

Gary grinned. "I'm not a slacker like you."

"Well, this slacker needs a shower and a nap before he can do anything else."

"Come on, all you've done since going to the *Galina* was sit on your ass."

"You're right, and I'm worn out from doing it. Have a nice dive." Ryan went down the steps to the stateroom he shared with Gary and stripped out of his clothes before taking a shower. The hot water pounding his skin and washing away the salt and grime felt good. After pulling on clean clothes, he stepped to the galley and found Grandpa had made a pot of fish stew and left it to simmer on the stove. Unable to handle eating stew for yet another meal, he fixed a sandwich and washed it down with a beer before retiring to his bunk. He stretched out under the sheet, luxuriating in the air conditioning, and drifted off to sleep, hoping he wouldn't have to worry about wrangling wayward ships any time soon.

CHAPTER TWENTY-SIX

South Beach
Miami, Florida

At six a.m., there were few people on South Beach and even fewer in the water, which was where Emily Hunt was now pushing herself through the smooth Atlantic in long strokes. She was almost to the seawall at South Pointe Pier and the end of her two-mile swim. The water was clear and flat, with the waves just breaking on the sand. Swimming made her happy, and her mind shut off everything but the robotic motions of her freestyle technique.

As she approached the boulders of the seawall, she turned west toward the beach and drove hard for the shallows. When her feet touched sand, she kicked off and lunged forward, then gathered them under her again and started to run. She came out of the water and made a right on the wet sand. Rather than fixate on where her feet hit the ground, she focused on the day ahead and tried to make sense of the hunt for the captured freighter. Unlike with swimming, her mind drifted while running. It turned to DWR's work in Bluefields and the fact that the Caribbean's largest shipbreaker was just up the river from the sleepy town. And she thought about seeing Ryan.

Emily bent forward and sprinted as fast as she could. Her muscles screamed and her lungs ached, but she kept going, willing herself through the last mile at top speed. Finished with her run, she slowed and walked a block to her rental car. She toweled off and drove back to her hotel, showered, and put on slacks and a blouse.

She had spent yesterday working on other cases in her hotel room and this morning she was meeting the freelance sketch artist at the hospital. She had also used a mapping program to determine the distance the *Everglades Explorer* would have traveled at her cruising speed of six knots. Smith had told her the old ship would make ten knots when unloaded and that Spataro had ordered him to always cruise at six to conserve fuel. She'd drew a circle on the map to show how far the *Explorer* could have traveled at six knots and another circle to account for the increased speed. The latter ring reached Jamaica and extended halfway through the Caribbean to Venezuela. Each day, the circles would get larger, and the ship would become harder to find.

She'd focused on extending the circles to the north, south, and west. While she doubted the hijackers would cross the Atlantic, she could discount nothing in the beginning, even though her gut told her they were taking it to the breakers.

According to her rudimentary charts, they could be in South America in two days, Central America in four, and the United States in three. Cuba was only a short run away. If they went to Cuba, she could call off the search, because Ward and Young would never approve an operation to recover the ship from there. They didn't cover any ships doing business in Cuban waters because of the U.S. sanctions and travel bans.

On her way to the hospital, Emily stopped for coffee and a breakfast sandwich for the captain. She knew how terrible hospital food was and wanted him to have something tasty to eat.

At nine a.m., she met the sketch artist in the lobby. Steve was a heavyset man in his forties, with long red hair styled in what she called an Amish bowl cut. Together, they rode the elevator to Smith's floor and found the captain picking at a tray of rubbery eggs and a brown gravy-looking substance over toast.

When Emily set the fast food bag on the table, the man's eyes lit up, and he reached eagerly into it. While he ate, he talked to Steve and tried his best to give an accurate description of the pirate who had taken his ship.

Two hours later, Steve had completed his sketch and held it up for Smith to look at.

He nodded. "That's the guy."

Emily leaned over to look at the picture with him. The man looked unremarkable, with pale skin, black hair, and rough stubble forming a beard and mustache. The nose was the most distinguishing feature with a wide flare in the middle. Now all she needed was a name to go with the face.

Steve and Emily bid their farewells to Smith and left the hospital as the captain's family came into the room. She drove north on I-95 and got off to follow surface streets along the Miami River. It was a longer trip than taking the freeways, but it was more scenic, and she liked to see the changes along the waterfront. She'd been here many times while investigating cargo theft or checking on ship repairs. High-priced condos sprawled west from downtown Miami, taking over the small industrial buildings until they would eventually displace the commercial fishing and crabbing docks, but they wouldn't be able to move the shipping docks, wrecking yards, and scrap metal vendors farther upriver. The Miami River would always be a hub of trade, and the people paying for the view would have to watch rusty freighters and smoking tugs pass by their wide windows.

Spataro Shipping was one of the larger shipping concerns on the concrete-lined waterway. Their office was in an old two-story, tan building made of concrete block. High rusty chain-link fencing with four strands of barbed wire at the top surrounded the lot. Cargo containers in a variety of sizes and colors sat in stacks four and five high, waiting to be loaded onto ships along the quay. Semi-trucks entered and exited the dusty yard. She counted five massive cranes. Numerous reach stackers and forklifts barreled along the waterfront, busily moving cargo, and adding an element of chaos to the orderly-looking shipping yard.

Inside, the building was lit with fluorescent tube lights that provided a reflective sheen to the cracked and worn laminate floor tiles. Lorenzo's office was on the second floor, and Emily introduced herself to the secretary and asked if Mr. Spataro was available. She told Emily that he was expecting her and to go on in. The corner office's single-pane windows overlooked the shipping yard and the river. A small pleasure boat was passing by, the driver and passengers gawking openly at the massive cargo vessels.

Lorenzo Spataro greeted her by rising from his desk. She refrained from shaking his hand because of the sweat-soaked handkerchief that he held and sat across from him.

"How is Captain Smith?" he asked.

"He says he'll be good as new soon and ready to go to sea."

Spataro nodded. "I may not have a ship for him to captain if we don't get the *Explorer* back."

"Have you begun looking for another ship to buy?" she asked.

With a sigh, he said, "No, but I suppose I'll have to. No luck with the captain, then?"

Emily removed the color sketch of the mystery man and showed it to him.

He shook his head. "I've never seen him before."

She replaced the sketch in her briefcase. "Do you have a file on the *Explorer?*"

"Certainly. I had Maria put it in the conference room for you."

"Before I look at it, can I ask you a few questions?"

Spataro nodded and wiped his forehead.

"Do you have any enemies?"

"Not that I know of."

"What about disputes with workers or customers?"

"I always have some sort of dispute brewing. We're dealing with sailors, Ms. Hunt. They're a temperamental breed. You know the saying: 'A bitching sailor is a happy sailor.'"

"I've never heard that before."

"Sailors never seem happy unless they're complaining about something, like working conditions, pay, et cetera."

"I see. Have any of these unhappy sailors filed complaints or sabotaged one of your ships?"

Spataro leaned back in his chair and adjusted the antique wire fan to blow on his face. "Years ago, I had trouble paying a crew because my client didn't pay me. He promised to pay after one more voyage, and I agreed. We made a run to the DR, and, once in port, the crew complained to the union and the government seized my ship. They auctioned it off and the buyer had her taken straight to the breaker."

"I've heard of that happening, but usually it's a lengthy process from seizure to auction."

"Someone bribed the judge and he issued an order for seizure," Spataro explained. "The police have to enforce it, and they were probably greased as well. Once a ship is sold at a maritime auction, the auction eliminates a ship's history, including debts and prior ownership. It's like we never existed, and I had no rights."

"I don't remember that happening," Emily said.

"I wasn't with Ward and Young then. That incident was the reason I started using your company. The premiums are more, but the coverage is much better."

Emily nodded. She knew Ward and Young had some of the highest premiums in the business. She changed the subject, and asked, "The Haitians didn't seize the *Explorer*, did they?"

He gestured to her briefcase. "That man doesn't look like a Haitian to me."

"Maybe they hired someone to steal it. Have you had any problems down there?"

"Never, and I'm sure if my fixer had heard about the ship being in a Haitian port, he would have called me."

"Could he have been in on it?"

"No," Spataro said flatly. "He and Capt. Smith are good friends, and I look the other way when Smith takes extra goods to sell down there. He and the fixer split the profits. Money buys loyalty in Haiti, and Robenson Girard is as loyal as any man can get."

"What about the charterer who holds the Haitian contract?"

"Again, no." Spataro leaned forward. "Ms. Hunt, the men who took my ship are pirates, plain and simple. They have no connection to me or to my charter parties."

"But why *your* ship?"

"I don't know, and I ask myself that every day. Those men deserved better than to be shot to death."

Emily stood and said she would like to examine the ship's file. Spataro nodded, and said he'd had his secretary, Maria, place it in the conference room. As she closed the office door behind her, he picked up the phone.

Maria showed her the conference room, a narrow dusty room with mismatched chairs, a scarred wooden table, and a coffee maker. She helped herself to a cup of coffee and sat down to study the file. The last person to charter *Everglades Explorer* was Archibald Taliaferro, owner of Taliaferro Exports. She made a note of his address before leafing through the rest of the file.

She saw nothing of interest among the receipts, bills of laden, contracts, and customs forms. The coffee left a bitter taste in her mouth, and she was hungry for lunch. Deciding there was nothing more she could learn there, she returned the folder to Maria and knocked on Spataro's door.

After being called inside, she said, "I think I have everything I need, Mr. Spataro. I'm going over to Taliaferro Exports."

"Tell him I'll have a ship ready to sail for Haiti next week if he wants to send anything."

The insurance investigator nodded. "I'll be in touch, Mr. Spataro."

Before going to Taliaferro's place, she stopped at a Pollo Tropical and grabbed a chicken Caesar salad. She ate in the car while thinking about where the ship could have disappeared to. She pulled a picture that showed an overhead view of the *Explorer* from her briefcase and studied it.

Malaysia Airlines Flight 370's disappearance over the Indian Ocean had spurred many innovations regarding the search for missing ships and planes. As with anything, time and technology had helped to refine search software, and now companies were claiming to be able to identify a ship either in port or on the open ocean by using artificial intelligence and algorithmic analysis. Emily had approached Kyle Ward about purchasing such software. He had taken the idea to the board of directors, and they had declined. Instead of purchasing the software, they would pay for the software developer to run a search if they deemed it necessary.

She dialed Kyle's number and reached his secretary, who said he was unavailable, so she left a message for him to call her back.

Finished with her salad, she drove to Taliaferro Exports. The building was a bland structure on the edge of Miami International Airport, where screaming planes accompanied the sounds of vehicle traffic.

She waited an hour to see Taliaferro. He was a light-skinned mulatto with a round face and a heavy dose of freckles across his cheeks and nose. He nodded when Emily told him about the theft of the *Everglades Explorer*.

"I was sorry to hear about it," Taliaferro said. "I enjoy working with Lorenzo and Captain Smith."

"Mr. Spataro said to tell you that he'll have a ship going to Miragoâne next week."

"That's wonderful news. Like I said, I contracted with Spataro Shipping to move goods to Haiti. I have relatives there, and I like to do what I can for them."

She watched his face when she asked, "Do you know who took the *Explorer*?"

He stared right at her. "No. I had nothing to do with it. My business depends on those ships."

"Thank you for your time, Mr. Taliaferro." Emily stood and handed him a business card. "If you think of anything else, please call me."

The exporter shook her hand, assured her he would call if he heard anything, and escorted her to the door.

Back in the hot car, Emily started the engine and let the air conditioning cool the interior. She leaned her head back against the headrest, closed her eyes, and concentrated on her conversations with Spataro and Taliaferro. She'd once taken a class given by a former Secret Service agent on how to read a subject's face for micro expressions or tells. Most happened in fractions of a second, but a trained individual could spot them easily. She wasn't as skilled as some, but she'd put her training to use on both Taliaferro and Spataro and was certain neither of them was lying to her.

What now? she thought. *While I'm sifting through data and interviewing possible suspects, the ship is getting farther and farther away, or it's getting chopped into little bits.*

Her phone rang through the car speakers. She'd connected it via Bluetooth as soon as she'd gotten into the car at the rental agency. She pressed the button on the steering wheel and answered the call with, "Hey, Kyle."

"How's Miami?"

"Sweltering. Is there any chance you could get the board to approve of Hobbins Group searching for my missing ship?"

"None whatsoever. As a matter of fact, they want you to end your search so they can pay the claim."

"Are you sure?" she asked, feeling let down that the board wouldn't back her up, but she knew they didn't want to spend unnecessary funds to look for a thirty-year-old ship that had reached the end of its service life five years ago.

"You know them. It's all about the bottom line."

"Yeah, I know. Thanks, Kyle."

"I'll see you when you get back. We can go to dinner."

She heard his golf club slice through the air. "All right. I'll call you when I'm back in Tampa."

"Love you, babe."

The call ended before she could respond. It was just as well because she didn't want to say those words back to him.

She booked herself on a flight back to Tampa the following morning. Rush-hour traffic was just beginning as she threaded her way toward a hotel near the airport. She told herself she'd get a bottle of wine and wind down, although the reality was that she'd keep working the case and she knew it. The men who had needlessly died aboard the *Explorer* deserved more than her abandonment of them, and their families needed closure.

After returning to the hotel, Emily called Spataro and told him of the board's decision. With defeat in his voice, he told her he would start hunting for another ship. She promised him she would keep looking for the *Explorer* in her spare time, which brightened his mood, and he agreed to fund her expeditions if she needed financial help. She thanked him and hung up.

Next, she spread her charts and files on the bed and desk. She checked the distance between her suspected destination of Bluefields against the time it would take for the pirates to steam there. At max speed, it would take them just under five days, meaning they wouldn't arrive there until tomorrow. She thought about calling Greg Olsen and having his people keep a lookout for the ship, but she figured they were too busy.

Her eyes fell on the sketch of the pirate leader. She reached for her phone again and dialed a friend in the Tampa police department. Detective Kaya Takao answered on the third ring.

"How are you, Emily? We need to get together for a glass of wine."

"I know, Kaya. I've been meaning to call, but I've been out of town. I was wondering if you could do me a favor?"

"Sure, but you have to promise me that we'll get together when you get home."

"Absolutely," Emily assured her.

"Good. Now what can I do for you? Do you have more criminals for me to arrest?"

"No." Emily laughed. "I wanted to know if you can run a sketch of a suspect through your facial recognition software?"

"Yeah, that's tricky. It's tough to get a hit, but we can try."

"Great. Want me to fax the sketch?"

"Fax? What century are you in, girl?" Kaya laughed. "Send it by email."

"Okay. I'll need to find a scanner. I'm sure my hotel has one."

"I'll watch for it. I've gotta run. I'll call you if we get a hit."

"Thanks, Kaya. I'll talk to you soon," Emily said, and she hung up.

She took the sketch to the hotel's business center where she scanned it and emailed to herself. Within a few minutes, her phone chimed with the incoming email, and she forwarded it to Kaya. She put the sketch back in her briefcase and walked to the restaurant to get dinner and a glass of wine. With her work done for the night, it was time to relax and enjoy her posh surroundings, despite having no one to share them with.

As she ordered her second glass of wine, her thoughts centered on the pirate leader and just who he was. If Kaya's people were any good, they would find out for her, but she had no clue how big of a lead the sketch would actually be.

CHAPTER TWENTY-SEVEN

Tampa, Florida

The American Airlines Airbus A319 landed mid-afternoon, and Emily took an Uber to her apartment. She had a cozy one-bed, one-bath unit on the third floor of a gated building with an easterly view of the Courtney Campbell Causeway and a cove of Old Tampa Bay. She tossed her briefcase onto the counter and dropped her travel bag on the floor beside her bed. The laundry could wait until after she'd swam laps.

She was in the middle of changing into her swimsuit when her cell phone rang.

"Hey, Kaya. How are you?"

"I'm good. Can you come down to the station?"

"Sure, why?"

"We got a hit on the sketch."

"Great." Emily looked at the clock on her nightstand. "Will thirty minutes be all right?"

"I'll see you then."

Emily changed into a pair of dark slacks and a white blouse before getting into her four-door Jeep Wrangler. She had to control her speed on account of wanting to race through the streets to see Kaya's results.

She downshifted the manual transmission as she approached a red light. When she came to a stop, she raked her hair back into a ponytail and pulled it through the band she kept on her wrist. Traffic seemed to get worse every day, and she hated it a little more every day.

The light turned green and she shoved the shifter into first, but not before someone several cars back beeped their horn. A small part of her fantasized about shutting off the motor and faking car trouble just to make the person wait, but she mashed the gas and shot away from the light. She was in a hurry herself.

At the police station, she asked to see Takao. A few minutes later, a short, attractive woman with jet black hair appeared and ushered Emily to a small conference room where two men in black suits were waiting. Both were average-looking, with no remarkable features. She suspected they were federal agents.

Kaya made the introductions: James Stickney and Charles Gordon were from the FBI. Both men shook Emily's hand and asked where she had gotten the sketch of her suspect and why she had asked Takao to run it through the system.

Emily explained about the stolen ship and that the sketch depicted the pirate leader. "Why? What's this all about?"

Stickney cleared his throat. "We're not at liberty to say, Ms. Hunt, but thank you for coming in."

"I came all the way down here and you're not going to tell me who this guy is?" she asked.

"As I said, Ms. Hunt, we appreciate your cooperation," Stickney said.

"That's it?"

"Yes, ma'am," the agent said. The two men stood and left the office.

"What was *that* all about?" Emily asked her friend.

"I'm going off duty now. How about we go get that glass of wine?"

"Okay, but first tell me what's going on."

Kaya led her out of the building to the street and they walked toward the Tampa Riverwalk. "After you sent the sketch, I tried to put it in the system, but I got a call from one of the tech guys who said there were some problems with it. He asked if he could play with it and I told him to go ahead, figuring you'd be okay with it."

Emily nodded.

"Anyway, he used some modeling software and came up with a 3D rendering. Then he ran the model against some faces of famous people."

"What?"

Kaya shrugged. "It's a common thing. They run the sketch against celebrities to match points like the nose or chin, and when the computer says it's a match, it builds a set of nodal points. It's sort of like doing one of those Facebook celebrity *who-do-I-look-like?* programs. To be fair, it's not the best way to do it and we don't use the facial data to make an arrest, only to develop suspects and work the case. The tech thought your guy shared facial features with an actor named Wentworth Miller."

"I've never heard of him."

"Neither had I, but the tech said he'd been binge-watching a TV show called *Prison Break*."

"I don't think I've heard of that either," Emily said.

Kaya smiled. "You're not alone. Anyway, once the AI seized on those nodals, the search took very little time to come up with a man named Masoud Sadiq, and that's when the FBI called."

The women arrived at the Hillsborough River and went into a restaurant. Both ordered a glass of wine and carried them onto a patio that overlooked the river.

"Why is the FBI interested in him?" Emily asked.

"Sadiq is a member of the Syrian Army."

Emily sipped her red wine and stared at the river. *Why would the Syrian Army steal a ship in Haiti?*

"Apparently," Kaya continued, "he's been heavily involved in the fighting in Iraq and Syria. That's all I could get out of them, and I wasn't supposed to tell you."

"Was he ISIS?" she asked.

Kaya took a sip of wine. "That would be my guess."

Emily took out her phone and searched for the man's name. There were no references to Sadiq, which didn't surprise her. If he were a member of a terrorist organization, he wouldn't want to broadcast his face or location to the world. She then searched for Wentworth Miller and thought he resembled the sketch, but she would have never put the two together on her own.

The two women made small talk until their glasses were empty, then walked back to the police station. After a quick hug and agreeing to get together again soon, Emily drove to her office. She needed to file a report on Spataro's ship and get the claim prepared so he could purchase another one.

It was late by the time she wrapped up her paperwork and went back to her apartment, where she took a long swim in the complex's pool and did laundry. Emily was settling on the sofa with her last glass of wine for the evening when her phone rang.

"Ms. Hunt, this is Lorenzo Spataro."

"What can I do for you?"

"After we first spoke, I offered a reward for anyone who

spotted my missing ship. There's a man in Bluefields, Nicaragua, who claims that it just turned up at the breaking yard."

Emily couldn't believe that a member of the Syrian Army would suddenly turn to stealing ships and selling them for scrap—if that was even who had stolen the vessel. The guy in the sketch could be someone completely different from Sadiq, whom they only suspected because the celebrity facial features might have skewed the results. Still, she couldn't discount a good lead. "Are you sure?"

"He's positive. You need to get down there now."

CHAPTER TWENTY-EIGHT

Everglades Explorer
Puerto Cortés, Honduras

The *Everglades Explorer* entered Puerto Cortés, Honduras, the largest shipping port in Central America, five days after fleeing Haiti. They'd encountered rough seas during the passage, but it had been otherwise uneventful, and Sadiq was thankful for it. After securing the ship to their assigned berthing, he went ashore and met with his contact who had the cargo manifests and transfer paperwork for a bulk load of ammonium nitrate in one-thousand-kilo bags and drums of diesel fuel, arranged by General Golnar and paid for through shell corporations.

The stevedores craned the bags into the *Explorer*'s Number One and Three Holds and loaded the diesel into the Number Two Hold. In addition to the cargo, the port workers loaded a single shipping container onto the deck, across the middle hold after they'd put the hatch cover in place.

Sadiq stood by the railing, checking his clipboard to ensure all was aboard, and once again cast his gaze to the dock for what seemed like the thousandth time. He looked up and down the long concrete quay, covering most of the southern edge of the peninsula that sheltered the port. At the western end were oil and gas terminals; closer to him were storage and grain bins. To the south, beside the causeway that crossed the Alvarado Lagoon, a sea of multicolored containers awaited shipment. He wondered if anyone thought his load was suspicious or if they even cared. He hoped not, yet he continued to scan the docks for anyone who seemed overly interested in him or his ship.

Mounted on the warehouses and on poles all along the waterfront were a multitude of security cameras. Sadiq knew that after his mission was over, the FBI would backtrack his movements and look at the endless hours of footage from the cameras. He stared directly into the camera closest to him and smiled. He wanted the FBI to know exactly who was responsible for the attack on their country. They were excellent at finding the evidence after an attack, but not at preventing them. Soon the world would bear witness to his plans, and when the Prophet Mohammed welcomed him into Paradise, it would be as a hero.

Once the crewmen had chained the cargo container to the deck, the ship needed to fill their bunkers to capacity with diesel and to replenish their freshwater tanks. A tug came alongside the *Explorer* and moved it to the fueling station. Sadiq knew this was a necessary step, but he was ready to get underway. They had a berthing scheduled at Port Everglades, just south of Fort Lauderdale, Florida.

The longer they were here, the easier it would be for someone to find them, if anyone *was* looking for the ship.

They had chosen this freighter because it was long past its service life but still in good shape. The engine ran smoothly, and her smaller size made her more maneuverable. They'd also chosen one of the most lawless places in the world to swipe her from. He doubted anyone cared about the mixture of Haitians and Hondurans he'd dispatched and dropped over the rails. And he doubted that anyone would miss this old rust bucket. Every year, at least two dozen ships disappeared around the globe. The *Explorer* would be just one more ship in a string of statistics.

He turned his attention to the container. It was in serious need of a paint job and covered in rust, which was part of the disguise. Inside were four Russian-built 3M-14T Kalibr cruise missiles in a self-contained launch system designed specifically to fit into a forty-foot-long shipping container. It was better known as the Club-K container missile system. The Russians had developed these weapons to allow for strategic strikes anywhere a semi-truck, railcar, or ship could carry the container. These Kalibrs carried a one-thousand-pound conventional warhead and had a maximum speed of six-hundred-miles-per-hour with a range of over one thousand miles. They were perfect for what Sadiq had planned.

There had been much discussion between Sadiq and General Golnar about going to Venezuela, where Club-Ks had been stockpiled in case of a U.S. invasion. The trip would only add two days to their total sailing time, but Sadiq fretted about being stopped by the U.S. Coast Guard if they had a blockade in place or were searching every freighter coming and going from Caracas. The U.S. was adamant about their sanctions against President Maduro, which was why one of General Golnar's proxies at the Egyptian embassy in Caracas had purchased the missiles and arranged for them to be transported via truck over the mountains into Colombia and shipped from Barranquilla to Puerto Cortés.

The tugboat blasted its horn, signaling the bunkers were full and the ship was ready to move. A pilot came aboard the *Explorer*, and Sadiq and his captain stood on the bridge wing to watch as the tug took them out to the main channel. Once they had passed through the channel buoys, the pilot set them on a course for Santo Domingo, the capital of the Dominican Republic, then went down the ladder to the waiting pilot boat.

"Set our course for Port Everglades," Sadiq told his captain. "In six days, we will have a new world."

The captain smiled. "*Inshallah*."

God willing.

CHAPTER TWENTY-NINE

Bluefields International Airport
Bluefields, Nicaragua

Insurance investigator Emily Hunt stepped down from the Bell 407GPX behind Shelly Hughes, Dark Water Research's chief operating officer. The jungle heat and humidity, even in the late Nicaraguan evening, felt almost oppressive. Her neck started to sweat under her long hair, and she pulled it aside to let out the trapped heat. Sometimes she thought about cutting off her bra-length mane, and this was one of them.

Erica Opsal, the pilot, climbed out the helicopter, and the three women walked to a minivan. They rode across town to The Oasis Casino and Hotel, which was a block from the waterfront in what was considered the downtown. It was a three-story building with a tan-and-white stucco exterior and a tin roof. Thick ornate columns flanked the casino's entrance and held up the overhanging second level, where guests lounged on the open-air patio, enjoying evening drinks.

Emily and Shelly took the stairs to the third-floor presidential suite where Greg Olsen sat at the table, staring at a laptop, and drinking a beer.

He grinned when the women entered. "I knew my favorite insurance investigator couldn't stay away."

"I'm killing two birds with one stone," Emily said by way of a greeting.

"What do you mean?" Greg asked.

Emily got a beer from the fridge and took a long drink. It felt refreshing to her parched throat. After getting the call from Lorenzo Spataro about the possible sighting of the *Everglades Explorer*, she had packed a bag and booked a flight to Managua. It had taken her eight hours and one stop in Atlanta to get to Augusto Cesar Sandino International Airport. When she was in Atlanta, she'd tried to book a flight from Managua to Bluefields, but she couldn't find any. She would have to take a bus or rent a car, and neither option appealed to her. Eventually, she had called Greg, knowing he was in Bluefields, and asked if he could help her get from the capital city to the port on the eastern coast of the small country. He'd sent the helicopter and offered her a room in his suite.

"I'm sure Emily would like to freshen up," Shelly said. "She's had a long day."

"I wouldn't mind taking a shower. Then I'll answer all your questions."

"*All* of them?" Greg asked, raising his eyebrows.

Emily shook her head. "About why I'm here. Some subjects are off limits."

Shelly shot Greg a look that told him to behave and motioned toward the spare bedroom. "The shower is through there."

Emily showered and changed into shorts and a tank top, then joined her friends in the living area once more.

Shelly handed her a glass of wine. "Now, other than looking at our wreck, why are you here?"

"I'm looking for a stolen freighter, and we had a report that it was at the breakers."

"Here?" Greg asked.

"Yes."

Greg rubbed his chin. "You said it came in yesterday?"

"That's what this guy told my client. Why?"

"We were out on the bay all day yesterday and I never saw a ship head upriver."

Emily asked, "Could it have come in when it was dark?"

He shook his head. "The channel is too narrow, and it would be tricky to navigate at night."

"So, you don't think the ship is there?" Emily asked.

"I'm not saying it didn't slip past me, but I don't think it is. How about this? Tomorrow, you go look at the *EPC* and then I'll have someone drive you upriver to the breakers. You can look for your boat and take a look at the *Galina Jovovich*."

Emily stifled a yawn. "That sounds good. I think I'll go to bed so I can get an early start." She set the glass on the coffee table and stood. She was positive Greg would send Ryan with her, and she needed a good night's sleep to face the man she'd tried to leave behind but thought about every day.

CHAPTER THIRTY

Peggy Lynn
Over the wreck of *El Paso City*

The divers were in the middle of recovering as many items from the cable layer as they could to lighten the ship before they raised her. Dark Water Research's fleet of recovery vessels had arrived on site, including *Fort Stockton*, another cable layer, *Texas Ranger*, a forty-meter crane ship capable of lifting eight hundred tons, and *Liberty*, a sleek-looking coastal survey vessel built by Damen Shipyards, which Ryan and Travis had both agreed would make a great salvage vessel.

Peggy Lynn was nearly fifty years old and, despite her retrofits and upgrades, she was showing her age. It wouldn't be long before they'd need to find another boat to replace her. That was a prospect that none of the crew wanted to think about, and they'd agreed that they'd use the old gal until she could no longer reliably take them to sea. Ryan had a feeling that when that day arrived, Capt. Dennis and Grandpa would finally retire, too.

In the meantime, they had work to do, and Ryan now stood in *Peggy Lynn*'s diver Launch and Recovery System, or LARS, basically a large metal cage raised and lowered by the boat's crane, with his Kirby Morgan helmet on, ready to make his second dive of the day. The new cable-laying ship, *Fort Stockton*, had an empty cable reel, and it was Ryan's job to unbolt the basket so the *Texas Ranger* could lift it aboard the waiting barge.

Out of the corner of the helmet's faceplate, he saw DWR's Bell 407GPX helicopter come into view. It had made the trip from the States on the landing pad mounted on the bow of *Texas Ranger*. Rick and Erica used it to make daily flights between Bluefields and the DWR fleet. Ryan figured they were bringing supplies, or one of the endless official government visitors, or engineers working on either the wreck recovery or repairing the fiber-optic cable Ryan had cut before the *EPC* sank.

"Ready to dive?" Stacey asked over the intercom, acting as tender.

Ryan took one last look at the descending helicopter. How had Rick and Erica gotten together? The two had made no bones about their dislike for each other last year, when they'd all been together on St. Thomas in the Virgin Islands. *If Rick could land a good-looking woman like Erica*, Ryan wondered, *why can't I? What's wrong with me?*

"*Focus*, Weller," Stacey slapped him hard on the back of the helmet.

Ryan gave her an okay sign with his fingers, and she pushed the button on the crane controller, sending the LARS plunging into the water.

Several minutes later, he was on the bottom, looking at the wrecked ship. He made his way through the muck to the cable basket, where miles of carefully wound cable lay partially in the mud and partially in the basket.

Travis, Gary, Ryan, and Anthony had spent all the previous day using a suction tube to dig channels under the fiber-optic cable. Stacey's job had been to run one-inch-thick steel cables encased in a heavy layer of plastic under the fiber-optic cable, forming a spiderweb around it and the carousel. With the subsea cable contained, they'd unbolted all but four of the bolts securing the carousel to the deck of *El Paso City* and used more cables to rig an attachment point for the crane hook.

Now, Ryan swam to the center of the spiderweb and instructed the crane operator on the *Texas Ranger* to lower the crane hook. When Ryan told the operator to halt, the hook hovered just above his head. He slipped the ends of the steel cables connected to the carousel over the hook.

"All right, Hugo," Ryan said. "Raise the hook."

The lifting block slowly rose, putting tension on the carousel's cables. Ryan told Hugo to hold, squeezed beneath the carousel and the *EPC*'s deck, and used a pneumatic impact wrench to loosen the four bolts holding the carousel to the deck. As the last bolt came free, the carousel shifted, swinging away from the ship. Ryan dropped the impact wrench and pushed himself out of the way, barely missing being struck by the carousel as it swung back and smacked the deck.

"You okay, Ryan?" Stacey asked.

Ryan took a moment to shake off the near miss before scrambling out from under the swinging carousel. "I'm good. Slack up my umbilical and we'll be ready to hoist the carousel."

He climbed the railing to stand on the port side of the cable-laying barge as she took in the umbilical's slack. "All clear, Stacey?"

"Roger that," she replied.

Ryan ordered Hugo to commence lifting operations, giving him a running commentary of everything happening with the lift, painting a verbal picture for the crane operator. As the crane lifted the subsea cable and carousel, clouds of particulate billowed up, obscuring Ryan's view, and he called the lift to a halt.

When the water had cleared, Ryan gave Hugo the command to lift. Once the cable cleared the water, it was no longer Ryan's operation, and he climbed back into the LARS. Stacey hoisted him straight to the surface and helped him strip off his gear as he walked to the recompression chamber, passing Gary, who was acting as the backup diver. They high-fived, and Ryan jumped into the chamber for his extended recompression stops. Grandpa blew him back down to eighty feet and started slowly bringing him back up.

As Ryan lay on the thin pad over the hard steel bench, he put his arm over his eyes and asked Grandpa to shut off the lights. The old man did so, and Ryan slid his arm down to his chest. His thoughts drifted to his conversation with Travis. He needed to figure out whether he was an operator or a diver. How could he pick just one when he loved both?

What did his future hold, and how could he expect a woman to live the same life he did unless she enjoyed it? Stacey loved diving and being a captain, and it had worked for her and Travis. Now Rick was dating Erica. Greg had asked Shelly to move into his house, and Ryan had accepted an invitation to be a groomsman for Don Williams, a DWR engineer, at the end of May.

Ryan rolled onto his side and punched the pad. His knuckles ached, but he slammed them into the pad again. Most of the people he knew were in committed relationships. He'd always been a bit of a loner, preferring casual dating.

Most of his relationships had an end date from the very beginning, like a piece of fruit gone rotten.

Everyone seemed to be moving ahead with life, except him. Maybe it was time for him to leave the salvage boat and do something else, but it wouldn't be returning to Wilmington and working for his father's construction company. His Lafitte 44 sailboat was sitting on the hard at Five Islands Yacht Club in Chaguaramas, Trinidad. He could catch a ride to Bluefields, drive across Nicaragua to Managua, and hop a flight to Trinidad. Once there, he could refit his sailboat and disappear into the endless blue, but would it make him happy? Would he just be in a different place with the same problems? There was a saying for that: *no matter where you go, there you are*.

Was he really ready for a wife and kids and a house, or was he just restless, or jealous? Those were questions he couldn't answer while lying inside a steel tube, or even outside of it. They had plagued him for a while now and, with the added pressure to figure out his next move, he felt like the walls were closing in.

A rapping on the outside of the recompression chamber interrupted his thoughts. He sat up, careful not to smack his head on the sides or roof like he'd done so many times in the past, and looked out the small porthole at the back of a head of purple hair. He pressed the button on the squawk box. "What's up, Stace?"

She turned and, with a smile, said, "You're not going to believe who just showed up."

CHAPTER THIRTY-ONE

Everglades Explorer
Straits of Yucatán.

Sadiq stood on the bridge, his hands clasped behind his back, as his crewmen stretched massive tarps across the ship's cargo deck, making her look like a covered grain hauler instead of a general cargo vessel. Once the tarp was up, the men welded a scaffolding of pipes to the aft section of the superstructure. They strung more tarps over the piping to add bulk to the rear.

He knew satellites could track them, but there was usually a gap in coverage, anywhere from thirty minutes to several hours. During this gap, they would change the ship's outline, throwing off anyone using a search program based on the ship's previous profile. Sadiq didn't think a stolen freighter would be worth the time and expense, but he carried out his orders just the same.

Sadiq had reason to worry, and he did. He should have

kept the captain alive to report to the shipowner. The man's disappearance from the aft deck worried him as well. Where had he gone? Had he died in the waters off Miragoâne? Had someone found him and reported his murder? What if there was someone looking for the *Explorer* right now because he had been careless?

He recounted their travels from Lebanon to the Dominican Republic via jetliner using British visas. From there, they had snuck across the border into Haiti and met their contact, a ruthless warlord who provided them with weapons and a vehicle. The ride to the port had been fraught with danger, with rebel checkpoints, looters in the streets, and men who had followed them until Sadiq had exited the truck, dispatched the driver with several well-placed shots, and disabled the truck with more rounds to the radiator and tires.

When they'd reached Miragoâne, Sadiq and his men had waited until dark in a stinking room above a tiny restaurant. They had feasted on goat, beans, and rice before slipping into the streets and making their way to the docks. After commandeering a boat, Sadiq and his men rowed to the freighter, caught everyone sleeping, and shot them on the aft deck with their suppressed pistols. They'd weighed down the bodies with scraps of steel and dumped them in the Jamaican Channel.

With the canopy in place over the deck, the missile technician opened the container and began testing the system. Sadiq walked down to the container and stuck his head inside the open door. The control panels were a complex series of buttons, knobs, dials, and screens.

"Ah, Brother Sadiq, come. I will show you how this works," the technician said in Arabic.

Sadiq stepped inside. A generator hummed deeper in the

container, providing power and air conditioning for the electronics.

"Press this button here," the tech said, and Sadiq complied.

A series of tests began running, flashing numbers and strings of code in Russian across the screens.

"It is running the function test. Once it is complete, we will link to the satellites. You have the coordinates, do you not?"

"Of course." Sadiq patted his pocket. "And the launch codes."

Five minutes later, a beep from the console drew their attention to a screen. "There, you see. Everything works perfectly. Now I will turn on the GPS."

"Will that broadcast our signal?" Sadiq asked.

"No. I have masked the outgoing signal for the test, but we will not have that luxury when we launch the missiles." He pressed a button and the computer system set about connecting with Russia's Global Navigation Satellite System.

The two men watched in silence as each of the four missiles began a digital handshake to confirm and test the system.

"We are set, Sadiq. Would you like to put in the coordinates now?"

The terrorist leader sat on a rolling stool in front of the keyboard. He pulled a folded piece of paper from his pocket and input the strings of numbers showing the latitude and longitude of each missile strike.

"If you don't mind, brother, what are the targets?"

Sadiq finished entering the last set of numbers and pointed at the screen. "The first is Port Everglades in Fort Lauderdale, Florida. The missile strike will bring the first responders to the scene shortly before we drive the ship into the port and detonate our bomb. The next two are aimed at the American naval base in Guantanamo Bay, Cuba, and the last is a special surprise for the Russians. They have a frigate in Havana called the *Admiral Golovko*. We will destroy it to show our displeasure with the Russians for helping the Americans to fight against us."

The technician nodded and stroked his beard. "It is a splendid plan, Sadiq. We will be martyrs for the cause. *Inshallah.*"

"*Inshallah*, brother." Sadiq's watch beeped. "Come. We must pray."

The two men retrieved their prayer rugs and assembled with the rest of the crew on the main deck, facing east and praying for the successful completion of their mission.

CHAPTER THIRTY-TWO

Texas Ranger
Over the wreck of *El Paso City*

As soon as Emily and Shelly were clear of the landing platform on the crane ship, the helicopter lifted off and raced back toward shore.

Emily was no stranger to ships. It was her job to know them well, and she had been on everything from a rowboat to a Panamax freighter, but the *Texas Ranger* boasted the biggest crane she'd ever seen.

The two women made their way to the accommodation ladder hanging from the side of the vessel. At the bottom of the steps, they boarded a twenty-five-foot SAFE Defender rigid hull inflatable boat, or RIB, with twin Mercury outboards. They took seats in the air-conditioned cabin, and the pilot ordered the lines cast off, then maneuvered the RIB away from the much larger vessel. He spun the wheel and threw the throttles forward, making a wide circle around the fleet of workboats. Emily was thankful for the specially designed shock-mitigating seats as they bounced over waves and wakes.

She looked eagerly out the window at the *Peggy Lynn*'s red hull and took deep breaths through her nose, slowly exhaling out her mouth, trying to control her heart rate. *Get it together, Emily*, she told herself. Never in her relationship with Kyle had she felt like a giddy schoolgirl ready to see her crush, which was the only way she could describe the butterflies in her stomach and her racing heart in anticipation of seeing Ryan. Emily gripped the bar on the seatback in front of her to stop her hands from shaking.

"You okay?" Shelly asked.

"Yeah."

Shelly nodded, but Emily imagined that she knew the real answer: she was both elated and terrified to see Ryan again. She needed to focus on her work and forget about the rest, but that was easier said than done.

The Defender came alongside *Peggy Lynn,* and the two women climbed aboard. They greeted the people on deck, all of whom Emily had met, except for Anthony and Gary.

"Ryan's in the recompression chamber," Stacey informed her. "Just in case you were wondering."

"Okay," Emily said, struggling to keep her voice neutral, even though she wanted to add snarkily, '*I wasn't.*'

"Come up to the bridge and we'll go over the operation," Stacey said.

Dennis politely asked if any of them wanted coffee or something else to drink. All declined, and Stacey explained how the ghost ship had collided with the *EPC* and the work they were doing to recover the ship. "We've already pumped out the fuel to mitigate risks to the environment, and with the subsea cable out of the way, we'll roll the barge upright.

Once we get a clear picture of the damage, we'll know what we're facing, but for now, the plan is to weld temporary plates over the holes in the hull. We'll pump out the water and stabilize her with lift bags while the *Texas Ranger* picks her up."

"What if you can't lift her?" Emily asked, examining the barge's deck plans.

"Then we'll cut off her superstructure and remove the rest of the equipment from her deck."

"The ship will be a total loss if you do that," the insurance investigator stated.

"More or less," Shelly replied.

"What do you think, Captain Law?" Emily asked.

"It's a sound plan." Dennis sipped his coffee and watched the men working on the subsea cable carousel, which now sat on the barge that *Star of Galveston* had brought out several days ago.

Shelly added, "We hope to get *EPC* up and send her to a dry dock for full repairs and refit."

"What about the cable?" Emily inquired, joining Dennis at the window.

"We'll take the carousel off *Fort Stockton* and put the *EPC*'s carousel on her. The tangled cable will take longer to lay, but hopefully it will unspool with minimum fuss."

Emily asked, "If it doesn't?"

Dennis shrugged. "That's not my department."

"How far behind are you on the job?" Emily asked.

"The entire operation was supposed to take ten days," Shelly said. "Right now, we're two weeks behind, and we're losing money every day."

"When can I look at the wreck?" Emily asked.

Stacey ran a hand through her purple hair. "You can do it now or wait until we roll her over."

"I have to do it now."

"I'll send you with Gary. All my other divers are doing their surface intervals."

Emily nodded, even though she would rather dive with Ryan. She trusted him underwater, and he'd saved her life when a swift current had swept her off a wreck and she'd breathed her tank dry. "Can we go now?"

Stacey leaned out of the bridge door and shouted for Gary to join them. The Marine ran up the stairs and stood in the doorway. "Emily wants to dive on *EPC*. Get a couple of tanks ready while she gets changed."

"Roger that," Gary said, and he went to prepare his dive gear.

Stacey took Emily down to her stateroom, and Emily changed out of her clothes into a red bikini before pulling on her wetsuit. Back on deck, she removed her Dive Rite harness and wing from her gear bag and strapped it to a steel tank Gary had prepared before she screwed her regulator set to the tank valve. He told her the tank would provide all the extra weight she would need.

"You have a seven-foot hose on your primary regulator," Gary stated, checking her setup.

"Ryan built this for me a long time ago."

Gary looked up sharply. "You're *that* Emily?"

Nodding sheepishly, Emily admitted that she was. She was already sweating in the wetsuit, and the interrogating look Gary was giving her was making her feel even hotter. A flush of red crept up her neck and colored her cheeks.

The bear of a man stuck his hand out. "Glad to meet you, despite what that jerk Ryan says about you."

Emily shook his hand and said, "Likewise. What *does* that jerk say about me?"

As she sat down on the dressing bench, Gary said, "He's never said anything bad about you. I just like busting his chops."

"Oh," was all Emily said before slipping on her fins and shrugging the harness's straps over her shoulders. She stole a glance at the recompression chamber, wondering how long Ryan would be in it. She didn't know why it surprised her that he'd said nothing bad about her. He had every right to.

"You ready?" Gary asked.

"Yes." Emily snapped her camera housing closed and clipped it to her BCD.

"Good. The current isn't bad today, so we'll make a free descent to the wreck, check out the damage on the bow, and come up the mooring ball rope located there. If you need something or want to cancel the dive, use the tank banger." He pointed at a small plastic ball on a piece of bungee cord wrapped around the tank. The snap of the ball against steel would create a loud bang, attracting the attention of anyone nearby.

"You don't have to worry about Em," Stacey said. "She's a great diver."

Emily gave her a thankful smile, then pulled on her mask, put the regulator in her mouth, stepped over the rail behind Gary into the glistening blue water. She felt self-conscious with Gary right beside her, but as they swam, he seemed to relax and give her more space. She took lots of photos of what she could see of the collision impact point, as the barge's position on the seabed hid most of it. The unforgiving sea was already trying to claim the wreck for herself, coating it in a layer of slime. Big silver barracudas lingered in packs along the wreck, their predatory snouts jutting into the current. A nurse shark lay in the sand close to the hull.

It was Gary who signaled for them to go up. Emily glanced at her computer. She had plenty of air left, but they were almost into their no-decompression limits. They swam to the mooring line hooked to the barge's bow and slowly drifted up to fifteen feet for their three-minute safety stop.

Emily snapped a few more photos and hooked the camera to the D-ring on the shoulder strap of her BCD.

Aboard *Peggy Lynn*, Emily stripped off her gear and used a freshwater hose to rinse the salt from it before she showered in Stacey's cabin. When she returned to the main deck, she found Gary, Stacey, and Travis sitting on the dressing bench, talking to Ryan.

She stopped for a moment, taking in her ex-boyfriend's six-foot frame clad in surf shorts, his muscles rippling under his glistening tan skin. The butterflies returned to her stomach. His hair was longer, and he appeared happy, laughing at something one of them had said. Then he looked right at her and smiled.

CHAPTER THIRTY-THREE

Ryan's breath caught in his chest as he smiled at Emily Hunt. She was more beautiful than he remembered.

She was there because her job was to investigate wrecks and accidents, and to ensure the companies weren't trying to scam Ward and Young, but it surprised him that she had come and not another investigator. He turned away, not wanting to show how much he still cared for her, although he was sure it was evident in the stupid smile that made his cheeks hurt. He'd watched her gear up through the tiny porthole in the recompression chamber, and when she'd cast a glance his way, he'd jerked back and slammed his head into the roof. The back of his skull still hurt, but nothing compared to the ache in his heart.

Emily walked over and sat down beside Stacey. Ryan shifted to his left, slowly moving away from the group, and walking to the bridge.

Dennis glanced at Ryan as he entered. "Avoiding the ex?"

Ryan shrugged. Dennis had married his Peggy, the salvage boat's namesake, shortly after he'd graduated high school, and they'd had three children together. The sea captain and Peggy had been together for over forty years before she passed away from cancer. The old man hardly talked about his marriage, children, or grandkids, but Ryan knew he missed them. Dennis also rarely offered relationship advice, and when he did, Ryan usually shut up and listened. Today, the older man just turned back to the window, watching the other ships at work.

Tomorrow, one of DWR's crew boats would arrive with more divers, and the work would begin in earnest on raising *El Paso City*, giving the divers on *Peggy Lynn* a much-needed break.

"You okay, Dennis?"

"I'm good."

"You sure? You haven't seemed like yourself lately." Ryan had noticed that he'd been more quiet than usual since breaking his arm.

Dennis continued to watch the ships and took a sip of coffee. Ryan wondered how much Jim Beam was in the cup. The captain's use of the alcoholic beverage to self-medicate had its ups and downs, and when Dennis got into a mood, he drank more.

"It's about time to hang up my spurs."

"I didn't know you were a bull rider," Ryan quipped.

"You know what I mean."

Dennis's tone told Ryan to quit making jokes; this was a serious conversation. "What are you talking about?"

"After this job." He took another sip and turned to face Ryan. "I'm giving *Peggy* to Travis and Stacey." Ryan's expression must have betrayed his disappointment because Dennis went on. "They love this old gal and they've made it their home. I'd give her to you, but you're always gallivanting off to do something or other."

Ryan nodded. "What about your kids?"

"They don't care about this old tub, never have. You know that."

He understood, but this was a double blow. First, Emily had shown up, and now Dennis was quitting. He felt like his world was spinning off its axis. "Have you talked to anyone else about this?"

"Emery. He's ready, too. He's eighty-five and having a harder and harder time getting around the boat."

"I've noticed, but I wasn't going to say anything."

"Well, don't," Dennis said bluntly. "This is our decision, and I don't want anyone to know about it until we're ready to tell them."

"So why tell me?"

"I wanted you to be the first to know." Dennis sipped from his mug. "Are you going back in the water?"

Ryan shook his head. "No."

"Join me." Dennis motioned to the bottle of Jim Beam on the counter by the coffee maker.

Ryan poured himself a healthy dose of whiskey into a coffee mug. "What are we drinking to?"

"To old friends who pulled me out of a funk and got me back to living. Thank you."

The liquor burned down Ryan's throat, and warmth spread through his rib cage. Neither of them had the words to express what the other meant to him, so they just shared a silent moment together.

Dennis filled in the gap. "It's like this, Ryan. I'm telling you because you deserve to hear it from me. You put together this crew, and we've had some good times and some bad. It was hard on all of us when we found out you were in prison, but we pushed on. We had work to do and it was good for us."

"I sense a 'but,'" Ryan said.

"Yeah, there's a 'but.' My sea legs aren't what they used to be. Travis is a damn fine leader, and Stacey reminds me of Peggy; she's smart and capable and a planner. You need yourself one of those." He patted the ship's wheel with love and reverence. "Those two kids will do all right with *Peggy*."

Ryan held up his mug. "Here's to your retirement. Fair winds and following seas."

Capt. Dennis Law clinked his cup against Ryan's, and they shot back the bourbon whiskey. Ryan filled his empty cup with coffee and took a sip. The first day he'd met Dennis, he'd had a pot of strong, bitter coffee brewing, and despite his attempt to change the man's taste in coffee beans, the coffee hadn't changed. Ryan figured that what he was drinking now could strip paint. He swirled the coffee in his cup, staring into the black void.

Just how I like it, he thought. *Black like my soul*. He felt little joy today. *Have all my negative thoughts manifested themselves today?*

He should have been elated to see Emily, but he had no idea how to handle the situation, or if he should even approach her. In the end, he decided it was safer to stand on the bridge and drink coffee. It was better to pine secretly than to be rejected twice.

Shelly Hughes stepped onto the bridge. "Ryan, grab your kit. Greg wants you on the beach."

Dennis turned and put a hand on his shoulder. "Good luck, son."

CHAPTER THIRTY-FOUR

Fifteen minutes later, when Ryan climbed aboard the RIB, he wore running shoes, gray cargo pants, and a blue moisture-wicking polo shirt bearing the DWR company logo of an old brass dive helmet surrounded by the words 'Dark Water Research' on his left breast. He carried his Walther PPQ on his right hip. He preferred this gun to the Glock 19. It fit his hand better, and he liked the fit and finish of the German pistol with its specially designed trigger for use if the gun became submerged in water. Plus, Ryan was an old sailor, and anything designed for the Navy just had to be better in his mind.

Shelly and Emily waited for him to drive them to town. He took control of the Defender and ran them to shore, having to negotiate around the heavily laden ferry traveling between El Bluff and Bluefields. Ryan made his way around it and cruised into Bluefields, looking for a place to dock the RIB. He found a slot at the municipal dock and saw Wyn loading his fishing boat for a charter. The two men exchanged pleasantries while the women walked up the street. Neither had said a word to him on the run in.

When Ryan had left Bluefields to find the *Galina Jovovich*, it had been early morning and the docks were nearly empty. Now, colorfully dressed men, women, and children crowded the sidewalks and streets, waiting for the ferry beside trucks overladen with luggage, giant bunches of bananas, and crates of oranges, pineapples, and papayas. Street vendors sold roasted nuts, cooked and fresh fish, lobster tails, and meals of meat, rice, and vegetables. The smell of grilled corn and roasting pork filled the air.

His gaze took in the people from one end of the street to the other. Most of the men wore blue jeans and soccer shirts; others wore only shorts. The women wore bright dresses, and many bounced babies on their hips. He paused to look over a set of low tables piled high with freshly caught fish. The proprietor rolled them in newspaper for his customers and squatted beside the curb, smoking cigarettes, and fidgeting with his blue straw fedora.

Ryan bought a glass of mixed fruit juice, squeezed while he watched, from a vendor with a rolling cart and sipped it as he walked to the hotel and up to Greg's suite. He found his friends gathered around the table.

"What do you need, Greg? We've got diving to do," Ryan said.

"I want you to take Emily to the breakers, so she can look at the *Galina* and see if her client's ship is there."

"What's the point of looking at the ghost ship?" Ryan said. "They'll break it and we'll get paid our claim."

"Someone once told me that every stolen vessel has a story to tell," Emily said, staring right at him. "In order to interpret that story, you have to treat it like a crime scene and put together the pieces of the puzzle."

Ryan snorted. It was a line he'd used when they'd first met, and he'd intended for it to convince her to go to Key West with him, not to be used as a mantra. Besides, the

Galina wouldn't tell any stories. She was just another derelict ready for the scrapheap.

Greg laughed. "That's an interesting thought."

"If you could feel it, I'd kick you in the shin," Ryan said.

With a grin, Greg jokingly pulled back his fist. "Want to see who can punch in the leg the hardest?"

"Calm down, boys," Shelly admonished.

"Seriously, I just want to see the *Galina Jovovich* for myself," Emily said, "and look for the *Explorer*."

Ryan knew he wasn't going to get out of this, and besides, it was a chance to be alone with Emily, so he didn't know why he was balking so hard. He nodded. "You ready to go now?"

"Yes," she said.

Ryan led Emily back to the Defender. After paying the bill for leaving the boat alongside the dock, they climbed in. He started the engines and eased them away from the crowded marina. They had to cross the shallow Bay of Bluefields to reach the shipping channel that led up the Escondido River, and as they idled out the channel, Ryan pulled alongside Wyn, who was also making his way across, and yelled, "Wanna race?"

Wyn laughed and bumped his throttle, his clients urging him on. Ryan did the same, and Wyn backed down. They both laughed, and Ryan waved as he drove away.

"It's always some macho bullshit with you, isn't it?" Emily asked.

"What? A guy can't have a little fun?"

Emily just shook her head.

When they were almost to El Bluff, Ryan turned the wheel left, cutting across the channel. He carefully monitored the depth sounder because he didn't want to look like an idiot by running aground. He passed the green marker for the Escondido Channel and straightened the Defender to run between the navigational beacons. Seeing no other traffic on the water, he pushed the throttle to its stop and the small boat leaped onto plane and shot upriver. They made the ten-mile run to the breakers in a little over ten minutes.

Idling into the ship graveyard, he pointed out the *Galina* and stopped the Defender alongside her. Emily tied the Defender's bow line beside a wooden ladder someone had afixed to *Galina*'s stern railing. Emily climbed up the ladder before Ryan had shut off the Defender's engines. He didn't care about touring the ship because he'd had his fill of her, but he followed Emily as she made her way through the derelict.

In the engine room, she snapped on a flashlight and shone it across the oily water sloshing in the hold. The noise of a generator and water pump made talking difficult.

On the bow, she examined the pile of cigarettes beside the crane's base and gave Ryan a recriminating glance. She'd never liked that he smoked and had asked him to quit multiple times. He shrugged and turned away, intent on getting this done as fast as possible and returning to work on *Peggy Lynn*.

Ryan waited for her to finish her tour while lounging on the Defender. Emily finally came down the ladder and Ryan watched her carefully, although he pretended to be disinterested. She looked good in her tan shorts and a pink shirt, under which she wore a bikini top, the tie strings dangling down her back.

"You ready?" Ryan asked, trying to take his mind off how much he wanted to kiss her.

She held up a camera. "I've got photos of the crime scene."

"The only crime committed here was by those idiots who turned the ship loose."

"The tow cable broke and the tug was forced to abandon the ship."

Ryan raised an eyebrow. He would have liked to learn how

the *Galina* got loose but started the Defender's engines. Emily cast the lines off. "Can you idle through the fleet so we can look for the *Explorer?*"

They toured the breaking yard, motoring past derelicts that looked well past their prime. Some had sunk and rested on the bottom with half their hulls underwater. At the end of the channel, marked by a row of buoys, he turned the Defender around and headed toward the main channel. She asked him to put in at the small dock in front of a rundown shack used as an office. Beyond it was a ship being broken apart. An army of workers swarmed over it with cutting torches, grinders, and jackhammers. A crane equipped with an electromagnet moved cut steel from piles beside the ship to waiting barges.

She tied the boat to the dock, and Ryan accompanied her to the shack, where she showed the manager several pictures of the *Explorer* and the man who had supposedly captured her. He said he hadn't seen either.

Back at the Defender, they got in and headed down the channel. Thick green jungle encroached on both sides of the waterway. A troupe of howler monkeys swung from low hanging branches and perched on the railings of the defunct ships. At the main channel, he jammed the throttle forward.

After a few minutes of silence, Emily said, "Greg told me you had to fend off pirates."

He shrugged. "It was just a bunch of poor Miskitos hoping for a big payday."

"What happened?"

Ryan kept his eyes on the river ahead, watching for sunken limbs or other debris floating in the water, and debated about telling her the whole gruesome tale. "Why do you care?"

"I was just asking."

Her asking about the attempted hijacking touched a

nerve with him. "It was dangerous shit. Shit you said you didn't want to be a part of, so if you really want to know, I'll tell you about the guy who caught fire when the fuel tank on his boat exploded and I shot him in the head to put him out of his misery. Do you want to hear what his screams sounded like? Maybe you'd like to dream about those, too."

She crossed her arms. "You don't have to be an asshole."

Ryan ripped the throttle back to neutral and the Defender came off plane, drifting with the current. He jabbed his finger at her. "You can't comprehend why I'm being an asshole? Let's start with the fact that you called Floyd Landis and told him you were breaking up with me and I was to never call you again. You didn't have the guts to say it to my face, and now you waltz in here like you're doing your job." He used his fingers to make air quotes around job. "You could have done everything from your desk a thousand miles away, yet here you are, out here in the sticks, mucking about."

It pleased him to see her looking thoroughly rebuked, and he turned back to the wheel, goosing the engines to straighten the boat between the channel's marker buoys.

"Thanks for making me regret that decision," Emily shot back.

"Screw you, Emily, and the horse you rode in on."

"Oh, you'd like that, wouldn't you?"

Ryan never let off the throttle as they approached the turn to the ferry channel to Bluefields. He threw the boat over hard, nearly pitching Emily from her seat. The starboard inflatable tube dipped below the surface. Ryan added power as they leaned into the apex. He brought the boat out of the turn and cruised to Bluefields. Not bothering to tie up, he just nosed the RIB into the weathered wood-and-concrete dock and told Emily to get the hell out.

She happily obliged and gave him the middle finger once she was on the dock.

Ryan stuck his tongue out as he backed the boat away and headed for *Peggy Lynn*. Before he was halfway across the Bay of Bluefields, his sat phone rang and he dropped the throttle to neutral to answer the call with a curt, "What do you want, Greg?"

"I need you back at the Oasis."

"I have work to do, Dad."

"And you work for me."

"How many times do we have to go over this? I'm an independent—"

Greg cut him off. "Don't yell at me because you and Emily got into it."

Ryan took a deep breath and gritted his teeth. As he blew out, he tried to force out his anger. "I'll be there in a few minutes."

He hung up, turned the boat around, and drove back to the dock. How had he expected her to react when he'd yelled at her? Had he really thought she wouldn't tell Shelly, or that she and Greg couldn't see that he had upset her? Greg was right. He shouldn't have been angry with him just because he was upset with himself for blowing up at Emily.

"What a mess," he muttered to himself.

Ryan walked back to the hotel suite and took a beer from the fridge. After opening it and taking a long drink, he asked, "Can I talk to you for a minute, Em?"

She rose and followed him out to the balcony. He leaned against the railing and looked east across the harbor. He could see the Defender riding easily along the dock. The ferry had come across from El Bluff, and people were disgorging from it. Another barge, loaded with cargo containers, floated along the commercial dock. A line of semi-tractors with skeletal trailers purposely built to carry the forty-foot steel cargo containers lined the street, waiting for a crane to lift the containers from the barge to the trailers. The town definitely needed a dedicated port for rail and truck transportation, to prevent dock hands and semi-trucks from crowding the town's narrow streets.

He turned from the harbor view to face Emily. "Look, I'm sorry about yelling at you out there. I just ... I'm sorry."

"It's okay. I kinda deserved it. I should have talked to you instead of using Landis."

"I miss you," he confessed.

She put a hand on his arm. He hoped she would say something similar, but instead she said, "I need your help."

CHAPTER THIRTY-FIVE

Ryan closed his eyes, took a slow breath in, and let it out through puffed-up cheeks. Emily had just asked for his help rather than telling him that she missed him or that she loved him. It wasn't what he had expected her to say, and part of him was deeply disappointed. All he had left to ask was, "With what?"

"I'd like to talk to you and Greg at the same time."

Ryan agreed, and they stepped inside. He got another beer from the fridge and sat at the table with Greg, Shelly, and Emily.

Emily removed a picture of the *Explorer* along with a picture of Masoud Sadiq from her briefcase and laid them on the table. "About six days ago, this guy stole this ship from Miragoâne, Haiti."

"Who is he?" Greg asked, picking up the picture.

"He is, or was, a member of the Syrian Army."

Greg glanced at Ryan who shrugged and sipped his beer, then asked, "Why would he steal the ship?"

"That's what I'd like to know," Emily said. "I had the *Explorer*'s captain do a sketch of the pirate leader, and I asked my friend at Tampa PD to run his photo through their facial recog database to see if they got any hits. After a lot of legwork, they identified him. Then the FBI showed up and started asking me questions about why I was interested in him."

"What did they say?" Greg asked.

"Nothing actually. It was my friend Kaya who told me he was a Syrian."

"Let me get this straight," Greg said. "Tampa PD identified this guy from a *sketch*? I didn't think that was possible."

"Technically, they used data points from celebrities and matched nodals to the sketch."

Greg grinned. "That sounds really sketchy."

Ignoring his friend's weak pun, Ryan asked, "So, what do you need help with?"

Emily wiggled in her seat and spent a moment straightening her photos. "First, I'd like to get the ship back for the owner. He feels responsible for the men the pirates killed, and—"

Ryan cut her off. "The pirates killed the crew?"

"Everyone but the captain. He was badly wounded, but he managed to roll off the back of the ship to escape. Some Catholic missionaries patched him up and helped get him medevacked to the States."

"You think there's something more to it than just theft?" Shelly asked.

"This is probably wild conjecture on my part, but I've spent a lot of time thinking about why Sadiq would want to steal a ship." She paused and looked around the table, her gaze settling on Ryan. "I think he might be planning a terror attack."

"I've heard worse theories," Greg said.

"Hold up," Ryan said. "That's a pretty big jump, don't you think?"

Emily nodded. "I know it is. I've tried to get information on Sadiq from some of my sources, but it's like a black hole. Nobody is talking about him or wants to admit he exists. The only reason I know he's an actual person is because the FBI showed up and started asking questions."

"Do you think Ashlee can identify the ship with that program she built to help you find Mango's sailboat?" Greg asked Ryan.

Ryan shrugged. A serial killer had stolen Mango Hulsey's sailboat from its anchorage in Martinique, and Ryan and his former co-worker had spent hours flying in helicopters and airplanes, taking pictures of boats at sea, in anchorages, and at marinas. Ashlee Calvo had run the pictures through a bespoke computer program she'd developed, matching them against the top and side profiles of Mango's boat.

"Ward and Young subcontract a company who have their own satellite program," Emily said. "They built it specifically to do what you're talking about."

"So why don't you use that?" Ryan asked.

"My boss turned me down," Emily said. "The board would rather pay the insurance claim than spend money on burgeoning technology. It's expensive and time-consuming to search hundreds of square miles of ocean for a specific vessel, and I can't cover every port, breaker, and anchorage in the Caribbean by myself."

"Then it's case closed. We can all go about doing our jobs," Ryan said. "I need to get back to *Peggy Lynn*. We have a dive rotation to keep."

"What if he's planning a terrorist attack?" Emily asked.

Ryan shook his head. "What if he *isn't?*"

"Why are you acting like such a jerk?" Emily asked. "The first time you came to my office, you were concerned about finding boats stolen by pirates, and you were willing to do whatever it took to stop them, including almost getting yourself killed by a drug lord in Mexico. What happened between then and now?"

"Let's just say I lost some of my wide-eyed optimism." The truth was that if Ryan took this job, he'd never get to work on *Peggy Lynn* again, and while he sometimes found the work boring and the long days at sea hard work, it was better than being a carpenter for his father or one of Greg's flunkies at his private military contracting business. If he walked away from the crew he'd put together and the work they did, he'd have to start all over again and build something new. He was getting older and thinking about his life, legacy, and future. Whatever he'd built with Dennis and the crew would pass to Travis and Stacey, and that pissed him off the most. *He* should be the one to inherit *Peggy Lynn* if Dennis was going to give her away.

"Regardless of whether this guy is a terrorist or not, he's a killer and that should be enough of a reason to search for him," Emily said.

"What about your boss?" Ryan asked. "Is he going to give you time off work to chase this ship?"

Emily's shoulders dropped. "I don't think he will."

"Do you want to hand this investigation to us?" Greg asked.

"No. I'd like to be involved in it. I just need help because my employer has decided not to pursue this case."

"Whose jurisdiction do the murders fall under?" Ryan asked.

"Technically, they were in Haitian waters aboard a U.S. flagged vessel, so it should be a joint investigation between the Haitian National Police and the FBI," Emily said.

"Maybe that's what the FBI was doing asking you about Sadiq," Shelly suggested.

Emily sat back in her chair and crossed her arms. Ryan could read the defeat on her face. This conversation wasn't going the way she had hoped it would. In that moment, the disappointment in her eyes swayed him. This was an opportunity to work with her again, and he should be jumping all over it.

"Let's do this," he said, wanting to offer an olive branch to her. "We'll call Landis and have him poke the bear and see what shakes out with Sadiq."

"You mean shake the tree and see what falls out," Greg corrected.

"Before you boys go off half-cocked again, let's use the satellites and find the ship," Shelly reasoned. "You find the ship, you find Sadiq and turn him over to the FBI."

"That settles it," Greg said. "Ryan, you run point on this thing and help Emily."

"No offense, boss," Ryan said, "but I have a job on the *Peggy Lynn*. We're raising your sunken ship."

"I've got a hundred divers that can do that job, but only one guy I trust to do *this*. And that's you, my friend."

Ryan stood. "Can I speak to you in private, Greg?"

In the master bedroom, Ryan closed the door behind him and sat on the bed across from Greg who was doing a wheelie.

"What's really going on?" Greg said. "This isn't like you."

Ryan sighed and closed his eyes. Greg had always been there for him, and he deserved to know the truth. He focused on his friend when he opened his eyes. "This afternoon, Dennis told me he and Grandpa are retiring after this job. He's giving the boat to Travis and Stacey."

"Aw, man, I'm sorry. That sucks."

"That's only half of it," Ryan added. "Travis told me that I need to choose between being a member of the crew or working for you. He said they need unit cohesion, and I'm not providing it by running off to do other jobs."

Greg nodded and let his front wheels drop with a thud. "What are you going to do?"

"I guess with Dennis giving them the boat and you needing me to go forth and produce miracles, I have my answer."

"Which is?"

Ryan flopped back on the bed; his arms spread. He stared at the water spot around the ceiling fan, a tan stain against the white paint. He enjoyed doing salvage jobs and working with the crew, and he always figured that when Dennis retired, he would offer the boat to him at a cheap price so he could keep working. Now things had gone pear-shaped, and if he helped Emily, his days as a commercial diver on *Peggy Lynn* would be over. He'd need to move on to the next thing in his life, whatever that may be. Based on Emily being more concerned about needing his help rather than missing him, he knew his future didn't include her, and that sucked as much as losing the salvage boat.

But she'd been right about one thing: he had charged into more than one situation because someone needed justice. The men killed aboard the *Everglades Explorer* needed a champion, someone to defend their rights and punish their killer. Life had ground his wide-eyed optimism into hard-scrabbled truths. One of them was that he was good at finding men and ships and bringing justice to those who deserved it. Whether or not he wanted to admit it, he liked having a gun in his hand, and going after Sadiq put one there again. Scuba diving pitted him against the elements, but hunting deserving prey was the ultimate game, and he'd become hooked on it a long time ago.

Greg interrupted his thoughts. "I think you need to help Emily find this ship. It'll be good for both of you. If nothing else, you can clear the air of all the sexual tension."

Ryan sat bolt upright. "What's wrong with you? That woman doesn't want me."

"You guys keep tap dancing around each other like you're made of eggshells. Just tell her how you feel."

"I did."

"I don't mean scream at her because she used Landis to dump you. I mean, tell her how you *really* feel—that you still love her. It'll be good for you."

Ryan let out another sigh. "I don't know, man."

"Well, I see the way she looks at you."

"Is it the same stupid look Shelly gives you because I think you've got her drugged?"

Greg placed his hands on his wheels and pushed his body into the air. When his pelvis was free of the cushion, he swiveled it as best he could, using his arms. "I know what I'm doing, and she likes it."

"That's disgusting. You've been hanging out with Rick for far too long."

Shelly opened the door, saw Greg swiveling his hips, and rolled her eyes. "Am I interrupting something?"

"Just showing him how it's done, baby."

She scoffed. "Show him later. We have a meeting in twenty minutes at the engineer's office."

Greg dropped onto his cushion. "Roger that, babe." He turned to Ryan. "You guys figure this out. You made a good team before, and you can be a great one again. She loves you, buddy. Love her back."

Eager to avoid the subject, Ryan said, "Don't you have a meeting to go to?"

"It's a hard decision. We've all had to make them, but it'll work out. Shit always works out."

"Yeah, and it rolls downhill. Why do I get the feeling that I'm standing at the bottom?"

"Because you're the enlisted guy and I'm the officer," Greg said.

"Or, to put it in more relevant terms, you have the money and I'm cheap labor."

"You're not cheap," Greg said. "*Easy*, yes, but not cheap."

"Thanks," Ryan replied, with as much sarcasm as he could muster.

"You're welcome. Now, go talk to Emily and then tell me what you decide to do."

"When will you be back?"

Greg tapped his wristwatch. "If it's like the rest of these meetings, it can go on for a couple of hours. If you thought the U.S. had red tape, they ain't got nothin' on Latin American countries. Oh, and we don't have siesta time."

"I could use a nap myself." Ryan yawned.

"You can sleep when you're dead," Greg said as he wheeled himself out of the room. Shelly dropped a briefcase into his lap as they made for the door, and the two of them left the suite.

Ryan stared out the bedroom door at Emily, who was sitting on the sofa. She stared right back. With another weary sigh, he stood and walked out into the living room.

He'd made his decision, and he doubted Travis would have him back after this, even to scrub the shitters.

CHAPTER THIRTY-SIX

When Ryan closed the door to the bedroom, it was like closing a door on the past, on *Peggy Lynn*, her crew, and all the adventures they'd had together. He wasn't sure where his life would go, but there was a mission in front of him now, and all he needed to do was keep his head down, bury himself in the work, and good things would come. They always had, no matter what challenges he'd faced, and this would be no different.

"Well?" Emily asked.

"We need a chart so we can figure sailing speeds and distances."

Smiling, she went to the table, opened her briefcase, and removed a large map of the Caribbean. After smoothing it out across the table, she stood back to allow Ryan to examine the circles she had drawn. Rings in blue depicted cruising speed, and rings in red denoted max speed. Each had a neatly labeled tag showing dates and distances.

Unfortunately, the rings didn't give them a huge amount to go on. If anything, they seemed to indicate to Ryan that the ship could practically be anywhere.

"Let's call your satellite company," he said. "We can start in Miragoâne. The ship was probably there for at least two days, so they can match the *Explorer*'s overhead and side profiles. From there, it should be a simple matter of following the ship to see where she went."

Emily pulled a business card for her contact at Hobbins Group from her briefcase and handed it to him. "You'll have to call because I'm not supposed to."

Using his sat phone, he dialed the number and asked to speak with Paul Hutchinson. When Hutchinson came on the line, Ryan explained who he was, the company he worked for, and what he needed done. Hutchinson told him it would take at least a day to get started and could possibly take up to a week for them to complete the search.

"Is there any way you can speed it up?" Ryan asked. "The guy who stole the *Explorer* is a murderer, and we want to capture him before he escapes."

"I'll see what I can do, but I can't make any promises."

"I'll pay the overtime."

"I understand you want to get this done straight away, Mr. Weller, but I already have a backlog of orders and everyone wants them done yesterday."

"Is there anything I can do to help speed things up?"

Hutchinson sighed. "Yeah. I need a time machine and about a billion dollars."

"I don't have either of those," Ryan said.

"Then you're just gonna have to wait your turn. Send me the photos and spec sheets so I can get started as soon as we wrap up the next job."

Ryan wrote down Hutchinson's email address, finished the call, and said to Emily, "I'm not sure how fast he'll get it done."

"There has to be something else we can do," she said.

He picked up the phone again and dialed Ashlee Calvo at DWR's headquarters.

She answered on the second ring. "Oh my gosh, I am so ready. Are you ready? Another week and I'm outta here to get ready for my wedding."

"Calm down, girl," Ryan said.

"I am calm. What's up?"

"Can you get me some satellite time?"

"Sure, you'll just have to pay for time like everybody else. Why?"

"I need to find a stolen freighter. I know it was in Miragoâne, Haiti, six days ago. We need to track it from there. Can you run the program you made to find Mango's sailboat on satellite images?"

Ashlee laughed, and Ryan visualized her sitting in front of her bank of computer monitors. She had the brain of a super nerd in the body of a petite redhead.

"What's so funny?" he asked.

"Picture an iceberg, okay?"

"Okay," he replied dubiously.

"What you want me to do is the tip, finding the ship. Beneath the surface is years of work with artificial intelligence and specific algorithms to develop software, testing, standardization, and all kinds of other stuff. I'm getting married at the end of this month, remember, so I don't have time to do any of that."

"Yeah, I know, but—"

She quickly interrupted. "Lucky for you, I know just what you need. I came across a company who does exactly what you want."

"I hope it isn't Hobbins Group," Ryan muttered.

"I've never heard of them. I'm talking about MarineSat AI." She lowered her voice. "I've been freelancing with them."

"Good for you, but can they help us?"

"Sure. Let me guess, you need this done right away?"

"Well, the guy who stole the ship killed the whole crew and we need to find him."

"Okay. Send me the data points, dates, deck plans, photos of the ship, and any other information you have."

"I should have called you first," Ryan said. "You're a lifesaver."

"I should always be your first call. By the way, do you have a plus one yet? I need to finalize the catering."

Ryan looked over at Emily.

She met his gaze and mouthed, "What?"

Into the phone, Ryan said, "I'll get back to you about that. In the meantime, I'll send you an email. You'll get it in a minute."

"Let me know about the plus one, *soon*," Ashlee said.

"Yes, ma'am." Ryan ended the call and set the phone on the desk.

"What was that about?" Emily asked.

"Nothing. Ashlee and Don are getting married on Memorial Day weekend and I'm supposed to be a groomsman."

"Really? That's great. I bet you'll look great in a tux."

Ryan didn't look up from his phone, instead distracting himself with an alert from a social media site telling him that his sister had posted a picture of her children. "We're wearing khaki shorts and blue shirts. She's getting a little antsy because I haven't told her if I'm bringing a plus one or not."

"Well?" Emily asked expectantly, leaning back in her chair as if to put herself on display.

Ryan shrugged. "I don't have one."

"Give them my best when you see them," Emily said.

Something in her voice made Ryan look up.

She gave him a strange look that made him wonder if he'd done or said something wrong.

After a long moment of staring at each other, she said, "I have the email ready to go. Where do I send it?"

He came around the table, leaned over Emily's shoulder, and typed in Ashlee's email address. A strand of her hair tickled his nose and he could smell her shampoo. She turned her head, and he could feel her just inches away. Her breath on his skin sent a shiver up his spine. He wanted to kiss her. Maybe she could be his plus one? Was that what the strange look was about? Was she inviting herself along?

With the email sent, he straightened and walked to the fridge for a bottle of water. Eventually, the chase for this ship would take them away from Nicaragua, and he needed to be ready to roll when that time came. He took a long drink and screwed the cap back on.

"I need to run out to *Peggy Lynn*, pack a bag, and return the Defender."

"Okay." Emily closed the laptop.

Ryan was halfway to the street when he heard someone on the steps behind him and turned to see Emily. "Where are you going?"

"We're working together now. Where you go, I go."

"Like a babysitter?"

"No." She smiled coquettishly. "Consider me your plus one."

"What?"

She linked her arm in his when they reached the street. "Why is it you can read a criminal's mind and tell him exactly what he wants to hear so you can manipulate him, but you can't understand a word I'm saying to you?"

He shrugged. *What is she trying to tell me?*

"I'll throw you a lifeline. Ask me to be your plus one."

"What?"

"Are you deaf?"

He grinned mischievously. "*What?*"

She giggled and bumped him playfully with her hip.

At the dock, Emily cast off the lines for the Defender as Ryan started the engines, then she jumped onto the boat.

As he idled out of the tiny harbor, he put his arm around her. "If you're going to be my plus one, are we going as friends or ...?"

"Let's start with friends and see where it goes."

He tried to keep the grin off his face as he raced the Defender out of the Bay of Bluefields and across the slick surface of the Caribbean Sea. As soon as Emily had told him she wanted to be his date to the wedding, his heart had lifted. He told himself to play it cool. The past was the past.

Now all they needed to do was wrap up the search for the *Explorer* with minimal fuss, but he knew in his gut that it wouldn't work out that way.

The truth was that it never did.

CHAPTER THIRTY-SEVEN

As they approached *Peggy Lynn*, Ryan hailed the salvage vessel on the radio and asked if there were divers in the water. Dennis radioed back to say there wasn't and told Ryan to approach on the starboard side. Travis and Gary helped secure the Defender to the railing. Ryan shut off the engines, and he and Emily climbed aboard the bigger vessel.

"Can you gather the crew?" Ryan asked Travis. "I need to speak to everyone."

"Yeah. Give me a few minutes, and I'll get them all on deck."

In his stateroom, Ryan pulled a duffle bag from the hanging locker. He haphazardly threw clothes and gear into it. There were a lot of things he couldn't take with him, like his guns, commercial diving gear, wet- and dry suits, and other miscellaneous items he'd collected. He would have to get all those later or have Greg take them back to Texas on the Hatteras.

Travis stopped in the doorway. "We're ready for you."

Ryan shouldered the bag, carried it to the main deck, and tossed it into the Defender. He turned and looked at the crowd of expectant faces. "You guys know that Travis told me to make a choice between being here full time or working freelance missions for Greg." He paused and glanced around, trying to gauge their expressions. "This is one of the hardest decisions I've ever had to make. As you can see, I've packed a bag. Greg has asked me to help Emily look for a missing freighter whose crew was murdered by pirates. I've enjoyed my time here and we've done some incredible jobs together, but everything comes to an end, right, Dennis?"

"Why are you throwing me under the bus?" the older man asked.

"Because we've all decided to leave."

Dennis muttered an unkind word about Ryan's parentage under his breath as he faced the crew. "Ryan's forcing me to say this before I wanted to, so here goes. Emery and I are retiring at the end of the month. I'm gifting *Peggy Lynn* to Travis and Stacey. I know you guys love this old gal as much as I do and that you'll take good care of her."

Stacey wiped tears from her eyes as she hugged the old sea captain. "You don't have to go."

"It's time, Stacey." He patted her on the back.

"I know, but I don't want you to go."

"We don't want to go either, whippersnapper," Emery said with a catch in his voice. "But these old sea legs just don't work like they used to, and I'm not much help on deck."

"What are you going to do?" Travis asked.

Dennis said, "We have families we haven't seen in years, and I'd like to connect with my grandkids."

"To fair winds and following seas," Gary said.

"Thank you kindly, shipmate," Grandpa said.

"I hate to break up the party," interrupted Ryan, "but Emily and I have to get back ashore."

"I'll drive," Stacey said. "I could use a stiff drink."

Ryan said, "We planned to catch a ride on the chopper."

"You're too late," Travis stated. "They've made their last flight of the day."

Dennis cleared his throat. "I'm giving you all the night off. Go ashore and be back here first thing in the morning."

"Hell, yeah," Gary shouted, and there was a rush to the Defender as the crew piled into its cabin and strapped themselves to the shock-absorption seats.

Ryan shook hands with Grandpa and Dennis, who said they'd see him at Don and Ashlee's wedding. "Looking forward to it," Ryan replied.

The Defender raced through the fading light back to Bluefields, and the crew stormed the bar at the Oasis Casino and Hotel. Ryan carried his gear bag up to the suite. He dropped it on the couch and started back to the bar, but Emily stopped him.

She crossed her arms and cocked her hip. "You know, you still haven't asked me."

"Asked you what?"

Throwing up her hands in exasperation, she said, "You *are* dense."

"I'm confused. What am I asking you about?"

"The wedding. A girl likes to be asked properly."

"What?"

"You already tried that, buddy."

Why was he so surprised that she wanted to go with him? His mind raced back through the afternoon, connecting the dots. The annoyed look when he didn't respond right away to her question, the coquettish smiles, the arm looped in his. Slowly, it dawned on him that she had been angling for this from the moment he'd gotten off the phone with Ashlee.

Ryan smiled and chuckled. He walked over to her and put his arms around her waist. Looking down into her blue eyes, he said, "Emily Hunt, will you go to Don and Ashlee's wedding with me?"

She gazed back at him with a coy grin. Sliding her arms around his shoulders, she replied, "I thought you'd never ask."

He leaned into her and they paused, foreheads resting against one another, their lips just millimeters apart. It seemed like every bit of tension they'd created over the years was pushing them apart, while, at the same time, their passion for one another was pulling them together. It was a moment that Ryan would never forget, and then her soft lips brushed against his, and he drew her in closer.

When Emily pulled away, she gazed up at him again. "Do you always kiss your friends like that?"

"Just the ones I really like."

"Greg's a lucky guy." She kissed him again, then pulled away. "Come on, friend. I think your crew is waiting on us."

They had a few drinks with the old gang before they retired to Greg's suite. Ryan found the paraplegic sitting on the balcony, swatting mosquitoes, and drinking a beer. Ryan sat beside him with two fresh beers. "It's done. I'm no longer a crewman of the *Peggy Lynn*."

"How does that make you feel?"

"Cut the psychological bullshit," Ryan said.

"Are you ready to hunt a ship?"

"Yeah, I packed a bag and Emily is my plus one to Don and Ashlee's wedding."

Greg smiled.

"Oh, shut up."

Greg pressed his fingers to his chest and said innocently, "I didn't say a word."

"Did you call her down here?"

"No, sir. I called Kyle Ward and told him about the *EPC* and the ghost ship. She came on her own, to ask you for help."

"Uh-huh," Ryan muttered around his beer bottle.

"Contrary to your opinion, I had nothing to do with this other than to suggest the two of you work together."

"That was more than enough."

"Something happened or she wouldn't be your plus one."

Ryan snorted. "We'll see."

CHAPTER THIRTY-EIGHT

After a restless night on the suite's uncomfortable sofa, Ryan had gotten up and gone outside. He was thinking about going for a run but decided against it when the wave of heat and humidity hit him. He went back upstairs and brewed coffee in the room's small pot, poured himself a cup, and stared at the charts and papers on the table.

During his sleepless night, Ryan had used Greg's computer to read about the Syrian Army, thinking he could get into Sadiq's mind, but what he read left him more confused than before. Since leaving the Navy, he'd rarely watched the news or even read the headlines. Keeping up with the latest world happenings and military news had dropped on his priority list, so he'd had to do a fair bit of reading.

Syria was a hot mess. There were more countries poking a stick into that bee's nest than he could count. The major players were the United States, Russia, and the Syrians themselves. Then there was an entire laundry list of Muslim extremist groups.

In a bid to defeat ISIS, the U.S had buddied up with

Russia to combat them. Putin's goal was to retain control of his country's only warm-water port in Tartus and the airbase near Latakia. They faced multiple threats from the Syrian Free Army, or SFA, The Nasar Front, and ISIS, all of whom were splinter groups of the original Syrian Arab Army, or SAA, and the splintered factions received support from the likes of Turkey, Iran, and Lebanon.

Fighters from around the world had converged on the country to support the jihadists or felt empathetic toward the refugees who had fled the country looking for peace outside the violent regime of Syria's president, Bashar al-Assad, who was responsible for a string of human rights abuses, including the use of chemical weapons against his own people.

The U.S. claimed they had all but wiped ISIS out, but other reports indicated that the group was still functioning despite its many setbacks.

All of which begged the question: whose side was Sadiq on, and what were his plans for the stolen freighter? The more Ryan tried to come at the problem from different angles, the more it added up to two things. One: Sadiq had had enough of the fighting and had struck out on his own. But what exactly was he going to do with a stolen freighter, and why had he killed the crew? Most modern-day pirates wanted to ransom either the ship or the crew, or both, yet the shipowner had heard nothing from the pirates.

The second option, as Emily had suggested during her pitch for help, was that Sadiq planned to use the freighter to stage a terror attack. That option raised even more questions. What was the target? In this part of the world, the obvious answer was the United States. When would he attack? How would he exploit a ship to make it the best weapon possible?

Ryan poured another cup of coffee and returned to the table. He was deep in thought about the Syrian Arab Army and terror attacks when Emily interrupted him by slipping her arms around his waist. He wrapped his hand around hers.

"What are you thinking about?" she asked.

"How I would use a ship as a weapon."

"And what would you do?"

"Turn it into a bomb and detonate it in the biggest shipping port I could find."

"Do you think that's what he plans to do?" she asked.

"I don't know. I guess we need more information on him. If we can figure out what makes him tick, then we might be able to find him."

Shelly came out of the other bedroom and poured herself a mug of coffee. "Greg will be out soon. He said to order breakfast."

They ordered room service and ate on the balcony because Emily's papers covered the table indoors.

Greg joined them as they were finishing, and Ryan sat with him, sipping coffee.

"What's the game plan?" Greg asked, after swallowing a bite of scrambled eggs.

"Find more information on the pirate leader. Ashlee is working the satellite angle, and I also think we need to go to Texas and put together a team to take the ship once we find it."

Greg leaned forward over his plate and hooked a fat glob of egg with his fork. "I'll have Chuck fly you up today."

"Great. I'll call him and set it up."

"I had him file a flight plan last night." He rolled his wrist to look at his chronograph. "He should be getting the plane ready now. Happy hunting."

Why his friend's forethought surprised him was beyond Ryan's comprehension. He should have known that Greg would have already scheduled a flight to Texas. It was the next logical step, but still, the man was ahead of him. He stood and slapped Greg on the back. "I'll see you later. Good luck with the port project."

"Call Landis when you're on the plane and ask him for help. If he can ferret out information on your boy, then it might help you find him."

"I had a similar thought," Ryan said.

"Don't do anything I wouldn't do," Greg advised.

Ryan grinned. "That leaves me with plenty of leeway."

CHAPTER THIRTY-NINE

Trident Headquarters
Texas City, Texas

It was late in the afternoon when Ryan parked Greg Olsen's midnight-black Chevrolet 2500 HD truck in front of an office near downtown Texas City, Texas. There were three buildings in the block of commercial offices, each painted light gray with stripes of blue and red around the top. Every office had a glass entry door, a small picture window in the front, and a roll-up garage door at the rear. This was where DWR had housed their clandestine operations when Greg's father had run the DHS ops, and Ryan had worked here before going on the run from the Aztlán Cartel after they had placed a bounty on his head. Now, Greg ran Trident from the building, and owned a gun store and shooting range in the adjoining spaces.

As Ryan and Emily walked to the door, a stocky man of Samoan descent with a gleaming bald head and a big grin swung it open. As usual, he wore tan cargo pants, combat boots, and a blue Columbia fishing shirt. Wiley X sunglasses hung from a strap around his neck.

"This must be good for you to call in the cavalry," Roland "Jinks" Jenkins said.

Inside, Ryan introduced Emily to the retired U.S. Navy senior chief and former member of SEAL Team Six.

"Nice to meet you, ma'am," Jinks said.

"I'd like you a lot better if you stopped calling me 'ma'am,'" Emily said. "I'm not that old."

Jinks laughed. "Force of habit. Landis is waiting for you."

Ryan pointed for Emily to go into the office, closing the door as he and Jinks followed her inside. Not much had changed since the last time Ryan had entered this office to meet with Landis. Two of the four televisions on the wall played news footage and sports highlights, while the other screens were black. There was a brown leather sofa, a solid oak desk, and, behind the desk, a set of floor-to-ceiling shelves and cabinets containing a variety of books, binders, and pictures of Greg's family. One of the photos was of him and Ryan in Afghanistan, the day before Greg had suffered a shrapnel wound to his back that had left him paralyzed.

Landis sat behind the desk. He was a gruff gentleman on the cusp of retirement from Homeland after spending decades as an Army Ranger, a member of the Las Vegas Police Department, and the FBI before transitioning to the DHS liaison job. His steel gray hair was still in the same buzz cut he'd worn for years. He'd lost a few pounds around the waist, and his shirt no longer strained at the buttons. He gazed at Emily and Ryan with watery blue eyes that seemed to take in everything at once.

Ryan shook his hand. "Thanks for coming."

He tapped the desk. "That's what liaisons do. Now, let's have your file."

Emily handed it over, and the DHS agent flipped through it while she recounted her time with Lorenzo Spataro and the steps that she'd taken to look for the *Everglades Explorer* to date.

"What did you learn about Sadiq?" Ryan asked.

Landis pushed a folder across the desk, and Ryan picked it up. The DHS agent leaned back in his chair and interlaced his fingers before drumming his thumbs against his stomach. He gave them a basic rundown of Sadiq's history and finished with, "The reason the FBI came calling is because he's on the terrorist watchlist. Apparently, he left the SAA and joined ISIS after a U.S. cruise missile strike killed his father."

Things began to crystalize in Ryan's mind. Sadiq wanted revenge.

"Did you talk to the FBI agents who approached me?" Emily asked.

"I did, and they asked what my interest was in the case," Landis said. "I told them that my liaisons at DWR were helping you look for the freighter, and they asked to be kept in the loop if you found anything of significance."

"Are they looking for Sadiq or the ship?" Jinks asked from his seat on the sofa.

"Not actively," Landis replied.

"What does that mean?" Ryan asked.

"They think the sketch and subsequent hit in the database were a fluke because the tech used suspect methods in rendering the image and in pinpointing facial nodals."

"I can see that," Emily said.

"So, they believe Sadiq is still in the Middle East and not on a freighter?" Jinks inquired.

Landis nodded. "The question now is: is this really Sadiq? Unless we have definitive proof that Sadiq is in control of the freighter, the FBI won't want to hear any more about it."

"Which means we have to figure out who this guy really

is," Ryan said. "If he's not Sadiq, we need to know who he is and what he's doing with a stolen ship."

"Where do we start?" Jinks asked.

"I'm waiting for Ashlee to get back with me," Ryan said. "She's working with a satellite tracking company to find the ship."

"How long will that take?" Landis asked.

"Let me call her and find out." He pulled out his cell phone and dialed Ashlee's number.

When she answered, she said, "I was just about to call you."

"I'm putting you on speaker."

They heard Ashlee take a deep breath before she said, "I don't have anything yet. It's taking longer than I thought it would."

"How long will it take?" Ryan asked.

"Hopefully, tomorrow."

"Okay, Ash. Keep in touch," he said and ended the call.

Landis stood. "I need to get back to my office, and rush hour is going to be a nightmare. Call me if you get something concrete on Sadiq."

Ryan shook hands with the DHS agent and promised to keep him in the loop. He stood, stretched, and turned to Emily. "I'm hungry. Let's go get something to eat."

"Sounds good," she replied.

"See you tomorrow, Jinks."

Jinks nodded and headed back to his office, which was a cubical near the front door.

Emily followed Ryan outside into the warm Texas evening. "It will be hot for Don and Ashlee's wedding," she said.

"Yeah, fortunately we're wearing shorts. I guess they're doing a beach theme."

Emily grinned coquettishly. "But you'd look even more handsome in a tux."

"Get in the truck." He opened the passenger door, and she stepped onto the nerf bar and into the seat. Ryan closed the door and ran around to the driver's side. A moment later, he had the truck started, and they pulled out of the parking lot.

Fifteen minutes later, he stopped beside a small, tan clapboard building with blue trim and a large red triangular sign that read Boyd's Cajun Grill Express. They slid out of the truck and joined the other people waiting to order food. The line snaked out the door amid the outside seating area. As they waited, Emily scrolled through messages on her phone, and Ryan breathed the salt air mixed with the pungent odors of cooking seafood and acrid crude oil. Texas City was one of the largest petrochemical refining and manufacturing centers in the United States, and Dark Water Research had built its headquarters there because of the deep-water port and easy access to the Gulf of Mexico. Ryan liked the small city, maybe because his friends lived there, but it wasn't the same as living in the Caribbean with its clear blue water.

Once they reached the counter, Emily ordered shrimp tacos, and Ryan ordered the crawfish basket with fried okra. They carried their fare to the pickup, and Ryan drove them onto the five-mile-long Texas City Dike, created when the city had dredged the Texas City Channel. The dike helped prevent sediment from filtering into the upper bay. From the end of the dike, they had a view of the Galveston skyline and the tip of the Bolivar Peninsula across the blue-brown waters of the bay.

Ryan stopped the truck in a dirt-and-gravel lot. They ate on the tailgate while watching barges, oil tankers, and pleasure boats move past. A dredge worked in the channel, a constant operation to remove the silt and keep it clear.

Emily sat cross-legged on the tailgate, the breeze blowing the strands of her hair across her cheeks. She kept brushing it off her face as she ate. Ryan finished his crawfish, which Emily said was disgusting when he popped the tail into his mouth then sucked on the crawfish's head before chewing. He explained that all the juices were in the head, and it made the meat taste much better. She remained unconvinced.

When they finished eating, he deposited their trash in a can, and they strolled hand in hand along the narrow strip of beach, watching fishermen surf cast or toss lures along the rocky shelves from their boats.

Emily took off her shoes and waded out on a narrow sandbar, picking up shells. He watched her smile with each discovery and delighted in them with her. She walked to the end of the sandbar and back, and after she put her sandals back on, Ryan took her hand again and stopped her. "I have to tell you that I really like being here with you and working together again. I understood why you broke up with me, but it broke my heart. I really thought we'd make a go of it ..." He trailed off, scuffing his foot in the sand.

Emily could see he was struggling to choose his words. She put a hand on his cheek and caressed it with her thumb. "I'm sorry, too. I should have been brave enough to tell you face-to-face, but I wasn't, and I've always regretted it."

He smiled and turned his head to kiss her palm. "Em, this could get dangerous, real fast."

"I know."

"By searching for this ship, we're putting ourselves in harm's way."

"This is what you do, Ryan." She let her hand drop from his face. "I realize that now. Demanding that you change would be trying to control you, and you'd be unhappy and resentful. I couldn't live with that. I think it was part of why I cut you out of my life, because I knew you would want to change, not for yourself, but for me, and at some point, you would go back to doing dangerous things, because it's in your nature." Her eyes shifted away from his. "That, and you were having an affair with that Haitian vodou woman."

Ryan grinned, ignoring everything else and fixating on her comment about his relationship with Joulie Lafitte, which only happened because Emily had dumped him. "So, you *were* jealous?"

"Yes. Yes, I was, and you have no right to make fun of me."

He suppressed his grin. "I'm not."

They walked slowly, both watching the setting sun reflecting off the water.

"What were you saying when you trailed off earlier?" she asked.

"I don't remember," he lied.

"Yes, you do. I told you I was jealous. Now you can tell me what you were going to say."

He stood there, staring into her beautiful face, her brilliant blue eyes searching his, a bemused smile on her lips. "I was going to say that I thought you were the one, and I figured we would get married and have a family."

Emily smiled coyly. "Ryan Weller, is that a proposal?"

His cheeks turned crimson and he stammered as he tried to find an answer that would both appease her and get himself off the hook. While he had once wanted very much to marry this beautiful woman, he hadn't imagined ever delivering such an awkward proposal. "I-I ... I mean ..."

She crossed her arms and gave him a pointed look before turning for the truck.

"Okay, yes," he called after her. "It was a proposal if you want it to be. I hadn't planned it to be, but ..." She kept walking. "Hey, wait!" He charged after her and blocked her path. "I thought we were telling each other the truth?"

"You really wanted to ask me to *marry* you? Why?"

"Because I fell in love with you during our trip to Marathon, and I've never felt for another woman the way I feel about you, Em. I love you. I want this to work between us."

Once again, she avoided his gaze by staring at the horizon, keeping her arms wrapped around her body. Then she nodded. "Okay." She thrust a finger into his chest. "Not to marriage, I mean." She took his hands in hers. "Let's see how it goes. I'm not promising anything."

He put his arm around her shoulders, and they walked to the truck, a smile on his face.

As they drove away from the dike, Ryan swung the truck into a small parking lot and hopped out.

"What are you doing?" Emily asked.

"I want to see what this anchor is doing here." He pointed at a large white ship's main anchor with several historical plaques on either side of it.

Emily leaned out the truck window. "What's it say?"

"On April 16, 1947, the French freighter *Grandcamp* exploded and killed 576 people, injured five thousand, and destroyed ten million dollars' in property. This ten-thousand-pound anchor landed here, a half mile away from where the ship exploded."

"Holy cow."

"Yeah. Wonder what made it explode?" He climbed back into the driver's seat, put the transmission in drive, and headed toward Greg's house on Tiki Island.

Emily pulled out her phone. While Ryan drove, she summarized as she read. "It says the *Grandcamp* was carrying ammonium nitrate stored in paper sacks. The longshoremen reported that the bags were hot to the touch while loading. Apparently, the manufacturer made the ammonium nitrate into pellets coated in paraffin, and between the warm day and the heat in the ship's hold, the pellets started to smolder. The pressure inside the hold blew off the ship's hatches, and the hull plates bulged at the seams. The water around the ship got so hot that it boiled and turned to steam. Eventually, the heat and pressure caused the ammonium nitrate to explode. It knocked the wings off two airplanes flying nearby, and people felt the shock in Louisiana, two-hundred-and-fifty miles away. The explosion of the *Grandcamp* caused another ship to catch fire, which was also loaded with ammonium nitrate. The detonation blew that ship's propeller over a mile away."

Ryan turned onto the freeway, and they rode in silence before Emily said, "It's mind-boggling to think how dangerous the chemicals are that farmers use to grow crops."

"And it washes into the lakes and oceans, causing algae blooms and dead zones that kill all living life underwater. I wish they'd put a stop to using all those chemicals on the fields."

"Unless you have more money than the farm lobby, you won't change anything," she said.

"You're right. You know they ship that stuff all over the world? It wouldn't be hard to turn a ship into a floating bomb with it."

"Please tell me you're joking."

"I wish I was," he said, but he didn't know how prophetic his words would be.

CHAPTER FORTY

The next morning, Ryan parked himself behind Greg's desk and checked his email. There was a note from Landis telling him Agent Stickney had called, asking for an update.

Then his email inbox chimed with a message from Ashlee. MarineSat AI had come through with the images of *Everglades Explorer*.

He stepped into the small cubical farm and called for Jinks to join him and Emily in Greg's office. Back at the desk, he read aloud the email Ashlee had written. "'We tracked your ship on its regular route from Haiti to Puerto Cortés, Honduras. However, it was spoofing the AIS to mask its identity along the way. In Puerto Cortés, it took on a load of cargo and fuel before it headed out. Instead of heading for the next stop on the itinerary, it turned north, and we lost it. There was a gap in the satellite coverage so we couldn't get the sequential imaging like we did with the earlier voyage. We're working on finding it now.'"

"Do they know what cargo they loaded and who the charter party was?" Emily asked. She'd pulled her hair into a ponytail and sat with her long legs crossed at the knee. Ryan kept stealing glances at her. While they'd spent the night at Greg's house, it hadn't been together, and that had disappointed him.

After some Internet research and conversation, she'd retired to Greg's room, and Ryan had ended up on the back deck alone with a six-pack of Stella Artois, his thoughts, and the mosquitoes. He'd tried to concentrate on the ship and what target they would hit, but his focus always slipped to the beautiful woman in the bedroom. When he'd finally gone to bed, it had taken him a long time to fall asleep as he stewed over thoughts of terrorist ships and reminisced about the wonderful times he and Emily had once shared.

She looked up from her laptop and caught him staring at her. "What?"

"Nothing."

"Well, stop it. You're creeping me out."

He waggled his eyebrows suggestively, and she shook her head in mock disgust.

Ryan dialed Ashlee's extension at DWR headquarters. When she answered, he asked her if she could get the ship's cargo manifest and security cam footage from the port.

"I'm working on it now," she replied. "Can your Homeland guy help if I need it?"

"I'm sure he can," Ryan said.

"Okay. I'll call you later."

While he'd been on the phone, Emily had leaned over his shoulder and started to scroll through the images. Most of them were low resolution photos, showing the ship in Miragoâne and progressing across the Caribbean to Honduras. MarineSat AI had digitally cleaned and enhanced the photos of the ship in port, but they still left a lot to be desired.

She clicked through the whole batch of twenty-five and

ran through them a second time. Ryan liked the feel of her body pressed against his, and her thick blonde mane smelled of lavender and coconut as it fell across his cheek. He wanted to whisk her back to Greg's house and forget about searching for the freighter.

Unfortunately, he had to put his amorous plans on hold because they had a job to do. He consoled himself with the thought that there would be plenty of time for loving her when they were done. Then, maybe he could put this life of danger and intrigue behind him and live happily ever after with Mrs. Emily Weller. *That has a nice ring to it*, he thought.

Ryan shifted his attention back to the images on the computer, where Emily was looking at the photos from Puerto Cortés. The sequential images showed cranes loading bags and transferring barrels on pallets from the quay. There was a break while the satellite circled the earth, and in the next series of photos, the ship sat beside the fueling dock with a cargo container traversing her Number Two Hold.

Ryan leaned in close to look at the standard forty-foot container, painted green and streaked with rust. Emily clicked to the next photo, but something caught Ryan's attention.

"Go back," he said.

She did, and Ryan used the zoom function. "There's something weird about that container. Look at this section across the top. It looks like there's a break where there shouldn't be one."

"What does that mean?"

"I don't know," he said, then motioned for Jinks to come over.

He pushed back from the desk and allowed Jinks to lean in close to the monitor. After a moment of examination, the former SEAL said, "It could be something or it could be nothing."

Ryan zoomed in and out on the picture, trying to find

distinguishing features about the container. He worked backward and forward in the photo sequence, zooming in and out with each one. Finally, he shook his head. The overhead views made it hard to see anything other than a standard container.

Ryan leaned back in the chair. For this op, he had to depend on others to do the leg work when he normally put boots on the ground and chased leads himself. This high-tech spy shit was for the birds, but it was how they did things now. Even the CIA had given up using human intelligence and gone almost exclusively to signals intelligence with a basement full of analysts doing exactly what he was doing now, looking at drone and satellite photos. While they still had spies, the agency often used foreign governments or PMCs like Greg's to run their counterintelligence and black operations.

"Here's what we know," he said. "The ship is heading into the Gulf of Mexico. Let's get a team together so we can be ready to board her as soon as she's within the range of your helicopter. We'll get the ship back for Spataro and catch some pirates. Everything else is conjecture, and we've wasted enough time on it."

"Roger that, boss," Jinks said with a grin. "What do you think? Fast rope insertion from a helicopter?"

"Yeah." Ryan nodded. "Perfect."

Jinks pulled his phone from his pocket on his way out the door and started calling his team, half of which were at the shooting range next door.

Ryan and Emily ordered lunch. They sat together on the couch while they waited for it to arrive. Eventually, she asked, "Are you going with them?"

"Not if you don't want me to."

Emily slipped an arm around his and held his hand. "You should go."

"What about you?"

"I'm a big girl. I can handle myself. I can see it in your eyes. You're jealous."

"Yeah, but it's time to let the other guys lead the way."

"Not on this one," she said. "You're an EOD tech. If Sadiq has a bomb on board, you'll need to disarm it."

"Are you sure?"

"Yes." She nodded in affirmation. "I've thought about this a lot over the last year. What you and I do isn't that different. We both chase criminals and put ourselves in danger to help others." She tried to smile lightheartedly, although she wasn't all that convincing. "I was angry because your job affected my way of life, and I couldn't stand not knowing if you were safe." She squeezed her eyes shut. "I'm sorry, Ryan."

"It's okay." He could see she was on the verge of crying and he didn't know what to say, so he put his arm around her.

"About four months ago, I was on a stakeout with my friend Kaya. She's a cop with Tampa PD. Her husband is ex-military and now a firefighter. She told me that on any given day, they can walk out the door and never see each other again because of what they do. She said it makes her love him more." Emily wiped a tear from her eye and laughed. "So, after that long story, I'm telling you to go do your job, and we'll make it work."

He pulled her close and kissed her forehead. "I love you, babe. We'll figure it out, I promise."

She wiped her cheeks with her hands and stood. At the desk, she blew her nose on a tissue.

Jinks walked in and tossed a sub sandwich to Ryan, then turned to see Emily's damp eyes as he passed her a salad bowl. "What did he do now? You want me to kick his ass?"

Emily smiled. "No, but I'm sending him in the helicopter with your boarding team."

"Sweet. All the guys will be here in an hour. We'll need at

least another hour to load out. I've got the pilot checking the chopper, and I've got gear for you in the back."

He sat down beside Ryan and they bumped fists before they opened their sandwiches.

"Jinks." When he looked up, Emily continued. "If something happens to him, I'll *kick* your ass."

"Yes, ma'am."

Ryan was halfway through his Italian sub when his phone rang, and he wiped his hands on a napkin before he picked it up. "Hey, Ashlee. Tell me you have some good news."

"It took a little digging because the port's record system is *way* out of date, but I found the manifest. I had to match manifests to quay numbers and loading times because the pirates renamed the ship *Evergreen Express*."

"Outstanding, Ash. Can you send it to me?"

"It should already be in your inbox. You owe me one big wedding present."

"I think I saw a toaster on your registry."

"I am not amused, Weller."

He laughed, then turned serious again. "Did you get a tracking number for the container they loaded?" he asked.

"There's one on the manifest."

"Can you backtrack it and see where it came from?"

"That's not my area of expertise, but I know someone I can farm it out to."

"Great, you're the best, Ashlee. Don's lucky to have you."

She laughed. "Darn right he is, and you still owe me."

"Call me when you have something," he said and hung up without hearing her response.

The computer chimed with an email. He went to the desk and swiveled the computer to read the screen as he didn't want to disturb Emily while she ate her salad. He squatted in front of the desk and opened the attached document, a scan of a handwritten bill of lading. It was written in Spanish, but it only took him a minute to translate it.

"What's it say?" Emily asked.

"If I'm reading this right, they loaded ammonium nitrate and diesel fuel in the holds, and the cargo container is labeled as electronic equipment. It says the destination is Santo Domingo."

"But we know that's not right," she said.

"The destination isn't, but the manifest checks out against the photos we have of them loading the cargo."

"Did Ashlee say anything about finding the ship's new track?" Jinks asked.

"No. I'm sure she's working on it, along with everything else I've asked her to do."

"Could we put an alert out on the cruisers' network?" Emily asked. "Maybe someone will spot the ship and we can get a fix on her."

"Most cruisers avoid the shipping lanes at all costs and give a wide berth to any freighters when they're near them," Ryan said. "Besides, if they're spoofing their AIS, the *Explorer* will show a different name."

"It was just a thought." She was about to take a bite of her salad when her fork stopped halfway to her mouth. "Ryan, do you remember what I read to you about the *Grandcamp*?"

"Yeah, it was the ship that exploded at the docks here. Why?"

"What if Sadiq mixes the diesel with the ammonium nitrate? All he would need is a way to detonate it and he'd have a huge bomb. The amount they loaded on the *Explorer* is about the same as what the *Grandcamp* had on her."

"That's the same way that Timothy McVeigh blew up the federal building in Oklahoma City," Jinks said. "So, if you put this all together, you have an ISIS terrorist on a ship loaded with ammonium nitrate and diesel fuel. This is *bad*."

"What's his target?" Emily asked.

Ryan went to a framed map of the Gulf of Mexico and Southern United States that Greg had hung on the wall beside the office door. "Ashlee said the ship turned north. If this is an ISIS terror attack, their most likely target would be a port in the U.S."

"If I were planning the operation," Jinks said. "I would want to hit something that would do maximum damage to the infrastructure."

"I agree," Ryan said

Jinks typed on his phone and, a moment later, said, "Houston and Miami are the largest ports in the area we're concerned with."

"But that leaves out a bunch of smaller ports," Emily said. "What about collateral damage? Terrorists like to make a statement and kill lots of people, right? Jinks, what's the busiest ports for cruise ships?"

Jinks typed on the phone again. "Port Everglades. It's the largest in the States, and number three in the world." He continued reading. "It's also the largest petroleum and container handling port in Florida."

"The *Explorer*'s home port is Miami," she added. "So, if it suddenly showed up on radar there, it wouldn't raise any suspicions."

"Don't ships have to schedule a berth?" Ryan asked.

Emily snapped her fingers. "If they changed the name to *Evergreen Express,* maybe they're using that for their docking date."

"But why schedule it?" Jinks asked. "I wouldn't tell anyone I was coming and just ram the ship right into the port."

"If they had a clear dock, they could get closer to the petrol holding tanks and refinery," Ryan said.

"How do we check to see if they have a berth scheduled?" Jinks asked.

Ryan had beat him to the punch and already had his phone to his ear to call Ashlee.

Emily interrupted him by saying, "Most of the ports list their docking schedules online with ship names, types, scheduled dates, and berthing numbers."

Ryan pulled the phone down to end the call, but Ashlee picked up before he could. He told her he'd had a question, but Emily had answered it. Then he asked, "Any luck finding our cargo container?"

"Not yet, but we found your ship," Ashlee said. "They strung tarps over the cargo area and built an extension onto the superstructure. The changes threw the guys at MarineSat off, but we're sure it's her."

"Where's she at?"

"She's heading east, almost to Cuba."

Ryan thanked her and relayed the news to Jinks and Emily, who were already at work, searching for further information about the *Explorer*'s destination. Jinx had moved to take control of Greg's desktop computer, while Emily tapped away on her laptop. He pulled out his laptop from his briefcase and powered it up.

Emily grinned at him mischievously. "Since you were busy, you get the Florida Panhandle, Alabama, Georgia, and Louisiana. Jinks is on Texas, and I'm looking at Port Everglades."

Ryan groaned. He doubted that Sadiq would target a port on the Redneck Riviera, but he'd been wrong before. While New Orleans was a large facility and handled cargo and oil, the only other place he could think to target along those miles of coast was Ingalls Shipyard in Pascagoula, Mississippi, or the Navy base at Gulfport.

He found the work tedious. Five minutes into his search and he was ready to quit.

Then Emily said, "You guys aren't going to believe this."

CHAPTER FORTY-ONE

"What?" Jinks and Ryan said in unison.

"On May twenty-fifth, Port Everglades will host a record eight cruise ships and a reported sixty thousand passengers."

"Holy cow," Jinks said. "That's a lot of people in one spot."

"Not to mention the port workers, family members, vacationers, and other people who'll be part of the collateral damage. It'll be the largest death toll of any terrorist attack on U.S. soil," Emily said.

"Do we need to alert Landis?" Jinks asked. "He did ask to be kept in the loop."

"Let's wait," Ryan suggested.

Emily and Jinks both looked at him questioningly.

"We know the ship is loaded with diesel and fertilizer and it's not on its regular course. I think we wait for it to get into range of our helicopter and launch our raid."

"You're right," Jinks said. "In the meantime, let's collect more data and keep poking the bear." He sat down behind Greg's desk once again and surfed through the images of the ship.

"What are you doing?" Ryan asked when he saw Jinks was forwarding the emails from Ashlee to himself.

"I want to look at them on my computer. It's got a bigger screen."

Ryan checked his watch. Another half an hour and the rest of the team would arrive at the office. The noise at the gun range had died down. A headache was forming behind his temples. He rubbed them, walked to the team's work center, and found a cold can of Mountain Dew in the fridge. He leaned against the workbench and glanced around. The area consisted of workbenches, a large gun vault, and gear lockers containing everything from climbing gear to rebreather diving equipment for each man.

As Trident had expanded, Greg had added doors to the original workspace, so they now had direct access to the gun store and range on one side and to a storefront on the other side, outfitted with lockers, showers, sleeping quarters, a team room, and a small kitchen area.

After cracking open the soda can, Ryan took a long swig. The yearning for a cigarette was almost overpowering. He pressed the can against his temple.

"You okay?" someone asked.

Ryan looked up at a taller man with thick blond hair and a shaggy mustache.

The man stuck out his hand. He had the Second Amendment of the Constitution tattooed on his forearm in the shape of an AR-15 rifle. "I'm Scott Gregory. You're Ryan, right?"

"Yeah," Ryan said as they shook.

"Jinks said you needed gear."

"I know my way around."

"No offense, but I'm the quartermaster around here. I'll issue you the gear. We'll be wearing civvies under our kit.

Normally, cargo pants and tactical shirts or T-shirts. You got those?"

"Yeah, I got 'em," Ryan replied. Things had really changed since he had operated as a lone wolf out of the office. "You still got a KRISS Vector in the gun vault?"

"Sure do. You want that with a side of Glock 19?"

"With an extra helping of thirty-round mags." Ryan grinned. He had been in a funk a moment ago but was coming out of it.

"You got it, boss man." Scott pulled gear from a locker and stacked it on a workbench. "This is your kit. Get it squared away how you want it."

"Thanks." Ryan went to work adjusting the pockets on the load-bearing vest, tightening the straps on the drop leg holster, and checking his firearms. As he crammed rounds in magazines, he asked Scott if they had an EOD kit handy, and the man produced a standard issue Navy kit.

By the time Ryan had finished sorting his kit, all the team had come by, introducing themselves before checking their own gear. They were a mix of former Rangers, SEALs, and Air Force Pararescue, and they bantered about, using the usual black humor that accompanied every mission. Ryan hadn't realized how much he'd missed it.

He stepped out of the team room and fished another soda from the fridge on his way to the office.

"Hey, come here for a minute," Jinks said, waving him toward the cubicle.

"What's up?" Ryan asked, leaning on the divider.

"I forwarded our emails about the *Explorer* to a mutual friend of ours, Iceman."

"Why?" He knew only one man with that nickname. Larry Grove had earned it not just because he was cool under pressure, but because he also looked like Val Kilmer's character in *Top Gun*.

Jinks shrugged one shoulder. "He's at the ONI. I figured an extra set of eyes would help."

Ryan hadn't known that Grove had moved over to the Office of Naval Intelligence. "I thought he was still with SEAL Team Six." He and Larry had worked together on several operations when Ryan had been on active duty. Larry had also gotten the green light from the Navy to help Ryan with his first mission for the DHS.

Jinks smiled. "He got transferred when they promoted him to commander."

"He's a commander now?" Ryan questioned.

"Yep. Rumor has it they're looking to make him an admiral."

"*Holy shit*," Ryan said, dragging the words out.

"Yeah, no kidding. Our little tadpole is all grown up."

"What did he say about the container?"

"Here's the thing; I'm waiting for him to get back to me still. I called and left a message a few minutes ago, but we gotta hop so we'll be in position to take the *Explorer*, no matter what he says."

"I agree. I'm all set. Gregory hooked me up with a full kit."

"You going in those shorts?" Jinks asked.

"No. I need to run back to the house and change." He drained the last of his soda and tossed the can in the trash.

"Make it snappy."

"Roger that." Ryan leaned into the office and said to Emily, "I've got to go to Greg's place. Do you want to come?"

"Yeah." She closed her laptop, and he held the door open for her.

They climbed into the truck and headed south through town toward the freeway. Ryan hit the speed dial for Ashlee's number, and when she answered, he asked, "Any luck on the footage from Puerto Cortés?"

"No. They won't give it to me, and I'm not going to hack their system."

"Why not? It would help us a lot."

"I'm not doing that," she said, her voice rising in anger. "Everything we've done has been above board. I'm not a hacker, Ryan."

He tightened his grip on the steering wheel in frustration as he accelerated onto the Gulf Freeway. "Okay. Okay. Calm down," he said, more for his benefit than hers. "Any news on tracing the container?"

Ashlee rustled some papers, then gave Ryan a phone number to call, which Emily wrote on a slip of paper from her purse. "His name is Barry Thatcher. He's the guy I told you I was subcontracting with. I'll call you if anything changes here."

"Ash, I appreciate everything you've done. Thanks."

"Just show up at my wedding on time, goofball."

"I'll make sure he does," Emily chimed in. "Did he tell you he's bringing his plus one?"

"No," Ashlee said, annoyed. "Whose name am I putting on the guest list, *Ryan?*"

"Uh ... Emily Hunt."

"Thank you for letting me know, Emily. Your friend can be rather forgetful."

"You're welcome." Emily smiled at Ryan as if to say she knew exactly what Ashlee meant.

"I gotta go, Ash." He hung up, and had Emily dial the number for Barry Thatcher.

The man immediately told Ryan the container had come from Barranquilla, Colombia, on the *Caribe Princess*, a container ship. "Most likely, she was just the transporter. She makes a circuit around the Caribbean."

"What about the agent or the company that ordered the container?" Emily asked.

"The company who placed the order is a shell corporation based in the British Virgin Islands, which is owned by a shell corp in the Caymans, and it's owned by one in the Seychelles. I could keep chasing it, but I figure it will just be more dead ends."

"What about banking information?" Ryan asked.

"That's how I tracked the shell corps. Each routing number is tied to a post office box. Once the money was in the account, it bounced right out to the next one."

"Can you keep working it for me?" Ryan asked. "I know it's a long shot, but I'd like to see who paid for the container."

"Will do," Thatcher said, "but I make no promises."

"One more question. How're your hacking skills?"

"What do you think I've been doing?" Barry asked incredulously.

"Can you get me the security video of the *Everglades Ex* —I mean, the *Evergreen Express* at her berth in Puerto Cortés and any corresponding footage of the crew or agents."

"I'll get started. I told Ashlee this wouldn't be cheap, but she promised that you have deep pockets."

"I'm sure she did," Ryan muttered. "Call me on this number when you have something."

He thumbed the button on the steering wheel to end the call. Ryan pressed the pedal, and the big truck rocketed down the highway. If they got the proof Sadiq was on the ship and turned it over to the FBI, would they cut them out of the mission? Getting sidelined after doing all the work would suck.

Ryan could feel an energy building inside of him, propelling him forward with a focus and drive that always helped him to achieve his goals. Now it was telling him that they needed to have a sense of urgency about finding the *Everglades Explorer*. To him, it had escalated from a hunt for pirates and a missing freighter to how to stop an impending terrorist threat.

An hour later, Ryan and Emily met Jinks and the rest of the Trident boarding party at Pearland Regional Airport. A Sikorsky S-76D helicopter flown by a former pilot with the Army's 160th Special Operations Aviation Regiment, a support unit commissioned in the 1980s to handle the specific requirements of Special Forces operations, sat on a wheeled dolly outside DWR's hangar. Black Chevy Express cargo and passenger vans sat in the hangar, and the men were doing a bag drag from the vans to the helicopter, loading their gear and weapons.

They would fly in three legs to accommodate the Sikorsky's fuel window from Texas City to Gulfport, Mississippi, then on to St. Petersburg, Florida, finally landing at the Florida Keys Marathon International Airport in Marathon. The entire flight and refueling operations would take them no longer than seven hours, and hopefully the current crew of the *Explorer* didn't do anything rash in the meantime.

It was nearly eight p.m. when they'd boarded the helicopter. Ryan and Emily each carried a laptop computer and satellite phone to run logistics. As Ryan slid the helicopter's door closed, he glanced out at the dying light of the setting sun. He was going hunting once again, and this time, he had Emily by his side.

He settled into the seat beside her. Jinks flashed him a thumbs-up, and Emily squeezed his hand, her blue fingernails pressing against his tan skin.

The Sikorsky rose from the ground, reigniting the familiar sinking sensation in his stomach, not just because they were defying gravity, but also because he had a feeling that thousands of people would die if they failed to find and retake the *Everglades Explorer*.

Emily's left hand locked with his right, and he wondered what her fourth finger would look like with a diamond on it. Emily squeezed his hand again, bringing him back to the situation at hand. This wasn't the moment to get sappy.

He had to be at the top of his game.

CHAPTER FORTY-TWO

Marathon Airport
Marathon, Florida

As the thirteen-million-dollar dark-blue Sikorsky S-76D settled onto the tarmac on Vaca Key, the sun was just coming over the horizon. Ryan glanced at his watch. It was six-forty a.m, and the flight had taken ten hours instead of the supposed seven because of fueling delays in the dead of night and high winds along the western coast of Florida.

When the rotors came to a stop and the howl of the twin Pratt and Whitney turbo-jet engines had faded, Jinks opened the sliding door and everyone stepped out, stretching their legs and backs. The pilots went to the general aviation building to arrange for fuel and to pay the landing fees.

Ryan made a quick phone call, and several minutes later, a gray fifteen-passenger van pulled into the parking lot and stopped beside the gate in the airport fence. A stocky man with unruly blond hair slid out of the driver's seat. He wore tan cargo shorts, a white T-shirt with the logo for J.F. Green Builders on the pocket, and desert tan combat boots. Ryan walked over and shook hands with Joe Green, a man he'd worked for when he'd been hiding out from the bounty hunters the Aztlán Cartel had sent after him, shortly after Hurricane Irma had struck the Keys.

"How you been, Joe?"

"Doing good. Mugdha has everything ready for you." Mugdha was Joe's wife. They'd met online, and he'd flown to Mumbai to meet her. Now, she helped Joe run his construction company.

"Good. The guys could use some rest and hot food."

"You know her. She's always ready to entertain, even if it's for a group of your ragamuffin friends."

"Did she get her citizenship?"

"In December of last year. It was a nice Christmas present."

"I bet." Ryan turned to the group. "Guys, this is Joe."

Emily extended her hand and introduced herself.

Joe glanced at Ryan in surprise. He had known she and Ryan had just broken up when Ryan had worked for him, and he must have recognized the name. Ryan shrugged. "We're working things out."

"Come on, everyone." Joe slid open the rear passenger door, and the men groaned at having to ride in another vehicle after the lengthy flight.

"Don't worry, it's a short ride," Joe assured them.

After they arrived at Joe's house and sent the men into the kitchen to get breakfast, Joe and Ryan sat on the back deck with cups of coffee, overlooking the crystal-clear waters of the Gulf of Mexico and the nature preserve known as Shands Key. A gentle breeze fanned away the early morning heat and the mosquitoes.

"What's the deal with the Spec Ops team?"

"We're looking for a cargo vessel in the Florida Straits."

"Seems like overkill."

"It's a credible terrorist threat."

Joe nodded.

Ryan was glad the man didn't press him for more information. "I need to set up things so we can keep searching. We don't have a precise fix on the ship."

"You know where my office is."

"Thanks, Joe. Let me know what I owe you."

Joe laughed. "You ran up a pretty big tab last time you were here. Can I backdate the bill?"

"Sure. Greg's the one paying, anyway."

"Lucky you."

Ryan left the contractor to sip his coffee and headed for the office. He motioned for Emily to follow him, and she carried two plates loaded with bacon, eggs, and toast, and set them on the desk. Ryan pulled their laptops from the carry cases, opened their screens, and turned them on. He found outlets for the cords, munching on bacon as he worked.

Once he had his laptop up and running, he called Ashlee Calvo. She had texted him during the flight to let him know that Barry had sent her the security cam footage from Puerto Cortés, and she was running it through the facial recognition software in search of Masoud Sadiq.

Instead of 'hello,' Ashlee answered with, "I'm supposed to be off work right now. I'm getting married in a week."

"Yes, I know, and I'm eternally grateful that you've taken the time to help me."

"I'll be eternally grateful if you're on time for the ceremony. Maybe I should plant a bomb and need someone to defuse it, then you'll be there with bells on."

He laughed. "I'll pack my bomb suit."

"I don't care if you show up in a clown suit, as long as you've got your wedding clothes on under it."

"Okay, I get the picture, Ash, but I've got work to do. We only have two days before this ship is scheduled to berth at Port Everglades."

"That's the bad news."

"What do you mean?"

"From the satellite photos, your ship cut Cuba's international boundary and got chased by a gunship. My guys at MarineSat think that, based on the GPS coordinates between photos and the increased wake, the ship is traveling at twelve knots. You're down to one day."

Ryan involuntarily looked at his watch. "Where's the ship now?"

"It should be coming abreast of you in Marathon shortly."

"Damn."

"I do have some good news for you. Sadiq is on the *Explorer*. The camera footage from Puerto Cortés caught him standing at the rail and holding a clipboard. Ryan, he looked right at the camera and smiled."

"Sick bastard," Ryan muttered. "Have you sent it to me?"

"On the way, along with photos of the other crewmen I could spot. I also included the last known coordinates of the freighter."

"Thanks, Ash." He hung up and relayed the good and bad news to the team crowded into the office.

"What's the plan?" Jinks asked.

"We have to board and stop it. *Now*."

"I think we need to call in some support," Emily said. She laid FBI Agent Stickney's card on Ryan's keyboard.

"Can you send me an email with all the information on it?" Jinks asked. "I'll pass it to Iceman."

Ryan emailed Jinks, Agent Stickney, and Floyd Landis at DHS. His phone rang almost immediately after sending it. He said, "Hey, Landis, I take it you got my message."

"Where are you?"

"Jinks and I are in Marathon, Florida, with the team. We're getting ready to move out."

"Hold for right now."

"Why? The ship is racing for Port Everglades."

"We need more assets in place."

"Jinks is calling a Navy buddy."

"I need to coordinate with the FBI, Coast Guard, and local police," Landis said. "We need to eliminate as much collateral damage as possible."

"We can get aboard and stop her at sea. That would be the best way."

"I'm ordering you to wait."

"Okay," Ryan said and hung up the phone.

He looked at the men staring back at him. "Time to move."

CHAPTER FORTY-THREE

National Maritime Intelligence Center
Washington, D.C.

Established in 1882, the Office of Naval Intelligence was the nation's longest-serving intelligence agency. In recent years, ONI had combined with Coast Guard Intelligence to form the National Maritime Intelligence Center, making it the nation's premier maritime intelligence service.

ONI had also split into four separate centers of operations, each with its own concentration of duties. The Kennedy Irregular Warfare Center, or IWC, provided cutting-edge analytical support to Navy Special Warfare and Navy Expeditionary Combat Command forces.

Cmdr. Larry Grove had landed at the IWC after his tour had ended with SEAL Team Six, what was now called the Naval Special Warfare Development Group, or DevGru. If he wanted to become an admiral, he needed to serve in the intelligence community, and he was thankful he hadn't gotten stuck in the Pentagon. He'd walked those marble tiles for intelligence and operational briefings, and he had no desire to work in the backstabbing, paper-pushing ruthlessness of the Concrete Carousel.

For Larry, becoming a SEAL had been a dream come true. He'd joined the Navy in the summer of 2002, having graduated from the University of New Mexico with a degree in civil engineering. After completing BUD/S, he had joined Team Five in Coronado, California, and, eventually, he'd been selected for DevGru and tasked with the most complex and dangerous assignments.

Over his eighteen years as a SEAL, he'd found motivation in thinking about the people who had died on 9/11 or watching the video of them jumping from the burning towers of the World Trade Center. It infuriated him to no end that people in the United States cared more about appeasing the terrorists than killing them, and that attitude seemed to have filtered into the nation's intelligence and law enforcement agencies.

As he stared at the email, he had just received from Roland Jenkins confirming that Masoud Sadiq was aboard the *Everglades Explorer*, he tried to figure out how a private military contractor had put together better intelligence than the FBI and Homeland combined. However they had gotten the information, he needed to act on it now.

An ISIS terrorist was driving a ship loaded with explosives straight for South Florida.

He picked up the phone and dialed an extension. A moment later, a man answered in the bowels of the building. Larry said, "Have you looked at the satellite photos I sent you?"

"Yes, sir. Based on what I see, that cargo container matches one the Russian firm Novator put on display at the

Moscow Airshow in 2013. Have you heard of the Club-K cargo container missile system?"

"I have."

"I overlaid known images of the system against the satellite photos and they're a match. I also looked at the video footage. The breaks in the container where the roof would raise to fire the missile are also a match."

"What about the photos of Sadiq?" Larry asked.

"A positive match. The FBI system says he's still in Syria, but I flagged his photo on a British passport as he entered the Dominican Republic."

"Thanks, Lieutenant."

"No worries, sir, glad to help."

Larry hung up the phone and dialed his aide. When he came on the line, Larry said, "I need you to call Admiral Anderson and let him know I'm on my way up."

"May I say what it's regarding, sir?"

"An imminent terrorist threat." Larry ended the call and put his elbows on the desk before rubbing his face with both hands. He had a feeling that his commanding officer would admonish him for using ONI resources to support a private operation, but that was something to worry about later. He stood and opened the door that led to the adjoining bathroom and straightened his khaki service dress uniform in the mirror, ensuring his name plate, ribbon rack, and SEAL Trident were properly affixed and straightened. He tucked his garrison cap into his tan belt with a glance at the buckle to make sure the seam of his shirt matched the edge of the buckle and trouser fly-seam. With his gig line squared away, he left the office and took the stairs to the third floor.

Capt. Nathan Applebottom, Admiral Anderson's aide, stood as Larry stepped into the outer office. Larry had never liked Applebottom and, like many in the ONI offices, thought his name should be Kissesbottoms. Larry believed wholeheartedly that only individuals who had trained to perfect the mission of irregular warfare should staff the IWC. Yet, here he was meeting with an officer of the line who had been the captain of an Arleigh Burke-class destroyer. Larry felt that officers from the fleet were too rigid and too worried about politics and the chain of command to act on the kind of intelligence such as he was about to present.

The short, balding Applebottom rushed to the admiral's door. He knocked before opening it and announcing Larry's arrival. Larry took two steps into the admiral's office and came to attention before saying, "Commander Grove reporting, sir."

Admiral Anderson looked around Larry, and said, "Close the damned door, Applebottom."

The aide shut the door while Larry remained at perfect attention, eyes fixed on an oil painting of the USS *Constitution* mounted to the wall behind the admiral's desk.

"Sit down, Commander," Anderson said.

Larry relaxed and sat in the chair, waiting for the other man to speak.

Anderson leaned forward, placed his forearms on the desk blotter, and folded his hands together. "Commander, why are you looking for the freighter *Everglades Explorer?*"

He knew this moment had been coming from the instant he'd clicked the mouse to send the information packet on Sadiq and the *Explorer* to the admiral. "I was sent credible intelligence that suggests the *Everglades Explorer* may be involved in an impending terror attack."

"Against the U.S.?" Anderson asked.

"Yes, sir. The intel suggests the target is Port Everglades in Florida. The ship was stolen from Haiti, and satellite photos show the ship loading ammonium nitrate and diesel fuel in Honduras, plus there was a cargo container on deck which Lieutenant Blevins matched to the Club-K missile system."

The admiral laughed. "There's no such thing. You and I both know that."

"There are reports that the Iranians have purchased them," Larry argued.

Anderson leaned back in his chair. "Where did this information come from?"

"Sir, I received it from Trident, a private military contractor."

"You're telling me you put aside your duties and everyone else's in this building to look at information from an outside source?"

"Yes, sir."

Anderson exploded from his seat, jabbing his finger at Larry. "You're out of line, mister. I'm calling SOCOM to have you demoted. Do you understand me?" His voice lowered to a growl. "You'll never make admiral. Get out of my office."

Larry popped to attention. "Sir, Masoud Sadiq is a suspected ISIS terrorist, and he's on that ship. He's on the FBI's watchlist, and he's driving a bomb straight for us."

"*Get. Out.*"

He executed a perfect about-face and marched from the admiral's office. As he left, Larry noted that Applebottom had a smirk on his face. He knew he'd put his career in jeopardy, but his job as a SEAL was to protect the nation.

Back in his office, Larry sat at his desk and emailed the package of information to Capt. Steven Warner, then he dialed Warner's number at SOCOM. After Larry told him who was calling, he jumped right into the reason. He finished with, "Admiral Anderson threw me out of his office for bringing this to him."

"I understand why."

"Yeah, I know. I probably shafted my career, but we need to give these guys some support."

"Yes, we do. I'll make some calls."

"Can I give your number to Jinks?"

"You mean retired Senior Chief Roland Jenkins?"

"Yes, sir. He's working for Trident now and he's on the boarding team headed for the ship."

"Absolutely, give him my number. How soon does he plan to launch his raid?"

"Now, sir."

"Tell him help is on the way."

CHAPTER FORTY-FOUR

Marathon Airport
Marathon, Florida

Jinks's phone rang as the team headed for the van. He saw it was his former commander, Larry Grove, the man he'd emailed not more than fifteen minutes ago. He thumbed the button to answer the phone and held it to his ear. "Hey, boss."

"I've just sent the information to Captain Warner at SOCOM in Tampa. He's passing it up the chain of command. We've been watching Masoud for a while now, but he slipped our surveillance net."

"Well, we found him," Jinks said.

"So, it seems. I had the photos that you sent me analyzed. Ryan was right about something being off about the container. My guy says there's a high probability that there's a Russian Club-K missile system inside."

"Oh, shit," Jinks said. He climbed into the van and gave the team the news.

Ryan started the engine. "We need to go."

"Jinks," Larry said into the phone. "You need to stop him from launching those missiles. Our missile defense shield is designed for ballistic missiles falling from high altitude, not surface skimmers."

"You're not telling me anything new, sir," Jinks replied. "We're on the way now." He quickly outlined the plan to take the ship for Larry's benefit.

"SOCOM also alerted Homeland and the FBI, but we don't know how fast they'll move."

"Great, alphabet soup," Jinks muttered. He figured the more people with a finger in the pie, the longer this operation would take, giving Sadiq plenty of time to enact his plan.

"Any idea what he's targeting with the missiles?" Larry asked.

"No idea, sir, but we think he'll launch right before going into port."

Jinks felt his phone vibrate with an incoming call. He pulled it away from his ear and recognized the Tampa area code. "I've got another call, sir, I'll talk to you soon." He swapped calls and put the phone back to his ear. "This is Jinks."

"Senior Chief, this is Captain Steve Warner, SOCOM."

"How can I help you, sir?"

"I'm helping you, Senior. I've called in a few favors and have the USS *Little Rock* headed toward Sadiq's freighter."

"Thank you, sir."

"Are you about to launch your operation?"

"Yes, sir, we're getting into the helicopter right now."

"Good luck, Jinks. Come home safe."

CHAPTER FORTY-FIVE

Everglades Explorer
Off Islamorada, Florida

The engineer had taken the limiter off the cargo vessel's engine and Masoud Sadiq's crew was racing for Port Everglades at nearly fourteen knots. They were still seventy miles away and, at their current speed, wouldn't enter port for another four hours. At this rate, they would miss their scheduled berthing time, but Sadiq didn't care.

The ship would still do plenty of damage when it exploded.

On the deck, the technician had opened the missile container and was preparing the Club-Ks. All he needed to do was raise the tubes into position, punch the button, and send them on their way with a blinding flash of smoke and fire as the liquid-fuel booster shot them from their launch tubes. Following ignition, the solid-fuel turbojet would kick in and the missiles would fly nap-of-the-earth toward their targets at six hundred miles an hour.

Sadiq leaned over the hold to watch the crewmen open the barrels of diesel and use a pump and hoses to soak the bags of ammonium nitrate in the Number One and Three Holds, while others planted plastic explosives to ignite the deadly combination of chemicals.

The brief battle with the Cuban gunboat had put them behind their arrival time. While he'd prepared for such an occurrence because he knew they would cut through Cuba's territorial waters, he hadn't planned for the battle to take as long as it had. The gunboat had approached, and Sadiq had slowed the freighter to draw them in. Then he and his men had fired RPGs into the boat and blown it up.

Once they had destroyed the Cuban boat, he'd instructed the engineer to make maximum speed toward Port Everglades. Whether Cuba would report the actions of the freighter or if anyone had seen it on satellite surveillance, he didn't know, and he didn't want to stick around to find out. He'd ordered the tarpaulin structure on the stern to be cut away and dropped overboard, then he'd directed the men to prepare the bomb and the missiles.

He turned away from the hold and the stench of diesel that wafted out and burned his nostrils. Today was a beautiful day to die for his cause. He was ready to see Paradise, but he wished he could see the caliphate return to rule the world. That would be Paradise on earth.

Sadiq's mission was an attack against the United States, but he didn't consider himself a terrorist. No, it was the Americans and the Jews who terrorized the world, forcing their capitalism and religion on others. The Americans worshiped oil, money, and the things they could purchase from the Internet more than they valued a relationship with the One True God. Even if they worshiped a god, it was the wrong one, and Sadiq knew the Prophet had sent him to rid the world of those nonbelievers.

The attack he was about to perpetrate would be a call of recruitment to join ISIS and make ready for the apocalypse. The End of Times would bring a massive battle against the rest of the world, centered in the town of Dabiq, Syria, a farming village surrounded by vast open plains. Once ISIS had defeated their enemies, the caliphate would rule over Iraq, Syria, and the rest of the Middle East, then conquer Turkey, and spread into Europe, instituting Sharia Law as it went. The infidels would be subdued.

Sadiq made his way back to the bridge and scanned the horizon with binoculars. He could make out the top of the Alligator Reef Light House, marking their passing of Islamorada Key. The ocean's colors amazed him. It was easy to see why the Americans swarmed here to spend their money, and Sadiq hated himself for finding pleasure in the scenery. He was here to do a job, to martyr himself, not for a vacation. Carefully, he turned in a circle to scan the entire horizon.

Something in the distance caught his attention. It was a black speck, low in the sky, but moving fast and coming straight toward him. He held his breath as he stared, transfixed, at the helicopter as it grew larger with each passing second. Were they coming for him? How had they found him? He should have kept some of his RPGs to thwart a boarding team, but he had exhausted his limited supply on the gunboat.

The pain in his chest grew from not breathing. He exhaled, then drew in a breath, slow and steady to prevent the binoculars from shaking. The helicopter was coming fast and low. Sadiq contemplated blowing the ship right where it was after firing the missiles, but he had to take a chance on repelling the helicopter. He had positioned the clacker to detonate the bomb near the bow, where he planned to stand as the captain drove the ship at full speed into its berthing. He would retreat there now, and if things did not go well, he would take these infidels with him.

But first he needed to prepare. He had only eight men with him. One of them had to remain in the engine room, and the tech had his own work. He picked up the walkie-talkie and ordered his two best men to the roof of the *Explorer* to fire on the helicopter. Then he said to the tech, "Prepare to fire the missiles."

CHAPTER FORTY-SIX

USS *Little Rock*
Andros Island, Bahamas

USS *Little Rock* (LCS-9)—the fifth ship in the Freedom-class littoral combat ship line—cruised around the north end of Andros Island and entered the Florida Straits, making way for Key West. She wasn't the first to bear the *Little Rock* name, just the newest, and Commander Michelle Spearing was her captain.

"You have a phone call on the secure line, Captain," Petty Officer Richard Coker said.

Spearing levered her slim five-foot-eight frame from the shock-absorbing seat on the ship's bridge. "I'll take it in my quarters."

"Aye, ma'am."

She walked to the small suite of rooms designated for her private use, closed the door, and picked up the phone. "Captain Spearing. How may I help you?"

"This is Captain Steven Warner, SOCOM Command."

"What can I do for you, sir?" Spearing pulled off her ball cap bearing a patch of the ship's coat of arms and tossed it on the desk. She ran a hand through her short, curly black hair and scratched the back of her head where the cap's Velcro tab always rubbed.

"I understand you're on your way to Key West."

"Yes, sir." The *Little Rock* had just taken part in an exercise with several submarines and was on its way to Truman Harbor.

"I want you to be on the lookout for a general cargo vessel named *Everglades Explorer*, renamed *Evergreen Express*. There's a credible threat that the freighter is carrying Russian Club-K cruise missiles."

Spearing felt the air leave her lungs and gasped it all back in.

"Exactly, Captain," Warner said.

"What do you want me to do, sir?"

"Get the HELIOS ready to fire. It might be the only thing that can stop the missiles."

"The HELIOS is for ship's defense."

"I'm sure you can figure out what to do if they launch."

"Yes, sir. Does Squadron Two and Fourth Fleet know about this?"

"They're being briefed as we speak."

Spearing nodded, even though her caller couldn't see her reaction. Her ship belonged to LCS Squadron Two, home-ported in Mayport, Florida, along with four other littoral combat ships. When deployed to the Caribbean, the *Little Rock* fell under the command of Fourth Fleet, which had no permanently assigned ships but controlled all U.S. Navy ships, aircraft, and submarines operating in the waters around Central and South America. As an operational member of the fleet, Spearing's orders should have come from Rear Admiral Carlton Billings.

She ignored the blatant disregard for the chain of command. "Do you have images of the ship we're searching for, sir?"

"Your people should have them now. There's a private military contractor about to board her. You are to render whatever assistance they may need until I can move assets into place."

"Roger that, sir," Spearing said, but the line was already dead.

Picking up her cap, she ran her thumb over the coat of arms before placing it on her head. This was her first command and her first combat actions aboard her. She would defend the ship and her country. It wasn't just an oath, but her way of life. Passing through the bridge, she said, "I'm heading to the CIC. You have the bridge, Ensign Davis."

The CIC, or Combat Information Center, was the heart of the *Little Rock*. From there, they could run all operations from steering the ship to launching weapons to gathering intelligence. Spearing wanted to make sure the HELIOS laser was up and running.

HELIOS stood for High Energy Laser with Integrated Optical-dazzler and Surveillance and was Lockheed Martin's newest incarnation of their laser defense weapons. The *Little Rock* was the first LCS to receive the "beam of death," as some liked to call it. Others called it Lightsaber, but unlike its *Star Wars* namesake, the laser could fire a visible warning shot like a tracer round. At one dollar a shot, the system was infinitely less expensive than the Sea Whiz fifty-caliber machine guns or the five-million-dollar-apiece SM-6 ship defense missiles. When coupled to Raytheon's SPY-6 radar system, the laser had proven effective at shooting down unmanned aerial vehicles, stopping small boat attacks, and, at short ranges, hitting an incoming cruise missile. It could also pinpoint targets for laser-guided missiles or be used to burn up targets.

As Spearing entered the CIC, her eyes had to adjust to the dim room, lit mainly by the glow of computer screens and red lights.

"Captain on deck," Lt. Cmdr. Gary Sharpe said loudly enough for everyone in the CIC to know that Spearing had entered the room.

"Theoretical question for you, Commander," Spearing said. "Can the HELIOS hit a target moving parallel to the ship?"

"What kind of target, ma'am?"

"Let's say a Kalibr cruise missile traveling at Mach 1?"

"It's possible." He rubbed his bald head, then adjusted the tan belt on his blue coveralls. "The system is designed to hit incoming targets, but I suppose we could do it."

"Good. Warm up the HELIOS and standby to fire."

"Is there something I should know, ma'am?"

"Listen up," Spearing said, commanding everyone's attention. "We have a possible cruise missile launch scenario from a container ship as it passes us. I need all eyes peeled for missile launch and be ready to shoot them down with the laser. This is not a drill. I repeat, this is not a drill. It is a credible terrorist attack against the United States. You, in this very room, are the tip of the spear. It's your job to detect and shoot down these missiles before they can reach their targets. Is that clear?"

A chorus of "Yes, ma'am" echoed through the CIC.

Spearing's heart thundered in her chest and her palms were sweaty. She wiped them on her pants and took several deep breaths. This would be the first true test of her ship, its systems, and its crew, and she hoped like hell that they passed with flying colors. "Watch for message traffic from SOCOM with pictures of the cargo vessel. Once they come in, plug them into the SPY system, and let's hunt these bastards down."

LT. KYLE NAGY was a proud member of Generation Z. Born in late 1995, the first year of the generation, he'd spent his youth playing computer and video games instead of Little League and basketball. To him, the games were the ultimate hand-eye sport. He could type over one hundred words a minute, had lightning-fast reflexes when palming a video game controller, and could work his way through a newly released video game in less than twenty-four hours.

All that made him a perfect laser weapons system officer. Nagy oversaw a crew of three who maintained the HELIOS in a constant state of readiness. He was also the man who pulled the trigger. Arrayed in front of his seat were multiple computer touchscreens which allowed him to operate and fire the laser. He reached out and pressed a button on the screen to slide the doghouse back from the HELIOS unit, mounted forward of the antenna cluster on the bridge roof.

Once the housing had fully retracted, he powered up the laser system and ran through the test functions to ensure it was ready to fire. Everything worked via a handheld control, just like his PlayStation video games.

The HELIOS laser cannon consisted of three main components mounted on a rotating base. The main fixture was the cannon itself, concentrating six fiber-optic lasers into a single beam; the second component was the radio frequency sensor which provided targeting data; and the third element was the target tracking sensor, allowing the laser to lock onto and track its target through any manner of gyrations. He tested each system to ensure its readiness.

As Nagy worked, the ship's 1MC—the shipboard public address system—blared, calling its crew to battle stations.

It was time for the *Little Rock* to earn her battle stripes.

CHAPTER FORTY-SEVEN

Sikorsky S-76D
Islamorada, Florida

Ryan Weller glanced around the helicopter's cabin at the stoic faces of the battle-hardened men. Each carried his choice of long gun and sidearm, and they were giving their gear a final check to ensure the Velcro was snug, the buckles fastened, and their gear pockets were snapped closed so they wouldn't lose anything on the rope slide down to the ship or during the ensuing battle. Ryan believed the men on board would put up a serious fight.

His KRISS Vector pointed at the deck and he subconsciously flicked the safety on and off. It was a habit he had developed in the Navy and it helped to calm his nerves, the thundering of his blood, and the adrenaline mainlining through his veins.

The helicopter's rotors had been spinning as they drove up in the van, and the team had climbed aboard quickly. It turned south into the wind as it took off, then swept northeast, angling directly for the last known position of the *Everglades Explorer*. Now they were chasing it over the vast blue depths of the Atlantic Ocean.

Ryan glanced down at his own kit, making one more pass over it. He listened through his headset as the pilot told them he had the freighter in sight, and that they would be over it in less than five minutes. The men began racking rounds into their weapons. Ryan chambered a round into his rifle and his pistol. He glanced at Emily, who had accompanied them on the flight but would stay in the bird while the rest of them fast-roped down to the ship.

"Two minutes," the pilot said.

Jinks and Scott Gregory slid open the doors, allowing the hurricane-force winds to sweep through the cabin. The men donned their leather gloves and prepared to make the drop.

"One minute," the pilot said.

The crew stood, and Ryan's eyes met Emily's. He smiled at her and mouthed, "I love you." She mouthed it back. He felt a tug at his heart to stay with her and out of harm's way, but that wasn't who he was. He needed to be in the thick of the action and take the fight to the bad guys.

The helicopter suddenly jerked sideways, and the men grabbed whatever they could to stay upright.

"What the hell was that?" Jinks yelled.

"Incoming fire," the pilot responded stoically.

"Scott, you and Stafford give us cover fire," Jinks shouted.

The helicopter nosed over and raced for the *Explorer* again while the men grabbed their firearms and braced themselves against the airframe. Stafford held a HK417 semi-automatic battle rifle and Scott pulled an M60 machine gun from a storage compartment.

As the helicopter approached the ship, Ryan saw the brass flying out of the M60 as Scott laid down cover fire from the rear seat. Stafford knelt in the open door, his hot brass blowing back to hit Scott. Ryan put his hand out and deflected Stafford's brass, so it hit the deck instead. He leaned forward and saw two men on the ship's stern returning fire.

One of them went down, and the second ducked behind the cover of the radar dome. The M60's rounds shattered the plastic and sparked off the spinning antenna. Then the antenna broke off and the terrorist's head snapped back.

Something else caught his attention: the launch tubes for the missiles were rising from the container.

"Get us over the ship, *now*," Jinks yelled at the pilot.

The Sikorsky slipped sideways, and the M60 chattered again.

"Go. Go. Go," Ryan screamed, kicking out the ropes as the helicopter slid over the bridge roof.

Ryan took his place in the line, and when his turn came, he gripped the rope and wrapped his feet around it, trapping it between his boots. Halfway down, the friction heat came through his gloves and then the helicopter lurched. He kept his eyes on the roof of the freighter's superstructure and saw the rope swaying. Below, Jinks and the others were already firing their guns at the terrorists.

The helicopter lurched again, and Ryan fell the last five feet to the deck, landing hard and feeling the shock through his shins and knees. He rolled to get clear of the rope and flattened himself to the deck to avoid the incoming gunfire. Another man fell beside Ryan, and he screamed as his tibia snapped.

Rolling again, Ryan saw the helicopter had pulled away from the ship and the two men still on the ropes dropped away, windmilling their hands and feet as they fell ten feet to the unyielding steel deck. Both men landed hard and rolled but seemed to be all right.

Ryan came to his hands and knees and scrambled backward to the railing around the rear of the superstructure. If he were Sadiq, he would send two teams; one up the portside stairs and the other up the starboard to trap the assaulters on the roof. With crossing fields of fire and minimized escape routes, the assaulters would be quickly gunned down.

He looked over the edge and saw a walkway less than ten feet below. Waving for Scott to join him, the two men eased over the side, holding themselves in place with their hands before dropping to the grating below. Ryan motioned for Scott to go to starboard while he went to port, hopefully flanking their enemy.

As he spun around the corner away from the safety of the solid steel bulkheads, Ryan shouldered his rifle. Two men were advancing on his position. Both had their guns against their shoulders, but Ryan's sudden appearance startled them, giving him a split-second advantage. He shot the first terrorist in the chest with multiple rounds. As he fell away, Ryan kept depressing the trigger, striking the second in the face and neck.

He leaped over the bodies, exchanging magazines as he did so, and ran down the steps to the main deck. Ryan kept running toward the cargo container. The missile launch tubes pointed straight in the air. Ahead, two men knelt by the container with guns to their shoulders, firing at him. Diving to the deck behind the Number Three hatch cover, he wiggled his way forward, trying to avoid the bullets that chattered off the steel and ricocheted away in loud whines as he tried to get into position to return fire.

Suddenly, the missiles launched in a deafening roar, ejecting from their vertical launch tubes amidst a cloud of white smoke.

Ryan's head rang as the four rockets raced skyward.

CHAPTER FORTY-EIGHT

USS *Little Rock*
Florida Straits

Before joining the Navy, the largest body of water Petty Officer Second Class Wayne Carter had ever seen was Wilson Lake, a nine-thousand-acre reservoir formed by damming the Saline River. He'd grown up in the tiny town of Bunker Hill, Kansas, with a population of ninety-five. Now he was an operations specialist for the SPY-6 radar, the most advanced radar system in the U.S. Navy.

As Carter sat before the radar display, a sense of urgency filled him. He tuned the knobs and rattled the keyboard to wring the most out of the state-of-the-art electronics so he could find the general cargo vessel *Everglades Explorer*. He zoomed out of the concentrated screen and connected with the Northrop Grumman E-2 Hawkeye carrying the Airborne Warning and Control System, or AWACS, radar dome. The AWACS allowed Carter to see over the horizon with his ship's radar. He could link the SPY-6 to any fighter jets, AWACS, and helicopters in the immediate vicinity to give him a three-dimensional radar picture of the battlefield.

Suddenly, the screen before him lit up with a missile launch warning. The radar pinpointed the launch site as being five miles away and began tracking all four missiles, showing them as tiny blinking dots on the screen.

"We have missile launch!" Carter screamed. "I repeat, we have missile launch."

CHAPTER FORTY-NINE

Capt. Michelle Spearing heard the missile launch warning blare over the 1MC and leaped from her seat. She grabbed a pair of binoculars and scanned the horizon, but she couldn't see the launch point or the smoke trails of the Kalibr missiles. Once they jettisoned from their vertical launch system, their thrust-vectoring boosters would align them on their proper flight paths, then the main engines would take over as the missiles followed the terrain to their targets.

"Fire the HELIOS," she commanded.

Ensign Davis relayed her instructions to the CIC and, a moment later, Lt. Kyle Nagy used his joystick controls to center the HELIOS crosshairs on the nearest Club-K as it skimmed above the water's surface. The target tracking sensor made minute adjustments to compensate for the variations in the missile's flight path and the pitch and roll of the ship.

Nagy lightly tapped the X button with his thumb and fired the laser. Through the black-and-white image on his screen, Nagy watched as the laser burned a hole through the missile's outer casing and exploded the missile in midair.

Cheers erupted from the crew members and Nagy expected the *Top Gun* soundtrack to start playing. Instead of celebrating with his shipmates, he spun the HELIOS and aimed it at the next rapidly fleeing missile. He had no targeting solution. The remaining missiles would soon be out of range, even if he dialed the laser all the way up to three hundred kilowatts and froze every system on the *Little Rock* as the HELIOS commandeered their electricity to fire.

"Shooting solution, Nagy," Lt. Cmdr. Sharpe barked.

"We have none, sir." Nagy put the controller on the desk and adjusted his glasses. He swiveled to look at the red-faced officer, who had the phone that connected him to the bridge pressed to his ear. "They're out of range."

Sharpe relayed the report to Capt. Spearing. He slammed the handset down on its cradle. "Intercept solution with the launch vessel, now!"

A few seconds later, Nagy heard a female OS call out that she was transmitting a new route to the navigator.

On the bridge, Ens. Davis said to the captain, "We have the solution, ma'am."

"Get us there now, full speed," Spearing barked. She had the binoculars glued to her face, still trying to locate the missiles, but all that was left to see were wispy lines of contrail smoke. The ship's twin Rolls Royce gas turbines spooled up, spinning the impellers of the attached waterjet propulsion system. The 378-foot ship had a top speed of twenty-two miles per hour, and Spearing wanted every ounce of speed she could get to intercept the vessel that had just launched cruise missiles against her country.

"What do we have on the SPY, Ensign?" Spearing asked the officer of the watch when the ship was on its new course and speed.

Davis picked up the phone again. This time, OS2 Wayne Carter replied that the other missiles were traveling south, and all indicators pointed toward impacts in Cuba.

"Where?" Spearing asked when Davis gave her the news.

"Their best guess is Havana or Guantanamo Bay, ma'am."

Spearing ran to the control panel and snatched up the satellite phone. She rang the number for the Fourth Fleet headquarters in Jacksonville. When the duty officer answered, Spearing demanded to speak to Admiral Billings, but he replied curtly that the admiral was in a meeting.

"You best get your ass into his office, *mister*, because we just had a rogue cruise missile launch in the Florida Straits. I need to talk to the admiral—*now*. Do you read me?"

"Yes, ma'am."

A moment later, Billings came on the line. "We received a flash alert from Space Command about the missile launch."

"We shot down one of the missiles with the HELIOS, but we were unable to stop the other three."

"Outstanding work, Captain. There will be a full debrief later, but right now I have to get back to my meeting."

"Thank you, sir." Spearing hung up and stared out the window. Her hands tightened on the console as the warship rushed through the choppy seas on a direct intercept with the *Everglades Explorer*.

CHAPTER FIFTY

Everglades Explorer
Florida Straits

The sound of an explosion somewhere over the northern horizon seemed to draw everyone's attention.

"What *the hell* was that?" Ryan muttered from his position behind the hatch cover.

Had the missile reached its target? They were too far from Port Everglades for him to hear the explosion.

More gunfire cut his thoughts short. The two men at the cargo container were firing again. He could swivel around and crawl back toward the superstructure, but there were men engaged in battle there. "Jinks, sitrep," he said into his bone mic.

"I've got two men down, one with a broken leg and another with a gunshot wound. We're pinned on the catwalk behind the bridge and Stafford can't engage with his sniper rifle because there's someone near the bow keeping our heads down."

Ryan rolled onto his side and assessed the situation. The terrorists had his assault force pinned down, and men needed medical attention. He was staring at the blue sea rolling past as the bullets whizzed overhead. He contemplated throwing a grenade, but it could potentially detonate the massive bomb they were riding on. The smell of diesel fuel was heavy in the air, and while he knew that diesel ignited at 125 degrees, he also knew anything could happen. "Mr. Murphy has come to play."

"Damn right he has," Jinks replied.

If they didn't get this situation under control soon, the terrorists could blow the ship and they'd have to continue this fight in the afterlife.

The helicopter suddenly came alongside the *Explorer*. He shook his head as he saw the blonde hair of the gunwoman whipping around in the breeze. Emily had the M60 out and was laying suppressive fire. He doubted she'd make much of a difference. It was hard for an untrained operator to shoot from a moving aircraft and hit a target, and between the pitch and roll of the chopper, the wind deflection of the bullets, the drop of gravity, and the speed of the two moving objects, it was even harder.

Even with all these factors, her bullets were forcing the attacking terrorists to take cover and to stop firing at him. He didn't have a fix on their position or where Emily's rounds were striking, but he needed to move. He waved toward the bow where the shooter was hiding, and she concentrated her shots there.

Jinks said over the radio, "The guy on the bow is dead. Our guys are headed to the engine room. The bridge controls are jammed."

Jumping up, Ryan put his submachine gun to his shoulder

and advanced on the two shooters near the container. He shot the first one in the chest and head, then swung his gun to the right and took out the second man with another double tap of bullets to the skull.

As he approached the container, Scott said, "I'm coming up on your right."

"Copy that," Ryan said, and the two men moved to the container's open door. Scott took the lead and clicked on his gun-mounted flashlight as he stepped through the door. He shot a man sitting at the console, then stopped to examine the screens.

"We need to keep moving," Ryan said. "There may be more tangos."

"Just a minute," Scott said, holding up a finger. He pointed at the screen. "These are the coordinates of the three remaining missiles. Two are headed for our base at Guantanamo Bay and the other is going to Havana."

"You copy that, Jinks?"

"Yeah, I'll get Captain Warner on the horn right now."

Ryan and Gregory moved forward to the bow, finding the dead terrorist draped over his machine gun. Ryan pulled him off the gun and photographed his face with his phone. He suddenly recognized the man riddled with bullets, all angled down from the helicopter. Emily had taken out one of the FBI's Most Wanted. "Jinks, Sadiq is dead."

"Hooyah," Jinks said and the other SEALs echoed him.

"Hey, you're an EOD guy, right?" Scott asked.

"Yeah."

"You might want to look at this."

Ryan squatted beside Scott, who pointed at a switch with a thick cable of detonation cords running from it.

"Suppose that's the clacker?"

Ryan pulled a pair of ceramic wire cutters from his pack and clipped the det wires one by one. He pocketed the switch so the FBI could examine it later. "We're still not out of the woods yet. This ship can blow up at any minute, and I don't know if he laid traps for us."

"Great," Scott mumbled. "I wonder why he didn't detonate after the missiles launched?"

"Let's hope he came to his senses," Ryan said.

"Self-preservation?"

"Who knows. I'm just glad to be standing here, but we need to get off here as soon as possible."

As they moved back toward the superstructure, he captured the likenesses of the other dead terrorists. He also peered into the holds to see a spiderweb of det wires leading to chunks of plastic explosive.

One of the team radioed that they had cleared the compartments and were now entering the engine room. A moment later, he told Jinks that the terrorists had been smashing the controls as they'd shot them.

Ryan and Jinks met in the ladderwell down to the engine room, and together they examined the controls.

"Way to muck up a perfectly good operation," Jinks lamented.

"Let's shut off the fuel flow," Ryan said to the other team members, and they started working on the problem.

Jinks put his hand to his ear and listened to his radio, as did Ryan. A Navy ship was hailing them.

"Tell them to stand clear," Ryan said into the radio as he jogged up the stairs with Jinks on his heels.

"Captain wants to speak to you," Stafford said to Jinks.

Jinks motioned for Ryan to speak to the captain, and he took the mic. "This is Ryan Weller on the *Everglades Explorer*. Over."

"Mr. Weller, this is Captain Michelle Spearing on the USS *Little Rock*. I'm ordering you to shut down your engines and heave to. Prepare to be boarded. Over."

"Negative, Captain. The engine controls on the bridge are jammed, and the ones in the engine room are smashed. We're working to shut off the fuel. Over."

"We're coming alongside. Prepare to receive my boarding team. Over."

"Negative again, Captain. This ship is full of ammonium nitrate and diesel fuel, and it's rigged with explosives. I request that you stand clear. I repeat, stand clear. Over."

"I'm sending a boarding team to assist. Over."

"No. This is a dangerous situation, and I do not want your ship or your team involved. Over."

The annoyed authority in Spearing's voice was loud and clear. "This is the United States Navy. You will be boarded and surrender your vessel. Over."

"I don't want to get into a pissing match with you, Captain, but I'm a trained U.S. Navy Explosive Ordnance Disposal technician, and have a contingent of ex-SEALs, Rangers, and PJs with me. I ask that you stand clear and wait for further instructions from your group commander. Over." He turned to Jinks. "Who do you know that can make this woman understand the situation and back down?"

Jinks took out his satellite phone and dialed a number.

"Captain Warner, this is Roland Jenkins. I need you to tell the captain of the USS *Little Rock* to stand clear until we can get the ship stopped and the explosives disarmed."

"Roger that. What else do you need?"

"We need to figure out how to dispose of this cargo."

"I'll talk to my bosses. Oh, you might want to know that the *Little Rock* shot down the missile headed for Port Everglades, but the other three struck targets in Cuba."

"What did they hit?" Jinks asked.

A pit opened in Ryan's stomach.

All eyes on the bridge were on Jinks as he listened to Warner. "Two of the missiles hit our base in Gitmo. They wiped out the prison completely and the third hit the *Admiral Golovko*, a Russian frigate docked in Havana harbor."

Jinks asked Warner, "What's Putin doing?"

"Right now, nothing. I need all the intel you can give me on who launched those missiles and I need it right now."

"I have pictures of the dead guys," Ryan said. "Where does he want me to send them?"

Warner rattled off the email address and Ryan punched it into his phone, emailing images of the dead men and a picture of the bomb in the Number Three Hold.

When Jinks told the team that the missiles had hit the prison at Gitmo, Scott smiled. "Guess they sent a bunch of their own to see Allah. Hope all seventy-two of their virgins are fat and ugly."

The men's laughter ended as the constant rumble and vibration in the deck died away, signaling the engine had finally stopped.

The radio crackled again. *"Everglades Explorer*, this is Captain Spearing. I am standing by to render assistance if needed. Over."

Jinks retrieved the mic and said, "We are dead in the water and are proceeding with render safe procedures for the explosives. Over."

Ryan and Jinx walked to the hold and stared at the massive bomb.

"That's a bit of an overkill," Jinks said. They climbed down the ladder to the sacks. Their feet sank into the wet material, leaving deep depressions. They began clipping det wires with ceramic pliers and removing the detonators from the explosives.

Fifteen minutes later, Scott stuck his head over the edge of the hold. "Hey, boss, Warner is on the horn again."

The two men climbed out of the hold and walked to the

bridge. Jinks took the phone and held it to his ear. "This is Jinks."

"Command has decided to blow the ship in place. They're clearing the shipping lanes in the Strait. The *Little Rock* is sending a boat to pick you up."

"We don't have any remotes for the detonators."

"Don't worry about that," Warner said. "Get your team off the ship."

"Roger that."

Jinks pocketed his phone and picked up the radio mic. "USS *Little Rock,* this is *Everglades Explorer*. We are prepared to receive your boarding team. Over."

"Roger, *Everglades Explorer*," a man's voice responded. "Boarding team is on its way. Over."

Jinks let the mic drop and used his bone mic to call his men to the bridge. Then he said, "How the hell are they going to blow up this ship?"

"Probably with a missile," Scott said. "You know those boat turds like to blow stuff up every chance they get."

Ryan clapped his friend on the back. "Let's not worry about it. Let's get off this floating death trap. I need a shower."

Jinks rubbed his skin, which was red from the diesel fuel. "Yeah, me too." He pointed at the approaching small boat, its bow throwing sheets of water into the air every time it slammed into a wave. "Guys, we need to transport our wounded to the boat. Get the emergency stretchers." Once the injured operators had been secured on the stretchers, Jinx administered a shot of morphine to each of the wounded. "Sleep tight, boys," he said. "We're about to blow this popsicle stand."

CHAPTER FIFTY-ONE

USS *Little Rock*
Florida Straits

It took several hours to clear eighty square miles of ocean surrounding the drifting freighter. Word had spread rapidly about the cargo ship of terror, and news helicopters and small boats had flocked to the area to get a firsthand look. Navy and Air Force fighter jets patrolled the skies while Navy and Coast Guard helicopters herded the news choppers and sightseers back to shore. Coast Guard cutters and police patrol boats floated in picket lines to keep the shipping lanes clear. It was a major operation, and Ryan was glad he was standing safely on the sidelines.

Once Ryan and the Trident team had arrived on the *Little Rock*, they'd surrendered their weapons and received clean blue coveralls, hot showers, and warm chow. Jinks and Ryan debriefed Capt. Spearing, who Jinks knew from his time at the Pentagon.

The Navy had decided to blow the *Everglades Explorer* where she sat because no one was sure how best to dispose of the diesel-soaked ammonium nitrate. The boarding team was lucky that it hadn't detonated while they were taking down the terrorists, and no harbormaster in his right mind would allow the ship to enter a port, where the damage would be catastrophic if she blew.

Spearing lifted the radio mic to her lips and called over the guard channel, "All ships and aircraft, stand clear and prepare for detonation."

A chorus of replies came back, letting her know the area around the *Everglades Explorer* was clear and ready for them to proceed. The boarding team and many of the *Little Rock*'s crew lined the rails, watching through binoculars, while Ryan and Jinks stood in the CIC with Spearing. They stared over Lt. Kyle Nagy's shoulder as he used his video game controller to align the sights of the HELIOS laser on the Number Three Hold of the cargo vessel.

"Fire," Spearing commanded.

Nagy pressed the X button and the laser worked its magic, burning a hole through the hull plates. Moments later, general cargo vessel *Everglades Explorer* detonated in a blinding flash. Even three miles away, the pressure wave buffeted the littoral combat ship, and deep in the CIC, they heard the explosion roll through the air.

Ryan slapped Nagy on the shoulder. "Welcome to EOD, where every day is a blast."

EPILOGUE

Burnet, Texas

Normally, Lake Buchanan was calm, but this Memorial Day weekend, it was a hive of activity as boats buzzed around the lake formed by damming the Colorado River. Sailboats leaned into the wind, their white canvas sheets stark against the blue water and the semi-arid landscape of Texas's hill country. The bright sunshine warmed the air to eighty degrees, and a light breeze blew across the water, keeping the wedding guests from sweltering in the high heat and humidity.

Ashlee Calvo's parents had built a brick-and-concrete, two-story home on the lake's eastern shore. It had a grand-arched entrance, and the rear of the home overlooked a small beach and the glistening lake beyond. Two large tents stood to one side, their side flaps rolled up to reveal chairs and tables within them.

Guests packed the two decks on the back of the house or

stood in little clumps in the yard. Ryan Weller, Greg Olsen, Mango Hulsey, and two other men wore khaki shorts and blue shirts, distinguishing them as Don Williams's groomsmen. Don wore khaki shorts and a white shirt, a burnt-orange Texas Longhorns ball cap pulled down over his mop of brown hair, and he had a new silver wedding ring on his finger.

Many in the crowd were Dark Water Research employees, including the crew of *Peggy Lynn*, who had taken a reprieve from their work on raising the cable-laying barge *El Paso City* and would return to Nicaragua once the wedding festivities were over.

The groomsmen, along with Grandpa and Dennis Law, sat in chairs in the tent's shade, talking about Ryan's latest adventure.

"I'd love to get my hands on that laser," Don said.

"I don't think the Navy will hand them out anytime soon," Ryan said, "but it was pretty cool."

Don grinned. "I bet it was."

The news broadcasts had carried nothing but stories about Masoud Sadiq's thwarted attack and the destruction the missiles had caused. Russia and the U.S. had been quick to respond, raining cruise missiles and bombs down on ISIS camps throughout Iraq and Syria. A contingent of troops were sent in to mop up, but no battle had taken place at Dabiq, and the apocalypse hadn't come.

"So, Emily killed Sadiq?" Mango asked.

"Yeah, she was pretty badass, backing us up with the M60 from the helicopter," Ryan said.

"You know," Mango said. "According to ISIS beliefs, if a fighter is killed by a woman, he won't go to heaven."

"No virgins for him," Grandpa quipped.

"Well," Greg said, changing the subject. "Looks like Texas A&M is reloading."

"Reloading," Don scoffed. "Not a chance. You're lucky

they changed conferences and don't have to face Texas anymore."

The men continued to banter about college football, and Ryan turned to look for his plus one.

Emily Hunt stood beneath the palm trees lining the sidewalk to the beach, talking to Shelly Hughes and Jennifer Hulsey. The breeze gusted and Emily's pale-blue sundress plastered to her body, silhouetting her figure, and tugging at her blonde mane.

Ryan excused himself from the group and walked across the lawn to the ice chests packed with beer, soda, wine, and water. He scooped out two Lone Star beers and carried them over to the three women. After twisting off the tops, he handed one to Emily and the other to Shelly, after she scolded him for not bringing her a beer. Jennifer declined when he asked if she wanted one because he was going back to the cooler.

Emily accompanied him as he dug out another beer. "What do you think?"

"About what?" he asked after taking a long drink.

"All of this?"

"What? The wedding? It's all right." He was glad it was over, and he was ready to eat some shredded pork from the pig that had cooked over coals all night in a pit beside the tents.

"No, this place. Wouldn't it be nice to have a house like this?"

"I guess, but I like living on my sailboat."

"You didn't picture us in a little white house with a picket fence?"

"Uh ... no. I pictured us living on *Windseeker*, sailing to exotic ports, and running naked on the beaches."

She laughed. "That's quite the fantasy."

"A man can have dreams. Are you the one I should be dreaming of, or do I need to keep searching?"

Emily laughed and took his hand. "Let's go get your boat and sail back to Florida."

"Really?"

"Yeah, I can take a leave of absence from work."

Ryan took a slow drink of beer. The suggestion that they go together had caught him off guard. He didn't know what would happen next with their relationship, and he wasn't looking forward to going to Trinidad to retrieve his boat alone. He'd toyed with the idea of putting it up for sale and letting Ramesh, the owner of the Five Islands Yacht Club where *Windseeker* sat on the hard, sell it, but he had too many personal possessions on board, including a cache of firearms.

The leave of absence meant it was only a temporary thing. Maybe along the way he could convince her to quit and they could sail on forever.

"Okay. What do we do when we get to Florida?" he asked.

She bumped him with her hip. "I think we can figure something out."

Ryan grinned lasciviously. "I hope we don't have to wait until we get to Florida to do *that*."

She kissed him hard. "You won't have to wait much longer."

"When do you want to leave for Trinidad?"

Emily held up her phone, the Internet screen open to the United Airlines page. "Tomorrow morning. I already bought the tickets."

ABOUT THE AUTHOR

Evan Graver is the author of the Ryan Weller Thriller Series. Before becoming a write, he worked in construction, as a security guard, a motorcycle and car technician, a property manager, and in the scuba industry. He served in the U.S. Navy as an aviation electronics technician until they medically retired him following a motorcycle accident which left him paralyzed. He found other avenues of adventure: riding ATVs, downhill skiing, skydiving, and bungee jumping. His passions are scuba diving and writing. He lives in Hollywood, Florida, with his wife and son.

WHATS NEXT :

If you liked *Dark Hunt* or any of Evan's other books, please leave him a review on Amazon.

If you would like to receive a *free* Ryan Weller Thriller Short Story, please visit www.evangraver.com and sign up for Evan's newsletter. You can learn more about Evan, his writing, and his characters.

Made in the USA
Monee, IL
19 April 2021